Praise for **KILLERWATT**, the first book in the Rhetta McCarter series, which was nominated for a 2011 Lovey Award for "Best First Novel" and an Indie Excellence Award Finalist for 2012.

"Oh, I love Rhetta McCarter! She's hilarious, smart, savvy, tenacious, loving--and just the teensiest bit stubborn. (Good thing, or her hometown would be in serious trouble.) **KILLERWATT** is a high-voltage, high-speed adventure--with humor, heart, and a frighteningly realistic story!" ~ *Hank Phillippi Ryan,* Anthony, Macavity and Agatha-winning author

"Feisty amateur sleuth Rhetta McCarter takes us along on a thrilling ride in her '79 Camaro as she tries to stop a terrorist plot that could mean lights out for the country...and for Rhetta! An exciting, fast-paced thriller from a promising debut author. ~ *Sharon Potts,* award-winning author of *In Their Blood* and *Someone's Watching*

"**KILLERWATT** is as fun and fast-paced as riding around in McCarter's '79 Camaro with the top down. Well-rounded characters and great writing make the frighteningly real terrorist scenario come to life." ~ D. Alan Lewis, author of *The Blood in Snowflake Garden*

From "Top Book Reviewers" *http://www.topbookreviewers.com*

"Hopkins has written a solid mystery thriller that will appeal to a wide audience. Her style takes a fun, light-hearted approach to a serious subject, which kept me reading it in one go. Even when my eyes were trying to close, I had to read the next chapter to see what would happen next to Rhetta. Hopkins has created a likable heroine that I could see become a series of books quickly. **KILLERWATT** is an entertaining read that shows how vulnerable we are. I hope it never really happens in my lifetime."

"I really enjoyed **KILLERWATT** and being introduced to protagonist Rhetta McCarter. She's spunky, smart, determined and opinionated - everything a reader wants in a leading lady and amateur sleuth. The book is set in Missouri and painted with such care you'll feel like you're zooming along the back roads, riding shotgun in Rhetta's prize Camaro."

"Sharon Woods Hopkins knocked this out of the park. She creates a suspenseful tale with well-drawn, believable characters."

P RAISE FOR *KILLERFIND*, NOMINATED FOR a 2012 Lovey Award for Best Series, and an Indie Excellence Award Finalist for 2013. Received First Place Winner of the Missouri Writers' Guild Show-me Best Book Awards, 2013.

"BUCKLE YOUR SEAT BELTS AND hang on tight! Rhetta McCarter's back behind the wheel—and you're lucky to be along for the ride!" ~ *Joanna Campbell Slan*, author of the critically acclaimed *Kiki Lowenstein Mystery Series*.

"AUTHOR SHARON WOODS HOPKINS REVS up the action in *KILLERFIND*, the second book in her Rhetta McCarter series. With a pedal-to-the-metal plot and plenty of hairpin turns, Hopkins delivers a mystery as muscular as her character's vintage Camaro. A long-buried body, a surplus of suspects, and a fresh murder thrown in the mix combust to create a roaring good read." ~ *Deborah Sharp,* author of the *Mace Bauer Mystery Series*

"*KILLERFIND* IS EVERY BIT AS satisfying as a summer ride on an open road with the top down. Sharon Woods Hopkins has created a fun and lively character in Rhetta McCarter, mortgage broker and car enthusiast turned amateur sleuth, and the supporting characters are just as well developed. Frankly, *KILLERFIND* is a killer find of a book!" ~ *Sue Ann Jaffarian,* author of the best-selling *Odelia Grey Mysteries* and *The Ghost of Granny Apples Mysteries.*

Sharon Woods Hopkins

Deadly Writes Publishing, LLC

KILLERTRUST by Sharon Woods Hopkins
Copyright © 2013 by Sharon Woods Hopkins

This is a work of fiction, and a product of the author's imagination. Any similarity to actual persons is purely coincidental. Persons, events, and places mentioned in this novel are used in a fictional manner.

Deadly Writes and the Deadly Writes image and colophon are trademarks of Deadly Writes Publishing, LLC.

Edited by Patricia Smith

Book cover and interior designed by Ellie Searl, Publishista®
www.publishista.com

ISBN-10: 0989345610
ISBN-13: 978-0-9893456-1-3
LCCN: 2013948302

www.sharonwoodshopkins.com
www.deadlywritespublishing.com
deadlywritespublishing@yahoo.com

DEADLY WRITES PULISHING, LLC
Marble Hill, MO

Acknowledgments

A HUGE "THANK YOU" TO my wonderful readers who show such love and enthusiasm for Rhetta McCarter.

A great big *thank you* to my early readers, Lyndie Kempfer and Sondra Gockel. Your input helped me so much!

Thank you to the real Rushia Coughenour who cheerfully became a corpse in this story.

Thanks to my friend Charlie Hutchings, Bollinger County Coroner, who patiently answered all my questions and only raised his eyebrows a couple of times.

Thanks to my chief mechanic and business partner, my wonderful son Jeff Snowden who keeps the real Cami tuned and beautiful, and to my delightful daughter in law, Wendy and my terrific grandson, Dylan. Love you guys!

Dedication

To MY BEST FRIEND, MY kindest and sharpest critic, to the person I admire the most: my husband, Bill Hopkins. Without you, there would not have been a *KILLERTRUST*. I love you.

Prologue

IT WAS EXACTLY ONE WEEK since he'd eliminated the final one. The killer shuffled into the opulent waiting area staffed by a sole receptionist. The young blonde seated behind a mahogany desk acknowledged the bent old man with a slight bow of her head. Her English was nearly flawless. "How may I help you, sir?"

"I'm here about Garibaldi."

Her small hand lifted the phone. She punched a single button. "There's a gentleman about Garibaldi." After listening a few seconds, she nodded, then said, "Yes, sir." Her tiny voice matched her stature. She returned the phone to its cradle. She glanced up. Her eyes met the old man's. "Follow me, please." She stood.

He followed her across the thickly carpeted reception area to a small room containing a single wooden chair and a tea service-sized table. She gestured. He sat. The lock tumblers on the door fell into place when she left, closing him in, alone.

Clutching a small object in his right hand, he used his left to roll up his right shirtsleeve to his elbow. There was barely time to rehearse his speech one more time—the speech he'd repeated to himself a thousand times on the trip—before the door opened.

A short, dark man wearing thick round glasses that made his eyes appear overlarge, stepped in and closed the door. There was scarcely enough space for both men. He stood in front of the seated man. He cleared his throat and pushed up his glasses. They had slipped down on a thin sheen of sweat to the end of his angular nose. "Let me see."

The old man displayed the object and his arm.

The dark man scrutinized both for an agonizingly long minute. He nodded slowly. "Yes, you have the proper credentials." His English was also excellent.

The old man exhaled. "Good." Dots of sweat popped out on his forehead and above his wispy grey mustache. He fingered his grey beard.

The short man's shoulders rose and dropped. He removed his glasses, rubbed his eyes a moment before replacing the glasses onto their perch. "There is no need to ask you for the account number. You are too soon. There is still one other." The dark man folded his hands across his stomach.

The old man gasped, shaking his head in protest. "No, you must be wrong. That can't be. I'm the last. The others are all dead."

Chapter 1

Thursday late afternoon, November 15
Cape Girardeau, Missouri

"THAT POOR MAN WASN'T CARRYING anything."

Rhetta McCarter ran her hands through her spiky, blonde-streaked hair as she repeated her eyewitness account for the third time. She stood eye to eye with the cop, who glared at her just inches from her face. She wondered how he was tall enough to make the force. Didn't they have to be at least five-foot four, or some such?

"When I first saw him, he was very much alive. He was standing in the median, waiting to cross Kingshighway. Looked like he was headed toward the Days and Nights Motel." She gestured in the general direction toward the new motel. The divided four-lane main thoroughfare through Cape Girardeau, Missouri had a faux brick median, replete with flowers, shrubs and weeds. "I'm telling you, Officer, I saw him plainly when I drove past, and he wasn't carrying anything. I saw both of his hands.

"That"—she pointed to a bottle of vodka protruding from a rumpled brown paper sack—"would have had to have been in his pocket, and I don't think it would've fit in those jeans, do you?" In spite of the cool air, the man lying motionless on the ground wore only faded jeans and a T-shirt. The half-full forty-ouncer, or liter if one used the metric system, lay tucked under his arm. It was much too bulky to fit in any pocket, even if he'd worn a jacket.

"I'm asking the questions here, ma'am, if you don't mind." He paused his patronizing questioning to straighten his shoulders. Undoubtedly, the habit sprang from being vertically challenged. The obvious bulk of a bulletproof vest under his shirt accentuated his overall square-ness. "Wait here, please."

The way he added the "please" made Rhetta want to smack him. She didn't answer. He glowered at her, then walked off. At least Rhetta interpreted the look as a glower. It was hard to tell with so many swirling blue and red lights creating an artificial aurora borealis on the side of the road. An ambulance skidded to a stop, ahead of the police patrol car. Seconds later, a brown and white Ford minivan emblazoned with *First News* in two-foot tall orange letters joined the gathering.

The late November evening darkness had now fully descended, bringing with it a flash of crisp air, hinting at the winter weather to come. While she waited, Rhetta rubbed her bare arms against the chill. She'd worn a short-sleeved blazer over starched linen slacks, and now her arms rippled in gooseflesh.

The summer and fall had been devilishly hot and dry and the unseasonable warmth had pushed on into November. Even this week before Thanksgiving, the daytime temperatures were still mild. The nights, however, were a different story. They previewed the cold winter weather right around the corner. Because of the summer-long drought, the deciduous trees along Kingshighway had long since parted company with their leaves. With their bare arms reaching skyward, they stood like skeletal sentries guarding the roadway. The parched grass in the adjacent county park hadn't needed mowing in weeks. The only green anywhere in the normally meticulous grass was in the form of the persistent weeds. Nothing seemed to deter their proliferation. The chill of the night air hadn't diminished the languishing smell of dust and dry leaves.

Another officer, taller and slimmer, bumped a wheeled measuring device over the rough highway shoulder, stopping occasionally to jot in a small notebook.

Rhetta crossed one leg over the other at her ankle, and leaned against the right front fender of Cami, her restored 1979 Camaro Rally Sport. She hoped the interview would finish soon. She also wished that she'd used the bathroom before she left the office.

After the Cape Girardeau County ambulance had loaded the man and zoomed off for Saint Mark's Hospital, the two uniformed officers finished working the accident scene. The milling crowd, which had assembled upon the arrival of the van carrying perky television reporterette, Kelly Davenport, from Cape's *First News*, thinned quickly when the anchor finished her report. The good citizens who weren't interviewed were undoubtedly disappointed that they hadn't had a chance at five minutes of fame. A hit-and-run accident garnered a lot of excitement in Cape Girardeau, a small city nestled along the Mississippi River. Especially on a slow news day.

Rhetta had managed to stay out of Kelly's line of sight, knowing if the reporter had stuck a microphone in front of her, she would've let her mouth overload her butt. She was majorly annoyed at the cops because they didn't seem to believe her account. The way they kept asking her to repeat everything, she felt they weren't taking her eyewitness account seriously.

A few onlookers straggled, watching the cops as they finished up. The taller officer sidled up to the shorter one, and both joined her near Cami's fender, shaking their heads in unison. "It's pretty dark, so I doubt you could make anything out, Mrs. McCarter," the short one muttered, and shook his head, either for emphasis or sympathy for her insistence on her version. She wasn't sure which way to interpret their actions. Either way, she was beginning to get ticked off.

She turned to him. "Officer, I'm telling you, he had nothing in his hands when he held them both up in front of him, like this." She demonstrated by throwing both of her own hands upward as though in surrender. "I remember because I thought that was a strange gesture."

Rhetta, a branch manager for Missouri Community Bank Mortgage and Insurance, insisted that when she'd left her office just over a mile down Kingshighway it was still plenty light enough to see clearly.

Her temper flared. "It happened just after I'd gone through the stoplight at Lexington. I couldn't help but notice the man standing in the middle of Kingshighway, waiting for his chance to finish crossing. He was on the island divider. I watched in the rear view mirror as he crossed the other two lanes of traffic." She put her hands on her hips in a move she hoped would convey her displeasure at the cops' reticence.

"If that's the case, and he made it across, when did he get hit?" The taller cop stepped toward her, taking over the questions. He tapped a pen against his notebook as he waited for her response.

She stood inches from his face, not backing down. "I told you. I watched him cross the street, and then watched traffic ahead of me. I glanced in the side view mirror to make sure he really was all right. That's when I saw a truck swerve to the shoulder, hit him, and speed away. I couldn't believe someone did that. I immediately called 9-1-1, then made a U-turn as soon as I could and drove back. I wanted to help." She stared pointedly at the notepad, which the cop flipped shut without notes, and returned to his shirt pocket.

Another police cruiser eased onto the shoulder to join the first. This one landed quietly, without lights swirling or siren screaming. A lone officer climbed out, spoke to the first two officers, then joined Rhetta, who was still propped up against Cami's fender. He was taller than the short cop, and nearly as tall, but more muscular than the tall cop.

"Good evening, Mrs. McCarter. My name is Sergeant Delmonti." He reached into his shirt pocket as he greeted her. "Did you know the victim?" he asked without preamble. His quiet professionalism instilled more confidence than the two previous officers had. He withdrew a notepad. The other officers had undoubtedly called him to the scene. He knew her name. Was he called because she was being recalcitrant? She hoped so. She was determined that the cops wouldn't talk her out of what she saw.

"Sergeant," she answered, and nodded her head in greeting. "No, I didn't. I just had the misfortune to witness what happened to him."

"Are you sure?" Delmonti flipped the spiral book back and forth, as though searching his notes, then began writing. Rhetta was happy to see him jotting onto the pages. The two other officers who had initially questioned her walked away, leaving the job of interviewing Rhetta to Delmonti.

"Of course, I'm sure. I saw it. The truck that hit him was a late model, dark color, maybe dark blue or black."

Delmonti shook his head. "We have that information. I was referring to the injured man. Are you sure you don't know him?"

Rhetta shivered, backed to Cami's driver's door, opened it leaned in and tugged a sweatshirt out from the back seat. When she turned, she saw that Delmonti had followed her to the door. He wore a sober expression with his blue uniform.

"I never saw that man before in my life." She draped the sweatshirt across her shoulders and shivered.

Delmonti slapped his left hand with the notepad, and removed something from under the page. Taking a step toward her, he proffered the item in his hand. "Then maybe you can explain how, even though he had no identification, he had your business card?"

Chapter 2

Thursday night, November 15

FOLLOWING A LIGHT SUPPER OF grilled chicken over penne pasta and a small glass of white Riesling from *Primo Vino!*, Rhetta began clearing away the dishes just as the news report came on. She grabbed the remote and turned up the volume on the kitchen counter TV. *First News* was running Kelly Davenport's on-site report of the accident. A camera zoomed in on a close-up of Kelly standing in front of St. Mark's Hospital.

The evening wind tousled Kelly's shoulder length ash blonde curls and she hunkered down into her trendy scarf. The reporter grasped the microphone and spoke directly into the camera. "Authorities tell us that the man struck by a hit and run driver late this afternoon in front of the Days and Nights Motel has passed away from his injuries. Police also report that no identification was found on the deceased man, who appeared to be in his late sixties. They are urging anyone who saw anything or who may have information about this accident to call the Cape Girardeau Police Department." A telephone number flashed across the screen before the breakaway to the newsroom.

"It was awful, Randolph," Rhetta said, turning off the TV. She gathered up the dishes and carried them to the sink. "I still can't believe I saw that truck hit the old guy. As soon as I saw it, I barreled to the next left turn opportunity—nearly a half mile farther down Kingshighway, now that they have those dividers. I swung a U-turn and raced back. The truck was pulled over onto the shoulder in front of where the man lay with a burly guy in a dark jacket standing over him. He stood there for a few seconds, staring down at the man. I saw a glow, and assumed he was using a cell phone to call the police. But when I pulled up, he bolted for his truck, and roared away."

"And of course, you told all of this to Delmonti?"

Randolph McCarter, retired circuit judge-turned-artist, obviously wanted to be sure that Rhetta had cooperated fully with the police. Rhetta had been known to have a less than stellar opinion of the cops.

"Absolutely!" Rhetta rose, gathered the dishes, and headed to the sink. "Even though the cops acted less than excited about my eyewitness account. Delmonti thinks the old guy was an itinerant drunk who stepped in front of a vehicle. I don't agree at all. The escaping dude even squealed his truck tires as he left. I couldn't make out the tag numbers. But I did notice that it had Missouri plates." She began rinsing the supper dishes and arranging them in the dishwasher. "I wonder why there was no mention of the truck on the news."

"Maybe Delmonti is keeping those details out of the media to see if any real witnesses come forward." Randolph wiped down the counter. "There was no mention of any liquor bottle, either."

"That's true. I wonder what's going on." Rhetta turned toward her husband, a dinner plate in her hand. "How could that poor man have gotten my card? I never saw or met him before. I'm sure of that." She turned and slid the plate into the dishwasher, closed the door and started the cycle.

"No doubt the police want to know why he had it, too. Whatever is going on is police business, Rhetta, and you don't need to get involved." Randolph had assumed that judge voice she hated. "Or maybe Delmonti feels that it was too dark for you to have clearly seen the truck."

"Now you're beginning to sound like the cops." She waved the dinner plate for emphasis. "By the time Delmonti got there, it had gotten darker, but there was plenty of light when I saw the man get hit. I was curious as to what he was doing crossing the highway, so I watched in the outside mirror, like I told Delmonti. It only took a couple of minutes for me to turn around and get over there. Although at the time it seemed like an eternity."

Her husband had not taken kindly to her previous entanglements with police investigations. She had already demonstrated an uncanny ability for getting involved with a dead body. Or two. She was garnering a reputation as a corpse magnet especially after she'd discovered a body under an old Camaro she had purchased last year. Now, another dead body had turned up. It was worse this time, because this dead man had her business card, and she had no clue how he got it. In fact, no one seemed to know who the unfortunate man was.

Rhetta grabbed four cans of cat food from the pantry and headed for the deck. "I'll feed the kids," she called back to Randolph. She jerked open the sliding glass door a little too hard; it bounced against the frame. Four feline faces stared at her. She closed the door, more gently than she'd opened it. After spooning the stinky mush into four bowls, the cats murmured appreciatively. She watched them snarf down the food— Pirate, Greystone, Jiggles and Smith. All had been strays adopted through the Humane Society, except for Greystone. Rhetta rescued him from a downspout outside her office. She said their names sounded like a law firm. The cats were their only children, their fur babies, as she liked to refer to them. Randolph was a widower when she met him, but he'd had no children. She had never been married, and was also childless.

She balanced the empty cat food cans in one hand and slid open the door back into the kitchen.

Randolph continued the conversation where they had left off. "More likely, the police are probably waiting for someone else to come forward. That way they can corroborate your account." If he'd noticed her display of temper, he clearly had the good sense not to mention it.

"You're probably right." Rhetta rinsed out the cans, opened the door into the garage, and tossed them into the trash. One missed the garbage can and clattered to the floor. "Crap," she muttered, and scurried out to retrieve it.

Back in the kitchen, she poured herself a cup of coffee and propped herself up on a stool at the island. "I can keep out of Delmonti's way. Believe me, I don't want to be involved either. But I'm worried about what will happen to him now. How long will he stay in the morgue?" She filled a cup for Randolph and slid it toward him. He pulled out another matching stool and joined her.

Randolph blew across the surface of his coffee. "The police will make every effort to identify him. They'll start by sending his fingerprints through the national fingerprint and criminal history system. If they get a hit, they'll try to locate any family."

"Where will his body stay while all this is happening?" She poured sweetener and skimmed milk into her coffee and stirred, the spoon clattering against the side of the coffee cup.

"Typically, unclaimed bodies stay at the morgue. At least while they track down family. They'll do their best to find next of kin, if for no other reason than the county doesn't want to have to pay for a funeral." He tasted his coffee.

"I totally get that you don't want me involved, Randolph. But, let's face it, I already am. I'm a witness. I practically saw it happen, for heaven's sake, and the poor man had my business card. Something smells fishy."

"What smells fishy is the cat food," Randolph said with a straight face, then hid behind his cup as he sipped again. His dark eyes flashed over the brim, and a lock of silver-streaked black hair flopped over one eye. Brushing it aside, he set his cup down and the corner of his mouth twitched. She knew he was trying not to smile.

She ignored his attempt at humor. "I don't want to appear overly dramatic, but something is way off kilter. Like why the guy that hit him pulled over. He obviously knew he hit him. What was he doing when he leaned over the man? I thought he was calling 9-1-1, but when I called, the dispatcher said no one else had called it in. As soon as I pulled over, he couldn't get out of there fast enough. I believe he ran him down deliberately."

Randolph sighed. "I'm sure there's a reasonable explanation, and we'll know it when they find the guy, or someone comes forward."

"Where's that cynical judge I married? What did you do with him?" Rhetta hopped down and made exaggerated searching motions around the kitchen. "The real Randolph would never believe that an undiscovered witness would come forward voluntarily."

"You win." He corralled her and wrapped his arms around her slim waist. "I admit it all seems very strange. Of course, I believe you saw exactly what you recounted. I just think there has to be an explanation, that's all." He kissed the top of her head.

When the house phone jangled, she slid out from his embrace to reach for it. She snatched up the phone on the third ring, yet the line was silent.

"Hello?" No answer. She glanced at the caller ID. *Blocked.* "Probably a freakin' survey robo call." She didn't wait to hear the message.

Chapter 3

Monday morning, November 19

KNOWING THE APPROACHING HOLIDAY SEASON would increase the temptation to eat rich and fattening foods, especially Mrs. Koblyk's cookies and cobblers, Rhetta had resolved to get back to running at least three times a week. Mrs. Koblyk was her well-intentioned neighbor who baked constantly and brought treats over to their house. Of course, the lure to partake in the sinful pleasures was often too much for Rhetta to resist. She ran a lot, just to try and keep up with Mother Nature, who seemed to have other plans for her. Especially when she indulged in Mrs. Koblyk's yummy treats.

Since hitting her forties, she noticed that parts of her anatomy had begun to shift. Mostly to her hind end. With that fact as a motivator, she peered at the clock that proved it was only five, and woke Randolph. He didn't share the shifting anatomy problem, but ran with her to keep in shape. They donned their running clothes and sturdy running shoes and headed to the park. After a brisk, three-mile run in the cool morning air, Rhetta was invigorated, but breathing heavier than she liked. She returned home for a quick shower, then a light breakfast. She wondered if her lungs would ever truly clear up. She had quit smoking—well, almost—but occasionally when she skipped running for a couple of days, she would get winded easily. Or was that due to advancing years? After all, forty-five was half way to ninety. Was she already past middle age? How many ninety-year-olds did she actually know? When she answered herself, she knew she was in trouble. She resolved to run more, and check out that new high dollar rejuvenating cream she'd seen advertised on TV.

Delighting in the clear day, Rhetta opened Cami's sunroof as a last homage to sunny skies, cranked up the satellite radio oldies station and sang along with The Beach Boys on her way to work. She wondered how much longer she'd be able to drive Cami this year before succumbing to winter. In past years, she always put Cami up for the entire winter and only brought her out Memorial Weekend. This year, she decided she might just drive Cami during the mild Missouri winter unless there was ice and snow. Then she was prepared to switch to her four-wheel-drive Chevy Trailblazer.

She and Randolph had first restored Cami a few years ago with the help of her mechanic and best friend, Ricky Lane, owner and chief mechanic of Fast Lane Muscle Cars in Gordonville, Missouri, a rural community outside Cape Girardeau. Ricky, short for Victoria, defined Cami as a resto mod, meaning it looked original to the model year on the outside, but under the hood purred a sleek LS 1 Corvette engine that delivered four hundred horses. The white leather interior was Rhetta's idea. Fast Lane had recently restored and painted Cami for the second time following a fire that nearly destroyed it. Rhetta shivered again when she remembered how close she'd come to losing her beloved car.

She grinned as she pulled up to work. She was early enough to nab the choice parking spot next to the employees' entrance. The area in front of the building was reserved for customers, but the first one into the building in the morning got the spot closest to the back door as a reward.

In the winter, it really was wonderful not having to slip slide all the way across the parking lot. Summertime, however, it was nice to get some exercise, so she didn't mind hoofing it some to get to her car. When she got there early, she liked to irritate her assistant, James

Woodhouse "Woody" Zelinski about it, since he prided himself on usually being the first one to work.

Even with a detour through Starbucks, she still managed to get to work before Woody.

Just as she set her tall cappuccino grande light on her desk and scooted her chair up, Woody sailed through the door, waving a newspaper. For a big guy, he moved with the grace of a hunting cat. ' It says here they've identified the victim of your hit and run. Take a look."

He tossed his coat on his desk chair, never missing a step on his way to Rhetta's desk. He didn't even chide her for taking his parking spot. Although they shared the small office, privacy dividers separated their workspaces. Their receptionist, LuEllen Cole, who hadn't yet arrived, manned a receptionist desk up front near the waiting area. Woody handed Rhetta the paper and pointed to an article. Although he outweighed Rhetta by at least a hundred pounds, he descended gracefully and soundlessly into a guest chair in front of her desk. He waited for her to scan it.

She adjusted her office chair from its low point, up to where her chin cleared the desk. The hydraulics on the chair were wearing out, and it lowered itself every evening, requiring her to adjust it in the morning or risk slamming her chin on the desk top.

She scooped up the newspaper and began reading the below-the-fold front-page column that he'd pointed to.

"Holy smokes!" she said. She yanked open the middle top drawer of her desk, grabbing the manila envelope that lay there, opened. She riffled through its contents until she found an official document bearing the seal of the United States Government. Inside the folded papers was a copy of a death certificate. Her eyes locked on the transcript:

Name: Caldwell, Alexander Franklin

Rank: First Lieutenant

Branch: U S Army

Casualty Category: killed in action, explosive device

Day of Death: 6 August, 1973.

Her father. She handed the certificate to Woody.

He read it quickly, and handed it back to her. He jabbed a finger at the newspaper lying on her desk. "I don't get it. This newspaper identifies the dead man as George Erickson." He tapped the paper. "It also says here that records indicate Erickson died in Vietnam on August 6, 1973." Woody picked it up and read aloud, "Further investigation is underway to verify the conflicting information." He set the paper down, and drilled a stare at Rhetta. "He supposedly died the exact same day as your father? Yet he died again in the accident?"

Rhetta returned her father's death certificate to the envelope, then tapped the newspaper. "There's something very weird going on here. How could the hit and run victim already be dead? "And even more curious, he was a soldier who died in Vietnam," she waved the manila envelope, "on the same day my father died." Rhetta's neck hairs stood on end high enough to tickle her earlobe.

Woody folded the paper. "Wait a minute. I'm thoroughly confused. You told me you saw your father at the hospital parking garage a while back. How can he be dead?" Woody rubbed his palm over his shaven head. His head rubbing was a gesture Rhetta knew well. It meant that he was upset or stressed. In this instance, it probably meant confused. She thought about rubbing her head, too.

"That's exactly what I'd like to know. At first, I wasn't sure I believed that old man who came to the parking garage when Randolph was in the hospital, even if he did give me my mother's locket as proof of his identity." She fingered the locket that she now wore on a silver chain around her neck. "How is he still alive when I have a death certificate?" She didn't tell Woody that the same man had called her on her birthday last month. She didn't know what to think about it then, and was even more confused than ever.

"What on earth's going on, Woody? I have a government issued death certificate here for my father, yet the man in the hospital garage claimed he was my father. Although he didn't appear very healthy, that man was very much alive. Now, another man dies, and it turns out he already died in Vietnam on the same day my father was supposed to have died. That means that obviously, those two men didn't die in Vietnam. So, why do they have military death records with the same day of death? What's going on? Who are they? Did they know each other?"

She stared at her assistant. "Woody, that dead man had one of my business cards. Do you suppose he could have gotten it from my father? And if he did, why?"

Woody tugged on his close-cropped whiskers. "There's got to be an explanation for this. You know, records at the end of the Vietnam War were probably pretty messed up."

She bit back a negative remark about her confidence in the government's ability to keep any accurate records. She had a strong opinion about how the government treated the military personnel who returned from the wars. Although Woody was a former Marine who served in Iraq and Afghanistan, and was a year older than Rhetta, sometimes she had to check herself from treating him like a younger brother. Woody had Post Traumatic Stress Disorder and the VA wasn't doing much to help him. She stifled her comment.

Rhetta stared at the paper. "Any which way I think about it, this doesn't make sense. It's too coincidental."

Woody sighed, and hoisted his tall frame out of the guest chair. She noticed his once dark chin whiskers had more and more grey peeking through.

He began pacing. "I know, I know, you don't believe in coincidences."

Chapter 4

Monday evening, November 19

"I DON'T BELIEVE IN COINCIDENCES," Rhetta said as she ambled around Randolph's studio later that evening. She'd changed clothes, donning well-worn jeans and an old sweatshirt. She offered to help sort through his paintings and help load them into his box-type art trailer that sat hooked up to his new bronze-colored four-door Ford pickup truck that Rhetta had christened "Artmobile II." The first Artmobile, an older Ford F100, had been a total loss when Randolph was run off the road the year before. Although he suffered a major head injury in that accident and was hospitalized, he recovered completely. The pickup, however, was a total loss. Randolph had a big art show coming up the weekend after Thanksgiving, so she volunteered to help him pack the trailer.

In addition to naming vehicles and pets, Rhetta even had a name for their detached garage. She called it "Garage Mahal," because the interior was finished out as nicely as the house. She finally named their home compound, *Daylily Dreamin'* from the abundance of wild daylilies that had surrounded the house when they bought it. In the spring and early summer, bright daylilies turned the entire front yard into waves of golden orange. She'd thinned them out to a manageable number, but they multiplied annually and bloomed gloriously.

Randolph had enclosed part of their barn into a well-lit studio where he spent most of his days painting. He had yet to name his studio. She had a name in mind, but wouldn't foist it on him. He might not like what she'd come up with after she read the article about him in a local paper called, "Trading the Bench for a Brush." Her private name for his studio was Master Strokes. She hadn't discussed it with him yet, but she rather liked the sound of it.

Randolph glanced at her over the top of his reading glasses as he carefully cleaned the brushes he'd used that day, massaging the bristles on each one with petroleum jelly to keep them moist and ready for the next paint.

"I agree, it's all very mysterious, but I'm sure there's a reasonable explanation." He lined up the brushes across a sheet of clean paper towel on his workbench. He was compulsively neat in his studio, as he was with his office desk. Rhetta's work desktop, on the other hand, always looked like the aftermath of a tornado.

Rhetta gathered two framed landscapes and disappeared into the trailer, which was parked alongside the barn door. They'd talked about how he'd never dreamed how successful his art career would become when he retired. His art was selling briskly at the Rivers West Gallery downtown and through Etsy, an online art site. Creating beautiful landscapes was his new full-time job.

She answered him while in the trailer, but repeated it when she got back to the studio when Randolph claimed he hadn't heard her.

"I said, I think I'm going to try to get to the bottom of this." She wiped her hands on a clean towel.

"That's what I was afraid you'd said. I don't see anything for you to get to the bottom of. The police are investigating the dead man. You don't need to do anything." He paused to give her a look she knew all too well. The look that said, "Mind your own business."

And, there was that tone she hated. It meant he was on to her, and suspected she would go snooping around. Again.

He added, "I guess if the man claiming to be your father should call you again, you could ask him about all of this. I'm sure if he knows anything about this George Erickson, he'll tell you all about it."

"Was that a sarcastic remark, since we both don't know anything about this man who claims to be my long-lost and already dead father? Especially since we don't have any idea when said father," Rhetta made air quotes as she said *father*, "may choose to call me again?" She hoisted a large canvas and trekked it to the trailer. "I know one thing for sure that I'm going to do, though," she said when she popped back into the studio.

"Oh, God, Rhetta, what does that mean?" Randolph shook his head.

She hugged his neck. "Don't sound so worried. I decided that I want to pay for that man's funeral if it turns out he has no family to claim him."

Chapter 5

RHETTA, RANDOLPH AND WOODY STOOD shivering alongside the gaping muddy hole. The day had started out overcast and cold and had not improved. Sleet and freezing rain pelted them as they huddled together, desperately trying to share an umbrella. The only other person in attendance was the elderly funeral director, Mr. DeBrock. He pulled his wool hat lower over his ears as he stepped forward to recite a generic prayer as the mechanical pulley slowly cranked the plain metal casket into the ground.

Rhetta batted away a freezing raindrop that mingled with the tear sliding down her cheek, then tugged her leather coat tightly around her.

Following the prayer, the director added softly, "May you rest in peace, George Erickson," and bowed his head.

Rhetta mumbled, "Amen," and stepped back. Randolph put an arm around her shoulders and hugged her to his side. Alongside her, Woody battled with an umbrella, but gave up as a gust of wind huffed it upward. He folded it and led the way back to her silver Trailblazer, which she had named Streak. It didn't streak anywhere, even with a great deal of effort. The six-cylinder SUV was peppy, true, but streak it didn't.

They piled in, with Randolph behind the wheel. He cranked the heat controls on high, and they sat in silence, letting the heater build warmth. The defroster quickly rid the windshield of the thin veneer of sleet.

"There won't be a marker, either, you know, unless we get him one," Rhetta said softly.

Randolph agreed. "It's only right that his grave be marked. Especially since he was a veteran."

"That's a good thing to do," Woody said. "It's for darn sure the government won't do anything. I checked into burying him at a veteran's cemetery, and no way. Said they couldn't assume he was a veteran, and besides, this man died in 1973."

Randolph glanced at Rhetta, who merely nodded. Then he slipped the SUV into drive. Woody seemed detached and yet, at the same time, upset by this death. Rhetta wondered what was bothering him. He had told her the VA wasn't paying for his medicine anymore. Was he having problems? Woody had been injured when an IED exploded under his Humvee, and he sometimes suffered violent flashbacks. She only sensed a time or two when she thought he might be heading toward a spell, but she'd never seen him in a full-blown episode. Now, she regretted the "out of sight, out of mind" attitude she was afraid she'd adopted. Just because she couldn't see Woody whenever he had problems, didn't mean that he wasn't suffering.

The ground, not yet frozen, was a slurry of mud and ice under the wheels. Rhetta had wheedled the cemetery into donating a plot, but it was in the very back, in a seldom-traveled area. Randolph shifted into four-wheel-drive, following the same ruts to leave as they gouged into the ground on their way in. She wasn't going to complain. At least the cemetery recognized that a Vietnam veteran deserved a decent burial.

Once they'd bounced onto the gravel road behind the cemetery, Woody spoke up. "I still can't figure out who that dead guy was, and why he had your business card. And why would somebody have run him down?"

"Me neither. The police have asked me that a dozen times." She twisted around to talk to Woody.

"You gotta admit it's pretty strange that you saw him get hit, and then the police find your card on him. Do you think there's any way that you could have dropped a card out of your purse when you rushed over to see about him?" Woody rubbed his hands together. "My hands are still cold," he added.

Rhetta sighed. "No. I left my purse in the car when I jumped out and ran over to see what happened. I remember grabbing my phone, nothing else." She held up her cell phone, which she had left on the console, to illustrate.

As she held the phone aloft, she noticed a missed call. She didn't recognize the number.

After dropping Woody off at his tidy bungalow on Whitener Street near the Southeast Missouri State University campus in Cape, Randolph deftly maneuvered Streak out of town and down the gravel county road toward home. The weather hadn't improved much, but the streets were clear.

Their house was once a turn-of-the-twentieth-century farmhouse that sat in the center of ten acres of picturesque creek-side property out in Cape Girardeau County.

After they married, Rhetta and Randolph spent months looking for the perfect place while living in a modest two-bedroom apartment. Rhetta had loved remodeling the old house. Installing modern vinyl siding in the clapboard style kept the outside of the two-story white home looking very much like the old pictures of it that Rhetta had found in the attic. Inside, however, it was beautifully modernized.

Their location afforded them privacy and country living, yet was only a few minutes from Rhetta's office. Their privacy wasn't total, however. Their elderly neighbors, Mr. and Mrs. Koblyk, lived in a neat cottage in a copse of pines right where the McCarters' driveway met the county road. Rhetta waved to Mrs. Koblyk, who appeared on her porch right on cue when she heard them approach. Mrs. Koblyk waved back, then scurried into her house. The Koblyks had emigrated from Hungary in the early sixties. Mr. Koblyk was long retired and tinkered, as he called it, fixing up broken toys, and repairing jewelry, while Mrs. Koblyk delighted in baking and sharing with the McCarters.

As they slowed to make the turn into their driveway, Mrs. Koblyk reappeared on the front porch holding a large plastic bag in one hand and waving them down with the other.

"Pull over, Randolph. Mrs. Koblyk is motioning for us to stop."

"She has something in her hand. Could be something good." He pulled into their drive.

As soon as he turned off the road, Mrs. Koblyk carefully descended the steps from her porch and greeted them when they stopped. Randolph rolled down his window.

"Hello today Mister Judge and Missus Rhetta," she said, her cheeks rosy against the cold. She wore only a hand-knitted cardigan over her skirt and blouse. Not enough to ward off the chill. She shivered as she handed Randolph the plastic sack, recycled from Walmart. "I bake for you the twisted poppy seed bread," she said, smiling broadly. Even after all the years in this country, Mrs. Koblyk still spoke with a broad Eastern European accent.

"Thanks," Randolph said, relieving her of the plastic bag. The contents felt warm. He sniffed. "It smells wonderful."

"I just get them from the oven. The poppy seeds, they may spill a little."

Rhetta stretched over from the passenger seat, and inhaled the delicious aroma escaping from the bag. "This smells heavenly, Mrs. Koblyk. You're such a dear." She wondered if she'd have to hit the treadmill in the morning. That depended upon whether or not Rhetta could hold her share to one slice.

Mrs. Koblyk waved her hand as though shooing away a fly. "It's nothing. Mr. Koblyk, he ask this morning for me to bake the poppy seed bread, so I say, why not? And I make extra for the judge, while I am baking."

Randolph grinned.

"Oh, of course, for you too, Missus," she added. *Of course.*

While Randolph parked, Rhetta headed for the family room, dropping her coat on a kitchen chair on the way. "I'm going to get a fire started, Sweets," she called out. "It's definitely fireplace weather." She placed the bag from Mrs. Koblyk on the kitchen counter. "I think Mrs. Koblyk is sweet on you," Rhetta added. Randolph merely chuckled.

The blinking red message light on the answering machine caught her eye as she loped across the kitchen. She changed course and veered toward it. She punched the "play" button. Her stomach knotted when she recognized the voice.

"George was murdered."

Chapter 6

WITH ONE ARM CIRCLING HIS wife's shoulder, Randolph used his free hand to hit "play" again.

"George was murdered," the wheezy voice began. "You know who this is. I can't talk about this on the phone, and it's too dangerous to meet in person. Go to your office right away, Rhetta, as soon as you get this message. I left a key for you in your mail slot. It fits a locker in the Cape Girardeau airport. What's inside will explain all of this. And, Rhetta? Don't try to find me. It's too dangerous." Then the line went dead.

"Damn," Rhetta said, punching Star 69, trying to call the number back.

"I'm sorry, but the number you have called is not in service..." Rhetta disconnected before the rest of the message finished playing.

She stared at the phone. "The phone he called from isn't in service. Imagine that." She shrugged away from Randolph, and sat on a stool. Her hands shook. She gritted her teeth. "Why? What's going on? What is he trying to drag me into?"

"Are you sure that's him?" Randolph said, enveloping her small hands with his.

"Yes. I'm sure. It's the same voice as that of the man who stopped me in the hospital garage claiming to be my dear old dad. I'd recognize his voice anytime. Wouldn't I love to know how he manages to claim being my father when I have my father's death certificate? If he calls again, I intend to ask him about that."

She visualized the contents of the large manila envelope tucked away in her top drawer at the office. She had memorized everything in it. She had proof positive that her father died during the Vietnam War. So who is this crazy old man claiming to be her father?

Rhetta pounded the counter with her fist. "I'm not going to do a thing that he asks. This guy is a cuckoo, and I won't be dragged into some lunatic scheme of his. 'Too dangerous to meet in person,' my butt. He sounds like a paranoid cold-war ex-spy from an old James Bond movie. I'm going to report this to the police."

Randolph kissed her cheek, and clasped her hands again. "I seriously doubt that there will be any kind of key at the office. If I'm right and there isn't, then definitely call Sergeant Delmonti, tell him about this, and that's that. Who knows? This may even be the guy who ran over poor George. If there is a key, whatever you do, don't go out to the airport. Call me right away. Then call Delmonti. This guy may be following you." He kissed her palm.

Rhetta shuddered. "You're right, as usual. I'm calling Delmonti anyway and telling him about all of this. The police may be able to piece this together." She slid off the stool and hugged her husband. "Right now, I'll get this fire going." As she passed the window, she glanced out, staring through slowly swirling snowflakes down the long driveway toward the road. Nothing looked out of place. No cars or vehicles lurked. Was he out there? Following her? Why?

And, what if there is a key waiting for me?

Chapter 7

Monday morning, December 10

THE DAY DAWNED CRISP AND bright, the sun sparkling like diamonds through the frost-coated trees. The dry dusting of snow glittered in the fields, as though fairies had sprinkled the tops of the weeds with magic sparkles. From her bed, Rhetta gazed out at the river birch trees stripped of leaves, but adorned with thousands of ice crystals. She loved living in the country. She stretched, then slid out from between the warm sheets and her husband's sleeping form, and padded to the kitchen to make coffee. Randolph meandered in just as the brew finished.

She and Randolph had spent most of the previous day packing up more art into the trailer. The Thanksgiving show had been hugely successful and Randolph had to gather more paintings for the last-minute Christmas shoppers who would be visiting the art galleries' open houses all this week.

"I'm going to the gallery early this morning. We have a buyer from Saint Louis coming in around ten, and I want to be sure I have all my stuff unloaded when he gets there. He's buying for shops from Saint Louis and Chicago." Randolph filled his coffee mug.

Rhetta saw his eyes light up as he talked. She brimmed with happiness that his art was finally getting meaningful recognition.

She never imagined when she met the handsome circuit judge at a Humane Society dinner auction that she would one day be married to this terrific man and he would become a successful artist. She had sworn never to marry, and he was a childless widower. Funny how life has such strange twists.

Because her own childhood had been too painful, she had decided not to have children. She grew up hating her father for abandoning them when she was a toddler. She adored her mother, but grew up very lonely, the result of her mother working several jobs to support them.

"I know they'll love your work, Sweets," she said as she refilled her own mug, a large ceramic one adorned with a picture of a black cat. She carried it with her to the master bedroom to shower and dress. She had thought about the mysterious key all the previous day, but didn't speak once of it to Randolph. He had her convinced to call Sergeant Delmonti, and that's what she would do. She wasn't going to rush down to the office because of a nut case phone call to check on any damn key.

She turned on the morning television news and stepped into the shower. Just as she soaped up, Randolph stuck his head into the steamy shower. "I'm leaving, see you tonight." He kissed her wet nose. She threw the soap at him. He ducked just in time.

An hour later, the cats had assembled on the back deck, waiting for their breakfast. She carried a bag of dry food outside and poured a portion into four separate bowls. Then she remembered that she hadn't carried out the trash, so she loaded three full bags into Streak and drove down to the barn where they kept the Dumpster, and wrestled the bags into it.

Finally underway, she decided to swing through McDonald's and get Woody a breakfast sandwich. Before leaving home, she had gulped down a breakfast shake, which was now sloshing in her stomach. She needed more coffee to settle the shake, so she ordered herself a tall coffee along with Woody's sandwich.

A few blocks before she reached the office, she remembered that she needed to pick up some postage. She detoured through the drive-through post office but couldn't remember what she needed, so she went on through without purchasing anything. She waved to the postal lady as she went by and received a strange look and partial wave in return.

Woody had not yet arrived when she got there, and a sense of dread washed over her. She realized that she had deliberately procrastinated, hoping she wouldn't be the first to get to the office in case there really was a key like the phone call had said. She unlocked the front door, slipped in quickly and braced her back against the door. Taking a deep breath, she dared a glance to the floor in front of the mail slot. Nothing. She let out a *whoosh* of air that she hadn't realized that she was holding.

"The old coot was jerking my chain after all," she muttered as she walked slowly to her desk, pausing at Woody's desk to set his sandwich down next to a small stuffed sock monkey that guarded his computer. "I'm glad I didn't make a fool of myself and rush down here yesterday." She balanced her hot coffee until she reached her own desk, then managed to set it down without spilling a drop. After hanging up her coat and scarf, she tugged open the bottom desk drawer and dropped her oversized purse into it. Then she went to the kitchen to make more coffee. One cup would never get her through the day.

The computers had booted up by the time Woody arrived. "Sorry I'm late," he said, huffing as he hurried to hang up his coat. "I had to take Jenn to work this morning. Her car wouldn't start." He spied the breakfast sack. "Did you get this for me?" He didn't wait for an answer, but began unwrapping the sandwich. "Thanks!" He munched hungrily, then strode to the kitchen.

Coffee cup in hand, he swallowed the last of the sandwich, then wiped errant crumbs off his beard as he made his way back to the front office. After he plopped into his chair and tossed the napkin into the trash, he swiveled toward Rhetta. "By the way, I came in here last night to meet new clients, a soldier and his wife, to take their application, since it was his only time off. The outside lights weren't on, so we better call that new maintenance man Jeff hired to help out. I think his name is Evan." He dusted crumbs off his neatly pressed white shirt. "Oh, and something else. I found a key on the floor by the mail slot and put it in your top drawer."

Chapter 8

R HETTA'S HEART SLAMMED AGAINST HER ribs. "What did you just say?"

"I came in here yesterday to take an application, and the outside lights weren't working," Woody repeated. "You probably need to call Jeff to get them fixed. I don't know how to reach that helper he hired. I think his first name is Evan. I don't know his last name."

Rhetta jerked the drawer open. It wasn't the application, or the prospect of calling Evan, a homeless guy with a long, ratty grey beard, that made her heart lurch. There, nestled on top of a sheaf of papers lay a small brass key attached to a rectangular plastic fob bearing a number: 127.

She clasped her hand around it, removed it, and then eased her drawer shut. She took a deep breath and closed her eyes. When she opened them, she scrutinized the little key, front and back. There was nothing to identify where it came from. Should she believe the phone call? Was this really a key to a locker at the airport? And, if it was, should she go and find out? Randolph had told her to call him if she found a key, in case she was dealing with a stalker. She returned the key to the drawer and reached for the phone.

"What's the key for?" Lost in her thoughts, she hadn't heard Woody edge up to her desk. She jumped at the sound of his voice.

"A locker at the airport." She peered up at him.

"Why?"

"What do you mean, *why*?"

"Why did someone leave you a key to a locker at the airport?"

"It wasn't just someone, Woody. I got a phone message yesterday from the man claiming to be my father. He says he left it for me, and I was supposed to go to the airport right away and find this locker. He actually wanted me to go last night." As she told him about the phone call, Woody rubbed his shaved head with both hands. Did the significance of this key upset him? Maybe, but not as much as it was upsetting her. With Woody's PTSD, sometimes it was hard to tell what might get to him. He didn't like talking about it, so she was reluctant to ask.

Just then, LuEllen flew through the door, out of breath and apologetic. "Sorry I'm late," she said, unwrapping a scarf from around her neck and slipping out of her wool jacket. "There's a bad accident on Mount Auburn near Independence. Both sides of the road are blocked and the traffic is getting majorly snarled." She gazed at Rhetta, who took a minute to answer.

"Oh, no problem, LuEllen. Just glad you're all right." Rhetta waved her hand dismissively.

LuEllen picked up her lunch tote and asked as she headed to the kitchen. "Anyone need coffee?"

Woody didn't answer, but Rhetta said, "No, thanks," as LuEllen disappeared around the corner. Rhetta picked up her conversation with Woody. "I'm not convinced. I think it's probably just someone's idea of a not-so-practical joke." She opened her top drawer and tossed the key into it, then slid the drawer shut.

"Aren't you going to go and check it out? I'll go with you," he added, and veered toward the coat rack. He shrugged into his coat, walked to the front door and waited.

Rhetta stared at Woody. He had just volunteered to go with her. This key business apparently piqued his interest, but she didn't question him just then. She'd use the drive time to the airport to quiz him.

She mobilized her senses. "First, I have to call Randolph. I promised I'd call him if a key showed up here." Rhetta couldn't quickly locate her cellphone. It had probably fallen to the bottom of her purse again. She lunged for the office phone and dialed Randolph's cell phone. The call went to his voice mail. "Sweets, there was a key dropped here yesterday. Woody and I are going to the airport to check it out. There's a number on the key, which I guess according to the phone call, is for a locker number. We're going to see if there's really a locker number 127, and what may be in it. I'll call you when we get there." She dropped the phone into its cradle.

Then she slid open the drawer and closed her hands around the key.

Chapter 9

Monday, late morning, December 10

RHETTA HIT THE REMOTE START so that Streak could idle and warm up before they climbed in. By the time they had buckled up, the vents gusted warm air. She turned down the satellite radio that blasted Cousin Brucie and the oldies, slid the SUV into gear, and merged with the southbound traffic on Kingshighway.

What snow had fallen overnight was gone, leaving the streets coated with a dirty slush mixed with mud. Rhetta wove through traffic and eventually eased onto the approach to southbound Interstate 55. The winter sun's brightness forced her to lower the visor against the glare. She fished around the console for her sunglasses, but came up empty. "Woody, can you hand me my sunglasses?" She waggled fingers at him as an invitation for him to rummage through the console until he located them.

He handed them to her. "Do you really think that was your father who called you? And showed up at the hospital parking lot last year?"

Rhetta thought about how to answer. She wasn't positive about the identity of the man who insisted he was her father. Maybe he was a stalker. After all, she had proof of her father's death. Then again, if he was a stalker, why was he so elusive? He wasn't actually doing much stalking, at least that she could tell.

"I don't know what to think. Last year, when he stopped me in the parking lot at the hospital, he gave me this locket." She fingered the locket at her throat. "It was definitely my mother's. Then he disappeared." She didn't tell Woody that the years of hatred toward the man claiming to be her father nearly boiled over the first time Frank Caldwell revealed himself to her. Luckily, she caught herself before she actually ran over him and killed him. That would have generated way too much paperwork. She sighed. She didn't actually want to kill him, but her anger very nearly made her do something very stupid.

She glanced at Woody. "I didn't tell you at the time, but he called me at the house on my birthday, after everyone went home from my party. He said he keeps tabs on me, which, frankly, gives me the creeps." She honked at a pickup that was trying to cut her off as she descended the ramp to the highway. The truck swerved aside. She thought she saw a middle-finger salute as she passed him.

Because the Cape Girardeau Regional Airport was located just a couple of miles south of Cape Girardeau, Rhetta arrowed down the exit ramp mere moments after getting on the interstate in Cape.

"How does he keep tabs on you?" Woody asked, as he glanced at traffic over his right shoulder.

"Beats me. That's why it gives me the creeps."

The airport had a dozen or so hangars that housed a few manufacturing businesses, and some accommodated several private planes. The airport's regional carrier, Cape Air shuttled to St. Louis Lambert International Airport where passengers could connect with major airlines and head out to any part of the world. In its own way, the little local airport served as a gateway to the world. As an added bonus, parking and security was much easier than dealing with the huge international airport in St. Louis, or even Memphis. Most people for a hundred miles around utilized the convenience of flying out of Cape. It made the airport a busy place some days.

Today, however, wasn't one of them. They breezed into the parking lot and snagged a space close to the main entrance.

"Maybe my father's watching us right now," Rhetta said after she and Woody piled out. She aimed the remote device and heard the Trailblazer beep, indicating the doors had locked.

Woody's head swiveled from side to side. "I don't see anybody paying us any special attention. In fact, I don't see anybody at all."

Rhetta glanced around. "Neither do I. I feel pretty stupid. I think someone's playing a joke on me, and is probably laughing his butt off as I run around trying to match a key to a locker." She extracted the key from her pocket and waved it at Woody. "All right, we might as well give them something to bust a gut at. Let's go find this locker." As she led the way, she barely avoided bumping into a thin man hurrying out the front door. A few strands of dark hair from his hatless head lifted in the chilly breeze. He wore the collar of his sheepskin rancher-style coat turned up near his ears. The coat covered him down to his knees, but Rhetta spotted blue jeans and brand name hiking boots.

"Woody, does that man look familiar to you?" When Rhetta looked at Woody for confirmation of her assessment, Woody was looking in the wrong direction. "Over there," she said and turned to point out the man. He was gone.

"Sorry, I guess I didn't see him." Woody followed Rhetta's gaze as she took in the parking lot. "What did he look like?"

Rhetta shrugged. "Medium height, thin. He reminds me of someone I know, but I can't place him." She needed to get a grip. She was imagining stalkers at every turn.

"Maybe he's one of those actors. I read where they will be coming into town today."

"What actors?" Rhetta stopped her march into the terminal, a tan brick building that was a clone of hundreds of other drab buildings from the seventies. "What are you talking about?"

"I read in the paper this week that some of the cast and crew from that movie that will be filmed here next spring are supposed to arrive in town this week. It was on *First News*, too."

"Now I remember. Kelly Davenport was all a-twitter about it. Sheesh. It will probably amount to a big zero, like when they filmed *Killshot* here. They had businesses and streets closed, and everyone was excited. Then when the movie finally came out, they had re-shot every single scene that had been filmed in Cape Girardeau. I think they used a studio to recreate the outdoor Mississippi River scenes. A total bust. I guess that's why I forgot all about it."

"That guy might have been one of the actors. They tend to slip in quietly, you know," Woody said. "It's not always paparazzi and glamour for these actors. A lot of them are almost nomadic, getting parts in movies all over, and living on the road.

"Yeah. Well, I guess we better find the lockers." Rhetta took stock of the airport's T-shaped layout, searching for the storage lockers. Not finding them, she approached an information booth in the center of the T and asked the young man working behind a circular desk where she might locate the lockers. He barely glanced up from his computer screen long enough to point to a hallway behind him.

"Straight down there, ma'am," he said, waving behind him, never taking his gaze from his computer.

"Don't you have to be at least sixteen to work in Missouri?" Rhetta said to Woody as she rounded the desk, arrowing toward the hallway the young man had indicated.

"I think so. Why do you ask?" Woody said, easily keeping pace with her trot.

"That kid back there," Rhetta said. "He doesn't look a day over twelve."

Woody's eyebrow shot up. "Uh, huh. Is that a sign you're getting old? The young adults look like twelve-year-olds?"

"That kid? There was nothing adult about him. He didn't even have facial hair under all that acne." They arrived at a U-shaped alcove lined with metal lockers much like the ones she remembered from high school. All of the painted grey lockers gleamed under the fluorescent lighting. They were lined up numerically with the lower numbers starting on her left and continuing around the U. Rhetta estimated there were about one hundred fifty total. All were closed, but some had keys sticking out, waiting to be rented. Off to the right, one locker stood ajar. Rhetta followed the sequence of numbers until she stood smack in front of the open one. In fact, it was obvious from the angle of the door, which listed forlornly, that it wasn't merely open. The locker door was jimmied off one of its hinges. Rhetta stared at the number on the front: 127. Then, she peered inside.

Empty.

Chapter 10

RHETTA'S HAND SHOOK AS SHE held the key aloft. She squinted to compare the number on it to the number on the locker. She didn't trust her eyes. She reached into her purse and felt around until she located the case for her glasses. She put them on and resumed examining the locker. The numbers were the same. Someone had found the locker before she did, and forced it open. Who? Why? Who else could have known about the locker? And what was in it?

She whirled around and marched back to the information booth. Woody continued examining the locker a moment before following her.

She waved the key at the attendant. "I want to file a complaint. Someone broke into my locker." His eyes tried to focus on the key as she waved it in front of him. "Have you seen anyone go to these lockers? Mine is number 127 and it's been broken open. The door is barely on its hinges, and, of course, it's empty."

She finally stopped flapping the key and the boy peered at it. "Lady, did you just ask me if I saw anyone go to the lockers? Shoot, that's just about everyone who flies. Most of the time passengers can't carry on all the stuff they think they can, so they have to rent a locker until they get back. There's always someone going back there." He rose, scratched at a patch of acne on his face and let himself out through the half door that sealed him in the information booth. Rhetta's first thought when he stood was that his height was due to a raised floor, but when he strode up alongside her, she had to stare up at him. She guessed he was even taller than Woody, who was a foot taller than her. Maybe this kid was actually older than twelve after all.

"Can you show me some ID and your rental receipt?" asked the young man, whose badge Rhetta noticed bore the name Haldane. *Who names a kid Haldane? Isn't that a poisonous gas?*

"I didn't bring a receipt. I didn't think I'd need it. I do have the key." She shook it at Haldane. She glanced sideways at Woody and caught him rubbing his head. She ignored the gesture and returned her attention to Haldane. "Someone must have done this today, or you would have noticed it, right?"

She hoped she'd put Haldane on the defensive and get him to quit asking her for dumb things like a receipt. He returned to his booth and tapped on the keyboard.

"Says here Number 127 was rented to…" He peered myopically at the name. "Frank Caldwell." He turned to Rhetta. "Are you Mrs. Caldwell?"

Rhetta's heart thundered against her chest bones at hearing the name. Whoever had rented this locker had used her father's name!

"No, actually, I'm his daughter. He asked me to pick up his stuff for him." That part, at least, was mostly true. She stole a look at Woody, but couldn't read his expression. When he saw her glance at him, he looked away.

"I'll file a complaint with security, notifying them that someone broke into this locker. You have to fill in a form and let us know what was in the locker." He rummaged around in a drawer and came up with a sheaf of papers. He selected one and slid it toward her. She stared at it, uncomprehendingly. The only thing that she knew for certain was that the man claiming to be her father had told her "what's inside will explain all this." She had no idea what, exactly, *all this* consisted of.

"I, uh, don't know for sure what was in there. He'll be flying back home in a couple of days. Can we fill in the report when he gets here?"

Haldane looked at her and tilted his head. She was sure he could see right through her charade. "That's fine, ma'am. He can take care of it then." He picked up the phone and she heard him call for Security.

"Great." She spun abruptly and sprinted for the door. Woody galloped after her. She heard Haldane call out, "Ma'am? You'll still need to report this to Security. Ma'am?"

Rhetta ignored him and fled to the door.

Once outside, Rhetta braked so suddenly that Woody had to skid to a stop to keep from piling over her. "What are you running away from?" he asked, stepping around her, and glancing over his shoulder.

Rhetta didn't answer. Instead, she held her hand to her forehead to shield her eyes from the sun and scanned the cars and vehicles in the parking lot. "I have a feeling that the person who broke into the locker was the guy I spotted when we got here. He looked at me kinda funny, making me think I knew him from somewhere. It has to be him." She swiveled her head around, continuing her search.

Woody followed her gaze. There was no one moving around the semi-deserted parking lot. Especially not the man Rhetta described. "I think he's long gone, if it was him," Woody said, and began ambling toward the Trailblazer. "I think you have a very vivid imagination." Rhetta followed, still gawking.

Rhetta fumed. "That settles it. I'm convinced this is some kind of stupid practical joke. I don't know who I ticked off, but I'm getting tired of getting jerked around." She aimed the remote device at the SUV and the locks snapped open. "Let's get back to the office, and get some real work done."

Chapter 11

IT STARTED SNOWING LIGHTLY ON the way back. Rhetta veered off Kingshighway into the drive-through at Rob's Roaster, one of her favorite delis. "It's close to lunchtime. Let's get a sandwich and take it to the office." She ordered a BLT on rye for herself. Woody ordered two meatball sandwiches, and balanced the food sacks and two large drinks on his lap as Rhetta navigated noon traffic. She remembered LuEllen had brought her lunch, so she didn't call her to ask about bringing something. Being gluten intolerant, LuEllen usually ate salads. Rhetta wished herself fat intolerant.

Two minutes later, she pulled into the parking lot and found no empty spaces near the front door. She waved at the full lot. "Crap. That DirecTV group in the basement is having a marketing meeting again and nabbed all the spaces. Where will our customers park? I think I should call and ask Jeff about this. They do this twice a week, every week and hog the parking lot all day. They should park in the back, since they're employees." She continued around to the rear of the building, and eased into a narrow spot between a service van and the Dumpster. A hand lettered sign taped on the van's door read, Evan the Handyman. She fumbled a minute in her purse, but came up empty handed. "Do you have your door keys?" she turned and asked Woody, who was looking out the window at the van. "Mine are all the way to the bottom of this freaking black hole of a purse." The futile trip to the airport had put Rhetta in a sour mood, so she decided now was a good time to call and discuss the parking issue with Jeff Patterson, owner of the building.

Woody handed the food bags to Rhetta, reached into his pocket, and produced his door keys.

"Well, well, Evan is in the building," Rhetta said, imitating the long-standing line, "Elvis has left the building!"

"Pretty suspicious-looking sign on his van," Woody jerked a thumb toward Evan's artwork. He didn't seem impressed with it. "It sorta matches his suspicious-looking ratty beard and homeless persona."

"I hope he at least knows how to change a light bulb," Rhetta muttered as she navigated the steps up to the back door. She gripped the railing with one hand, while carrying her bag with her sandwich in the other. The steps were slick from the newly fallen dusting of snow, and she didn't' feel like taking a tumble. "I guess Jeff hired him to be Tony's assistant? Or is Tony no longer working here?"

"Tony's still here. I see him occasionally. He attends the Post Traumatic Stress Disorder Peer Support Group meetings at the VFW."

"Why single out his beard? His hair is a rat's nest, too."

"What?" Woody slid his keys into the lock. "Whose beard?"

"Evan's. You said his beard was ratty, but his hair is a disaster too."

"That beard is so thin, it just doesn't look right. He should shave it off."

"Maybe he doesn't want to be clean shaven. Look at you, you have whiskers."

Woody stroked his own chin growth. "If my beard looked like his, I'd shave it off." He slid his keys into the lock.

Rhetta turned and pushed open the door with her backside. "I'm glad you're still going to the PTSD meetings. Are they helping?"

Woody said, "It's always slow going. So many of the guys are in denial. And of course, funding for the program is going to dry up before any of their problems are solved. Part of the VA cutbacks."

Rhetta swiveled toward Woody. "That's terrible. What can we do about it?"

Just then Lu Ellen called out, "Is that you, Rhetta?"

Woody hadn't answered her question. Rhetta thought he probably figured the question was rhetorical anyway.

"It's just us, LuEllen," Rhetta called back as she clomped down the hall toward the front of the office. Her fashionable brown leather boots tracked slush from her trek up the steps. She hadn't brought any indoor shoes to work. Woody, on the other hand, had slipped his boots off and tucked his feet into a pair of loafers. He'd hung his coat up on the rack next to two knitted hats that looked like sock monkeys. Rhetta grinned. Woody loved sock monkey puppets. He even entertained the sick children at the hospital with them. Rhetta wondered where he'd stashed his shoes, since he'd found them long before he'd gotten to his office, or had even passed the kitchen for that matter. He was always so prepared. She sighed.

"Where did you...?" She didn't finish her question about his shoes, since she had already arrived out front and Woody had detoured into the restroom.

Evan was standing in front of LuEllen's desk. His shaggy grey ponytail hung down past his shoulders from beneath a grubby black wool sock hat crammed down on his head. His grey beard was the usual scraggly mess drooping past his collarbone.

Woody had told her that Jeff allowed Evan to stay in the small apartment in the lower level that had once been a storage area that she called the Dungeon. As she recalled, it didn't have any windows. Evan's red plaid jacket barely buttoned over a bulging tummy. Strange how older men like Evan gained weight all around their middle, while their legs remained stick thin. His were no exception, their thinness made more prominent by the loose-fitting faded blue jeans he wore. His work boots had tracked in slush, and he stood in a small puddle in front of LuEllen's desk.

Rhetta sauntered over and stood in front of the desk. "Hi, Evan, how are you?"

"Good, ma'am," he answered, studying his feet.

"Can you help us out and change the outside light? Woody said it's burned out."

"Yes," was all he said.

Did he mean, "yes" it was burned out, or "yes" he'd change it? She shook her head as Evan shuffled away.

Rhetta turned to LuEllen. "How long was he here before we got here?"

LuEllen reached for a roll of paper towels in her desk drawer and circled her desk on her way to wiping up the puddle of slush that Evan left behind. She tore off a handful of towels and stooped to sop up the mess. "Just a few minutes. He said he thought you wanted him for something."

"I wanted him to fix the outside light, but I don't remember calling about it. Did I?" she added, addressing the question to Woody, who had returned from his detour to the bathroom. She didn't remember calling either Jeff or Tony. And she had certainly not called Evan. She didn't think Evan actually had a phone.

Woody lifted his shoulders in a shrug. "Don't know. Didn't hear you if you did." He filed past her and sat at his desk. He touched the mouse and his computer screen sprang to life.

"Hm. That's strange. Oh, well, just as long as he fixes it." She swiveled to watch Evan as he limped from the bowels of the building, paint-splattered metal stepstool in hand. He set it carefully, then climbed on to it, and reached for the light. Rhetta turned, set her purse down on her desk, then pulled out the chair. She sat quickly and gazed at her monitor, checking her email. When she looked up a few minutes later, Evan was gone.

"I'm glad Jeff gave him a place to stay," LuEllen said, dragging a large bag of trash past Rhetta's desk on her way to the back door. "He said Evan is a Vietnam vet who suffers from PTSD, and who has trouble holding down a steady job. He's such a tenderhearted man."

"Who, Evan?" Rhetta scooped up her trash bag and trotted after LuEllen. Evan didn't appear to be the tenderhearted type. He always looked unhappy, or maybe angry. Anyhow, she didn't think *tenderhearted* when she was around him.

"No, I mean Jeff is tenderhearted. Did you know he's letting Evan stay in the apartment downstairs in exchange for handyman help?" She made *tsk*-ing noises. "I hope he checked him out carefully. I wonder if Evan has access to all of our offices." LuEllen reached the back door and pulled it open. "Here, let me have your trash, and I'll go and toss it into the Dumpster." She reached for Rhetta's sack. "Hold the door for me. I didn't bring my keys."

Rhetta pushed open the door and held it while her head spun with what LuEllen said about Evan having served in 'Nam and suffering from PTSD. Woody didn't know him. He must not go to the support meetings. And did he truly have access to the offices? She needed to call Jeff. She doubted if Philip Corini, the new tenant, an accountant who recently moved to the area from Saint Louis, would like having Evan lurking around and possibly entering offices after hours.

Thinking about Corini made Rhetta shudder a little. She wasn't sure whether she preferred Evan or Corini. The accountant was slencer, medium height, of indeterminate age, with a comb-over the blue black color of a raven's feathers. His eyes were inscrutable, concealed as they always were behind oversized tinted glasses. She had spoken to the man a few times, mostly exchanges about the weather when she'd run into him as he retrieved his mail from the bank of mail boxes out front. He always looked her up and down several times before answering her. When she was within sniffing distance of him, she always detected a mixture of sweat and cheap aftershave, a combination that made her queasy. Being anywhere near him made gooseflesh explode on her arms, and her neck hairs stand at attention and salute.

"According to Jeff, Evan doesn't have keys to our offices," Rhetta said, hanging up. "But I did remind Jeff that our cable company friends are copping all the parking spots again with those stupid meetings. I don't know why Jeff rented the basement out to those guys anyway. It's too dingy down there for offices, anyway."

For heaven's sake, Rhetta, they're only here two days a week. As Momma used to say, don't get your panties in a knot. She regretted complaining to Jeff. She could almost hear Randolph chide her about her impatience. She pulled open her middle desk drawer, again. The manila folder was still there, taunting her.

Chapter 12

Tuesday, early morning, December 11

RHETTA COULDN'T SHUT HER BRAIN down enough to fall asleep. Having tossed and turned after going to bed, she finally turned on her bedside light and began a new mystery novel. After an hour into the plot, and learning from the eerie green glow of the LED clock that it was already well past midnight, she finally got drowsy enough to attempt sleep for the second time. Just as she lay the novel down and was reaching to turn out the light, the phone shrilled, making her heart pound and adrenaline surge through her like white lightning through a mountain man.

She hated middle-of-the-night phone calls. They never brought good news. Like the time her sick mother took a bad turn and the detached voice at the hospital summoned her. Every late night phone call brought that sickening memory streaming to the forefront, as though it had only been a few weeks instead of many years. Her stomach clenched. She groped on the nightstand for the phone to silence it before it woke Randolph, but instead, she sent it crashing to the floor loudly enough to wake the dead.

She rolled over the side of the bed and snatched it. Before she could speak, she heard a voice that she instantly recognized. Except it warbled like it was traveling though through a barrel of water. "Rhetta, I'm sorry if I woke you, but this is urgent." More warbling.

"Right now, sleeping is what's urgent to me." *Damn, now what?* "I'm going to hang up. I don't want to talk to you!" The surge of anger instantly replaced the knot of fear. She thought how good slamming the phone down in his ear would make her feel.

"That would be a big mistake, Rhetta. Please don't hang up."

Randolph propped himself up on his elbows as she untangled herself from the covers and stood. "Who is it?" he mouthed.

"My father," she mouthed back. Randolph groaned and lay back against the pillows.

The warbling stopped, replaced by a far-away sounding voice. "I'm using a satellite phone, so listen carefully. I don't have much time. You have to write this down. Do you have a pen?" His voice remained stonily calm.

Groping for a moment since she'd already removed her glasses, she finally located the pen and pad that she kept on her nightstand. "Hold on, Buster, I need to know some things, first. How can you be alive and bothering me when I have your death certificate?"

"I can't answer your questions right now. Just write down what I tell you. I'm taking a chance at even calling you on your house phone."

"What?" she said, unable to conceal the agitation in her voice. "I have to write something down but you won't answer a question? I don't think so."

He ignored her protest and continued, "I had a video for you, along with some paperwork, but it got stolen from the airport locker, so now this is the only way for you to see the video. It's vital that you see it. I started a YouTube account. Here's the login." He read off the information. "Read it back to me, please."

"A YouTube account? Are you freakin' kidding me? You call me in the middle of the night to give me a YouTube login? I'm going to hang up." She fumbled for the off button on the handheld, but couldn't find it without her glasses.

"Be still, Rhetta. I'm not playing games. Please read it back to me I need to know you have this information."

His serious tone made her change her mind about disconnecting. Instead, she grabbed the pen and scribbled the information, in large characters, then read it back.

"Go to your computer right now, and log in. I'm going to publish a video within the next five minutes, and then two minutes later I'm going to take it down. I can't risk anyone else seeing it."

"It'll take a minute for my computer to boot." Her feet found her slippers automatically. She always left them in the same place.

"That's about how long it will take to upload this. Do it now." He ended the call.

"What's going on?" Randolph asked as he slipped into his own house shoes and followed her to her computer.

"It's my father again. He said he's using a satellite phone, and gave me an account login for YouTube. He instructed me to log in and see some video he's posting."

"A YouTube video? What on earth?" Randolph padded up alongside her.

She powered her computer, then found a pair of reading glasses by her keyboard. The computer quickly chimed, signaling it was ready.

She opened a browser and typed the information he'd given her. "Invalid login" appeared on the screen. She closed the window and reopened it a moment later, and tried again. This time a video window appeared and she clicked on "Play." As it began to load, she clicked "save" and stashed it onto her hard drive.

A grainy color video flickered, revealing six men standing in a semi-circle, backs to whoever held the camera. The video bounced unsteadily, then captured an image of a man's arm obviously adjusting the camera. There was no way to discern a location, other than they were inside a dimly lit building. Light bounced from a single hanging light bulb. The camera light stretched out weakly ahead of the subjects, barely illuminating them.

"Frank, come over here," a gruff voice called out.

"Coming, hang on a sec." The man tossed the cigarette he was smoking to the floor and ground it out with his boot.

She recognized that man's voice.

She watched as the back of him joined the others. The film kept rolling. Frank had apparently set the camera down. All she could see was mostly the backs of everyone's heads and a couple of profiles. The gruff voice began speaking. "We are all Garibaldi Tontine," he intoned. All the heads nodded once. "I am Laurent Delor," he continued. A second man spoke, "I am Marcel Grisando." Following him, a man announced he was Cooper Worthington, then William Beshnarik, Alejandro Rodriguez, and George Erickson all identified themselves until finally, the voice she recognized. "I'm Frank Caldwell." Her stomach clenched at hearing the name. Her father!

Laurent wordlessly handed Frank a stainless steel cylinder roughly the size of a small vacuum bottle. Each man placed his right hand on top of it, like a baseball team grasping the top of a bat handle. They recited in unison, "We live and die together until there is just one. We are called Garibaldi Tontine." Then they turned and displayed their bared right arms to the camera. Rhetta peered at the screen, wanting a better look at the mark on their arms. The camera moved so shakily she couldn't identify the marks. The men stepped back, except for Laurent, who turned toward Frank.

"Because you are the youngest of us, I, the eldest, bestow this duty on you." Laurent ceremoniously opened the cylinder and placed a scroll inside, then carefully closed it back up again and handed it to Frank. "You will be the keeper. Our secret name is Garibaldi in honor of Guillermo Garibaldi, our fallen platoon leader." They all nodded solemnly. Frank accepted the cylinder. The men stepped aside. Rhetta could see well enough to read the date on the hand written banner tacked up behind them: August 6, 1973.

Frank turned sideways. Rhetta gasped, her hand flying to her mouth as she recognized a younger version of the man she'd encountered recently. It was her father, she was sure of it. The video faded out. Cold chills enveloped her. What about the man in the video who called himself George? Could it possibly be the same George Erickson who was killed by a hit and run? And the date on the banner—August 6, 1973—the same date as her father's death. And George Erickson's too, according to the newspaper article. Her hands shook. She needed to watch the video again. As she clicked on it, a window opened. "The content of this video is no longer available." She swiveled around to stare up at her husband, who had watched it over her shoulder.

"It's gone. I wanted to watch it again. He said he wasn't going to leave it up." She shook her head and turned back to the blank screen. "What on earth does this mean? Who is Garibaldi Tontine?" She sunk her head in her hands, and rubbed her temples. "Or what is Garibaldi Tontine?"

Randolph massaged her shoulders. She leaned back gratefully. "My clever wife downloaded it and saved it, remember? Let's watch it again. I think I may know what, if not who, Garibaldi Tontine is. I also need to see what that mark is on their arms."

Chapter 13

RANDOLPH HURRIED TO THE BEDROOM and returned with his glasses.

"I found it," Rhetta said. "Get settled in, and I'll play it again." When he stopped alongside her, she began replaying the video.

They watched again, silently. This time, Randolph clicked the mouse and froze several frames. "I want to study this strange mark on their arms." He scrutinized the blurry image of an unusual tattoo that each man bore on his arm.

"I'm convinced this man is the man claiming to be my father," Rhetta said, tapping the computer monitor on the image of Frank. Pointing to another figure, she added, "And I'll bet money this is George, recently deceased."

"I agree. Now we just have to figure out what's going on." Randolph minimized the screen and opened a new search.

"You said you know what this Garibaldi Tontine is?" Rhetta watched him open several browser windows.

Randolph pointed to a page from a legal website. "I know what Tontine means. It's an old type of financial trust that's set up like a reverse pyramid. I think some Italian named Tontine started this scheme back in the 1800s." He read from the open document. "It's an agreement in which investors receive annuity payments, with the special provision that when one participant dies, his or her share goes to the others, increasing the payments to the survivors. Generally, the last to die receives the remaining funds." He squeezed her hand. "Or, I should say, the survivors of the last to die get everything that's left. That could be a boatload. Tontines are illegal in the United States, by the way. I suspect it is indeed a Tontine trust. Sounds like they named it after their leader, a guy named Garibaldi. And that "Garibaldi" is also the password. The Tontine trust has to be established in a country that permitted this type of financial trust."

"What is it he wants me to know about this video? What is he trying to tell me? I'm so confused. I need coffee. Do you want some?"

"I do. I think sleep is out of the question for the rest of tonight." He took her hand and led her into the kitchen, and propped her up on a stool. He began assembling the coffee fixings.

Rhetta rubbed her temples. "All right, my super-smart husband. Tell me what you think is going on."

While the coffee brewed, Randolph joined her at the counter, carrying over the necessary enhancements to the coffee—sugar for him, sweetener and skim milk for her.

"I think that all these men are part of a Tontine Trust agreement, one I assume is named Garibaldi. I believe all of them deposited a sum of money to form this agreement. But where the money came from is anyone's guess. They could have all been involved in absconding with gold from the South Vietnamese. There was a lot of it missing after the war ended." He arranged the coffee cups in front of them. A plain white one for him, the black cat one for her.

"Where the story goes from there, or why it was started, is probably the reason your father wants you to see this so badly. It's possible that none of the original members of the Tontine are left. And if your father is so hell bent on you knowing about this, it must mean that he knows he's the last survivor and is trying to give you some information." The coffee completed its aromatic journey from the brewer to the carafe, and Randolph poured them each a cup. "And naturally, that's the part I don't like."

"Me neither, because now I'm mixed up with this. If there really is a Tontine trust, then if we assume each of those guys in the video is a part of it, then do my father's suspicions that George was murdered have to do with George's share? And if so, who murdered him?"

"That, my love, is undoubtedly what the cops have to find out. Whoever broke into the airport locker knows that your father is still alive, and probably wants him dead, so he can collect. He's probably the one who killed George Erickson. And now, because you know about it, I believe dear ol' dad put you in real danger." He sipped his coffee, then set the cup down and took both of Rhetta's hands in his. "One of the guys we saw on that video is a murderer."

Chapter 14

"WE NEED TO LET THE police know about this video," Randolph said, as he helped Rhetta clear away the coffee cups. "I think it's definitely connected to George Erickson's death. In fact, I'll make a call to the coroner and ask him if there was any unusual marking on George's arm like what we saw on those men in the video. We need to fill Delmonti in on what we just saw."

Rhetta nodded slowly. "I agree. Plus, if that mark is on poor George, then we'll know for sure that he is the same guy. Matt Clippard will tell you, won't he?" she added.

"Matt and I go back a long way. He's not like his predecessor, 'Stick-in-the-mud Sickfield.' Matt will let me know what, if anything was on George's arm. And if for some strange reason he didn't note it, the funeral director would probably notice it." Dr. Julian Sickfield, the county's previous coroner who held the job over twenty years, was well known for not sharing information.

Rhetta downed the last of her coffee as he continued. "We don't know exactly what kind of marks the men in the video have. They look like tattoos. I suspect the cops will have to enhance the video to see them more clearly. However, if George has no mark, then there's nothing to go on. Besides, there's no 'we' here, Rhetta. We turn this over to Sergeant Delmonti and let the cops solve it."

"Of course, Sweets. That's what I meant."

Rhetta watched him raise one eyebrow at her. She knew what that meant. He wasn't convinced that she would stay out of it. Her curiosity was epic. However, she didn't confess to him that this whole thing scared her, and that she'd much rather stay out of it and let the police solve the murder. This whole thing was getting too crazy, like a bad movie.

Instead, she said, "Old Frank said he thought he might be taking a chance even calling me on our home phone line. Do you think someone bugged our phone?" The thought of that made her head expand. Or maybe it was the lack of sleep and the introduction of caffeine into her bloodstream at such an early hour. "Do you know anyone who can check out our phones for us?"

Randolph's hesitation was enough to convince Rhetta that he believed their home phones might be compromised.

Then a thought hit her smack between the eyes. *How did someone know about the locker key number? Are my office phones tapped?* 'Sweets, maybe we better have him check my office, too. Someone knew that I was going out to the airport and what the locker number was. They had to have gotten that information from when I called you." The thought that her phones were no longer private made her ill. They discussed a lot of personal information with borrowers over the phone.

"I'll ask Billy Dan Kercheval. I just saw him yesterday, and he said retirement wasn't much fun in the wintertime since he couldn't fish. This will give him something to do beside sit down there at Merc's Diner and grouse all day."

"Good, the sooner the better. But Billy Dan retired from Inland Electric. How would he know about phone lines?" Rhetta rinsed out the cups and the coffee pot. "Anyway, Ricky should be keeping him too busy to grouse. Billy Dan and Ricky are still seeing each other."

Although, Rhetta mused, Ricky hadn't mentioned Billy Dan much lately. They'd been seeing each other on and off since last year. Were they in an off phase? She hoped not. She liked Billy Dan, and his quiet way helped keep Ricky calm.

Randolph sidled up beside her. "He started out working for the phone company before he went to Inland. He'll know what to do." He scooped Rhetta up and hugged her tightly. He traced her cheekbone with his thumb. "I don't like any of this, Rhetta. Promise me you won't get any more involved in this. If you hear from your father, you need to let Delmonti know right away. And me," he added, kissing her forehead

She hugged him back. He was the love of her life, and she would do what he said.

Deciding she was much too keyed up for any more sleep, she sought the quiet of the basement gym to exercise and clear her brain. She loved the rhythmical hum of the treadmill, where she could walk and think. She turned the machine on low and began walking. While she walked, she ran through everything she knew about her father. While she was growing up her mother had always told her that her father had left and wasn't coming back. Rhetta had not heard a single word from him until recently, when an old man claiming to be her father showed up in the hospital parking lot while Randolph was in the hospital. She increased the speed to a fast walk.

She had proof in her desk drawer that her father was dead. Yet this man came to her with evidence that he was not only alive, but was indeed her father. He gave her a locket that had belonged to her mother. Then he called with mysterious information, convinced his friend George was recently a murder victim by hit-and-run. *What does George have to do with all of this? And what does all this have to do with a Tontine trust?*

"Ow, crap, that hurt." Deep in thought, she didn't realize she had stopped walking until she went flying off the back, smacking her rear soundly against the wall. After considerable moaning, she pulled herself up and turned off the machine. The treadmill had a safety clip that she should have snapped to her shirt, which would have stopped it when she flew off. However, she hadn't worn it. Lesson learned. With her butt, arm and one leg aching from her collision, she gave up thinking and

limped upstairs in search of more coffee. She couldn't tell Woody what just happened. He'd never let her live it down.

The kitchen clock with giant numerals she could read easily without her glasses informed her it was barely 5:30. The aroma of bacon and eggs greeted her as she entered the kitchen. Randolph had already showered and cooked breakfast. The smell of eggs turned her stomach, but she joined him for wheat toast and bacon at the counter. She couldn't get used to eating eggs early in the morning. She preferred her eggs in an omelet, and for supper instead of breakfast.

"Sweets, I've been thinking about all of it," Rhetta said, limping to the table and reaching for the homemade strawberry jam, another gift from Mrs. Koblyk. "I can't wrap my head around this. How can this guy really be my father when I have his death certificate? Plus, we know that George Erickson died, too, the same day as my father, if the police information is correct. I'm getting the feeling that this is an elaborate hoax."

"That date is the same date as on the video. That is significant. But why?" Then Randolph eyed her suspiciously. "Why are you limping? I heard a thump downstairs. Did you fall off the treadmill or something?"

She waved her hand. "Oh, it's nothing. I think I turned my ankle."

He eyed her warily but resumed eating. "I'm not so sure it's a hoax," Randolph said as he finished mopping up his eggs with his toast. "I think Frank may be your real father. Somehow, I think George Erickson was trying to reach your father, and it got him killed. Or, he did make contact, possibly getting your card from Frank, which would explain how he came to have it when he got hit. Furthermore, I think it has something to do with their Tontine Trust. They may have all faked their deaths. That's why they all have the same date of death. I bet if we looked up the other members, we'd find their dates are the same."

"You may be right, Randolph. Something else bothers me. When or where or how would Frank have gotten my card?" She racked her brain. As far as she knew, he'd never been to her office. He did know where it was, so maybe he'd been in when she wasn't there. That could have been possible. She'd ask LuEllen and Woody.

Of course, she had plenty of business cards around the city. He could have picked up a card in a number of places, even the grocery store, where she had promotional information on display, along with her cards. "Now that I think about it, anybody could have picked up my card at the grocery store. I should have told Delmonti that."

Randolph stopped her. "There's too much coincidence, and neither you nor I believe in coincidences. That's why Sergeant Delmonti needs all of this information. You need to call him, tell him where in town your cards are readily available, then we can be done with all of this."

Rhetta finished the last of her toast, chasing it with a final swallow of coffee. "You're absolutely right and believe me I don't want a thing more to do with any of it. If that man really is my father, I don't want him contacting me again. I don't see any point in it. He wasn't around the whole time I was growing up, so he can stay away now."

She meant every word she told Randolph about staying away from all the intrigue. She slid off the stool and headed to the bedroom to shower and dress. She resolved to tell Delmonti about the YouTube video as soon as possible and end her involvement in this once and for all. She would call him as soon as she got to her office. Randolph would be pleased. She was pleased with herself for her decision. She began humming an oldies tune, and headed to the shower.

An errant thought skittered around in her head. *I sure would like to know how and why my father is mixed up in this, and now, me. What the heck is going on?*

A different little voice answered, "Mind your own business, Rhetta." That voice sounded a lot like her mother's.

She couldn't listen to her mother now, either.

Chapter 15

Friday morning, December 21

ALANGUID ORANGE SUN HOISTED itself slowly from a dark horizon into the morning sky on the shortest day of the year—the first official day of winter. Red-orange fingers of light seeped through the clouds, turning their edges from dark indigo to daylight golden. Rhetta watched it all from her kitchen window as she sipped her morning coffee. Randolph was still in the shower, and she'd turned off *First News* so she could relish the breaking dawn in peace and quiet.

Although there had already been one early round of snow and ice, the weather had turned unseasonably mild for the final week before Christmas. Rhetta picked out a multi-toned blue wool tweed blazer to coordinate with her navy slacks and donned her high-heeled boots. She didn't feel the need for a heavy coat. High afternoon temperatures were forecast to peak around sixty degrees.

By the time she arrived at the office, she'd had to root around her purse for sunglasses, and had even rolled the driver side window down enough to bring in some fresh air. And to dispel any lingering smoke odor that may have clung to her jacket.

She'd stopped at the Gas 'n' Go on the way in looking for coffee, even though she'd just finished the mug she'd taken with her from the house and would soon be at the office where she would put on another pot. She paid for her beverage, plus a bakery turnover for Woody and two crisp apples, one each for LuEllen and herself. And, before she could stop herself, she ordered a pack of cigarettes. While she was waiting to pay, she had watched the young woman working behind the counter climb down from the ladder from stocking up the cigarette bins with fresh packs. Smelling the new fresh cartons stacked up fueled an uncontrollable urge to smoke.

After paying for her sorry booty, she peered around to see if anyone she knew was in the convenience store. Not spotting anyone she knew, she dashed outside clutching her plainly wrapped package to her bosom. She stopped beside Streak, hands shaking, while she fished out the pack, tore into it, then lit up. Like a junkie she'd seen toking up in a movie recently, she inhaled deeply, closing her eyes while the nicotine rush spread through her body. After four more drags, she tossed the still-lit cigarette onto the asphalt, and stomped it out with the heel of her boot. She plucked the dead butt and tossed it, along with the rest of the unused package into the nearby Dumpster. Before she could make it to Streak's driver door, the foul odor of the full Dumpster hit her and she threw up. She glanced around to see if anyone was watching her. If anyone did happen to see her, they'd probably assume she was hung over or was purging. One look at her figure and anyone would know she wasn't thin enough to be purging.

Her truth was just as sad. She had just binged on cigarettes, causing her to throw up. She had fibbed to everyone, including her husband, telling everyone that she'd quit. Not only was she hiding the truth, she was lying to herself. Disgusted, she rolled the window down and prayed the smoke smell wouldn't linger on the sleeves of her jacket and gauzy print scarf.

Maybe it was the stress making her act out. She had heard nothing from Sergeant Delmonti in over a week. She'd shown Delmonti the video and told him everything she knew. He hadn't said much, only asked her if she could make him a copy of the video, which she did. He took plenty of notes about Tontine trusts.

Also, she had not heard anything more from her father. For that, she was glad. He had probably disappeared again, as was his pattern. After a sharp intake of air, she tasted the stale smoke at the back of her throat. She coughed, then groped around the console for the Tic Tacs she usually kept on hand. She found the plastic box and slid several out into her palm, then plopped them into her mouth.

She was reasonably sure that their phones weren't tapped. Last week, Billy Dan had checked the office and their home, and found no evidence of any phone tampering. Again, she was relieved, but now she couldn't figure out how anyone knew about the key at the airport. Her father must have told someone. Maybe someone he trusted. Her head began spinning about the key, her father, Tontine trusts, and hit and run accidents. No wonder she caved in and smoked. At least that's what she told herself.

She was alone in the office shortly after lunch when Evan shuffled through the front door. Woody had left around ten to meet Jenn and finish his Christmas shopping, and LuEllen had gone to the bank. If possible, Evan looked even more unkempt than usual. Rhetta met him near LuEllen's desk.

"Hi there, Evan. What's up?" she asked as she settled her haunch on the corner of LuEllen's metal desk.

"Jeff asked me to come by and give you this," he said, handing her a strange-looking key.

"What's this for?"

"It's a new key to the lock on the Dumpster. Someone broke the lock on the old one, so the trash company got us all new keys."

"Thanks." Rhetta tucked the key into one of LuEllen's desk drawers. Evan didn't leave. He clutched his grubby wool sock hat, fingering it, turning it over in his hands. Rhetta tried to avoid looking at his matted hair, but couldn't keep her eyes from darting to his head. His coat was even shabbier than the last time she saw him. And was that a lingering scent of alcohol that drifted her way?

"Sit down, Evan. Can I get you a cup of coffee?" She motioned to a guest chair in front of LuEllen's desk as she stood, ready to head to the kitchen if he said yes. He remained standing.

"No, no coffee. What is it you need?" He jammed the sock hat back on his head, and stuffed his hands into his pockets.

"Do you have any family around here?" Rhetta wondered if he had anywhere to go for Christmas. She had called Jeff and asked him to send Evan around to her office. She felt sorry for Evan, especially being a veteran. Besides, since she guessed him to be about the same age as her father, she wondered if he knew Frank.

"No, ma'am." From the dark look on his face, Rhetta worried she may have crossed a line.

"What will you do for Christmas?"

"Do?" He looked genuinely perplexed.

"Do you have somewhere to go for Christmas?"

"Here, ma'am. I'll be staying in my apartment." She had hoped he had family, since she'd heard from Woody that Evan was a Vietnam vet. He turned and began shuffling toward the door.

"Evan, I know it's none of my business, but I was wondering if I could ask you about your tour in Vietnam."

She saw his shoulders stiffen. He stopped, then slowly turned toward her.

"What about it?" His voice had an edge.

"My father served in Vietnam, too."

"That so?"

"I think he did until 1973. When were you there?"

"Until 1973, too, ma'am." He had reached the door.

"That's a coincidence. My father was Frank Caldwell, US Army. You didn't know him, did you?"

Evan straightened his back momentarily. Then, he slouched again, his hand on the door. "Maybe. There were a lot of us discharged about that same time. I don't keep up with any of them."

"My father wasn't discharged. He was killed. At least I have a death certificate. But someone claiming to be my father has shown up recently." She wasn't sure why she told him this, but she wanted a reaction from Evan. Maybe he'd heard of this happening to other veterans. According to Woody, Evan didn't attend the local PTSD support group. But then, Woody said a lot of soldiers didn't. Too many wounded warriors couldn't get help. Woody occasionally commented on that, and Rhetta agreed that the government should step up and do more.

"Sorry, ma'am, how do you mean he showed up? Didn't you say he was killed?" Evan's tone changed, and he tilted his head sideways.

Didn't he believe me?

"Yes, that's what his death certificate says. I really find it odd that I have a death certificate, and he's maybe not dead. Did the Army mess up a lot of Vietnam veterans' records?"

"Couldn't tell you, ma'am. Guess he's not dead if you seen him recently."

"Right, Evan. That's what my husband says, too."

"Anyway," Evan said, shuffling toward the door. "Don't think I knew him. I got shot, and sent home. Been messed up ever since. Happened to a lot of us." For the first time, Rhetta noticed his erratic gait was due to a limp in his right leg.

"Did you get shot in your leg?"

"Yeah, my leg. Don't lay any sympathy on me, 'cause I don't want it." He pushed open the door and limped out. Stung, Rhetta sat down hard.

Old Evan wasn't very friendly.

Chapter 16

"LuEllen, how old is Evan?"

LuEllen had returned from her errands, her fingers flying over her keyboard. She glanced up from her monitor at Rhetta's question. "I wouldn't know, why?"

"He was in Vietnam, so he's got to be what, sixty anyway, right?"

LuEllen stopped typing. "When did we clear out of Vietnam? Wasn't it around 1973, '74? If he was eighteen then, or nineteen, he could be late fifties, or if he was in his twenties, he'd be sixty or more. Why on earth do you ask?"

"No real reason. He came in here earlier and I was trying to talk to him. He said he got shot in 1973, so I was trying to guess his age. He looks to be in his sixties, I think."

LuEllen nodded and went back to the computer. "Thanks for the nice crisp apple. It was delicious."

"No, it was Gala."

LuEllen snickered.

Rhetta snatched up her phone and set off down the hall to the rest room. She always carried her phone with her. She felt naked without it. It vibrated in her hand a second before it rang.

"Hey girlfriend, what's happening? I saw where I'd missed your call." Ricky Lane always sounded chirpy. She was one of those people perpetually in a good mood. Although she was a Realtor, she had put her real estate license on inactive and was working full time at Fast Lane. She specialized in restoring sixties- and seventies-era muscle cars. She was the best mechanic around. She was also one heck of a body and paint expert.

She had always gone by her nickname, Ricky, but after about the millionth time some man had commented that he thought Ricky Lane, mechanic, was a man, she announced to everyone that maybe she should go by her real birth name, Victoria. She was met with resounding disagreement among her friends. Rhetta told her there would be no confusion once anyone met her.

Rhetta grinned. "I just wanted to remind you of our Christmas Open House."

"Wouldn't miss it. By the way, I have great news." Her voice practically bubbled through the line.

"What, you and Billy Dan got engaged?"

"No, silly, better than that." Her giggle was infectious.

Rhetta figured if it was better than romance, it had to involve muscle cars. She knew where her friend's passion lay. "You got a new car."

"Ding, ding, ding, give the girl a prize! Corr-rr-ect!" She laughed. "Well, you know. New for me. I bought it for myself for Christmas."

"Uh huh, and I bet it's a 1965 Mustang." She remembered Ricky scouring the countryside for a first year Mustang. "That you will paint red," she added, having heard Ricky expound numerous times about the correct red paint for whatever year car. To Rhetta, red was red. Not so to Ricky.

"Close. It's a 1967 Mustang Fastback, decent condition, just needs my magic worked on it. And yes, it will be Candy Apple Red."

Rhetta joined in her friend's laughter. "I guess you need a project, since you finished with Cami, and sold The Beast." The Beast was Ricky's 1979 Black Trans Am. She had listed the muscle car on eBay and on Craigslist and it sold on eBay for a great price. There were plenty of bidders on it, and Ricky realized a tidy profit.

Ricky, quieter now, said, "I'm gonna miss The Beast, but it went to a good home in Kentucky."

"And more importantly, the check cleared," added Rhetta.

Ricky giggled. "That, too."

"All right, what will you name this Mustang?" Ricky named her cats, too.

"I'm not sure. I'll have to be around it a while to tune into its personality."

"Tune in, that's cute." Rhetta snickered. "I'm confident it will reveal its true persona to you. Anyhow, be sure to bring Billy Dan, any time after noon. Lots of food, and I've already visited *Primo Vino!* and got your favorite Riesling."

"Sounds great, we'll be there." They disconnected, and Rhetta stuffed the iPhone into her blazer pocket. Randolph always chided her when she put the phone in a pocket, telling her that she'd lose it someday. Besides, her purse was in a drawer. She'd move it to the purse later.

She grinned when she pictured Ricky, her shoulder-skimming red hair tucked up under a ball cap and her lithe figure draped in green work coveralls. Although she was stunning when she dressed up, Ricky preferred jeans, work clothes and ball caps. Ricky was the garage-ista to Rhetta's fashionista.

LuEllen shut down her computer and began slipping on her coat. Rhetta glanced at the clock, and was surprised it was past quitting time. A quick peek out the window confirmed the hour. The sun had already set. She was irritated at herself because she hadn't gotten much done all afternoon. Although there weren't many new applications for home loans this time of the year, she had continuing education to finish by year's end, and another day had slipped by without her going online to read the material. She sighed and turned off the computer. She had a few more gifts to buy, then she'd head home.

After waving to LuEllen as she eased her red Kia Soul out of the parking lot, Rhetta stood on the sidewalk outside the door, shivering in the dark, riffling through her purse for keys. The night air was much cooler than morning had been. Noticing that the doorway was in total darkness, she glanced up. The outside light was out. Again. She remembered Evan replacing it. *Must have used a poor quality of bulb, or there's something wrong with the fixture.* "Crap," she muttered, groping in her purse. "I can't believe this danged light is out again," and buried her arm in her purse. "I'll call Jeff first thing in the morning." Closing her hand around a cluster of keys that would make a truck driver jealous, she pulled them out triumphantly. She had barely inserted the key into the door lock and turned it when a searing pain exploded in her skull.

She never felt the concrete meet her face.

Chapter 17

Friday night, December 21,

OH GOD, WHAT IS THAT AWFUL SMELL? Her stomach roiled. She nearly retched. She shivered violently. *Where am I? Why am I so cold?* The foul odor combined with bone-penetrating frigid air brought Rhetta around. When she tried opening her eyes, she realized they were already open. Lying on her stomach, head turned sideways, she was staring into absolute blackness. She had no idea where she was, except that she knew positively she wasn't in her bed. She was so cold she was shivering uncontrollably.

She strained to roll over but the effort produced a searing pain in the back of her head. She reached up and touched it gingerly, and felt a thick, sticky glob. She drew her hand back and the coppery smell of her own blood made her stomach clench. She struggled to remember what had happened. Her head began to spin. She felt the nausea rise again, and gulped to keep from retching.

She lay still, gathering her senses. It hurt to think. She was so cold, and her head throbbed. She couldn't see anything but she could smell rotting food. She felt the panic rise. Where was she? What happened? A familiar memory identified one particularly nasty odor as stale pizza. She gagged. Why was she lying with rotten pizza? Was she in a garbage can?

Taking a deep breath, and using all the strength she had, she managed to turn over and sit up. A wave of dizziness and nausea flooded her. She squeezed her eyes shut until it passed. The throbbing at the back of her head intensified. Trying to get her bearings, she thrust out her right arm and her hand slammed against a metal wall. Her ring connected with the side, clanging loudly. "Ow," she yelped. Slowly she tilted her head back and gazed upward, but saw nothing but blackness. With her left hand, she reached out, and soon felt another metal wall. She explored underneath herself, and felt plastic trash bags and crushed cardboard boxes. She was atop a mound of garbage. She tried to stand, but couldn't—the pile under her was too spongy and she was too wobbly. She slumped down heavily, realization rocking her. *I'm in the Dumpster. Dear God, what's happened?* Gathering all her strength, she tried again to stand, this time bracing herself against the side of the bin with one hand, and reaching above her with the other. She pushed against the metal lid, but it held snugly. She tried again, but it wouldn't budge. She visualized the key that Evan had brought them, which she'd left on LuEllen's desk. The lid was locked firmly in place. She began to feel woozy from the exertion, so despite the repugnance for where she had been sitting, she eased herself back down. This time she couldn't control the nausea. She turned her head and vomited.

Tears of pain, frustration, and disgust streamed down her face. How on earth would she get out? She fumbled around for her purse and her phone. After plunging her hand repeatedly into the pile of garbage around her and coming up empty-handed, she abandoned the effort. The sickening realization blanketed her like a bad smell. Her purse hadn't accompanied her into the Dumpster. Whoever had slugged her had stolen it. She'd planned to go shopping, so she had a good deal of cash in it, plus her credit cards. Then she felt her hands and realized she still wore her rings and her watch.

She tried to remember exactly what happened. She hadn't seen whoever sneaked up behind her and conked her. Because her purse was gone, she was sure the motive was robbery. What about her jewelry? She still had it on. Her ruby ring, a gift to herself for her fortieth birthday, had cost a bundle, even on sale. The diamond solitaire she wore next to her wedding band exceeded two carats. Why hadn't the thief taken the rings?

She began banging on the side of the bin, shouting for help, hoping that Evan or Jeff, or anybody would hear her. She'd even be glad to see that weird Philip Corini. Then, abruptly, she stopped, as reality slapped her upside the head. *If the thief threw me in here, it's probably because he thought I was dead. If I make a racket and he's anywhere around, he may come back and finish the job.* She began to feel sick and clammy all over again.

She tried to remember what day it was. *How long have I been in here?* Her teeth were chattering from the cold. She didn't know how long she'd been out and couldn't see well enough through the darkness to read the time on her watch. She tugged her blazer tighter around her for warmth. *I remember, now. I was going shopping. It's Friday. The garbage pickup isn't until early Monday morning. I have to get out of here! I may die before Monday. Oh God, was that the plan?* Tears trickled down her cheeks. *I don't want to die today.*

Especially not in a Dumpster.

Chapter 18

S HE HAD THRUST HER HANDS into her pockets in an effort to keep them warm. When she did, she cried, then laughed, giddy with gratitude.

She had found her iPhone!

"What did you just say?" Randolph asked. "We must not have a good connection. I could have sworn you said you were in a Dumpster."

"That's what I said. I'm in a Dumpster, and I think it's the one as big as a boxcar behind the office. It's locked. I can't budge the lid. Can you come and get me? Someone whacked me on the head and threw me in here. I think I was knocked out. I just now found my phone."

"Whacked on the head? Are you all right? What happened?"

Rhetta told him. At least all that she could remember of it.

"Did you call 9-1-1? Do you need an ambulance?"

"I did. The cops are on their way. I just need you to come and get me. I'm so cold and I don't feel good. I want to go home. Bring a ladder, or a stepstool and maybe a hacksaw." She tried not to sob, even though that's exactly what she wanted to do. By now she had worked herself up into a full-blown mad. She hated that she often cried whenever she got mad. She didn't want Randolph thinking she was going all girly on him and crying just because she was trapped in a smelly garbage Dumpster. Which, until she'd found her phone was exactly what she had done. Finding her phone was an answered prayer.

She didn't go to church as much as she should, but that didn't stop her from praying for a way out. She'd always heard there are no atheists in foxholes. She was there to attest that there were none in locked Dumpsters, either.

The egg-sized lump on her head throbbed every time her heart beat. And right now it was beating wildly. The pain reverberated like a drumbeat in her head. She yearned to get hold of whoever did this to her, and shake him 'til his teeth fell out. And then conk his noggin just so he'd know what it felt like.

"I can hear the sirens now, Sweets, so the cops should be here in a second."

"I'm on my way. I have a stepladder in the back of the truck. I'll drive down and get a hacksaw from the garage. Stay connected 'til the cops arrive. I sure hope they can get you out so you won't have to wait until I get there."

She heard him rustle around the kitchen, open and close the door. Then the familiar sounds of the Artmobile firing up.

As she listened to the comforting noises of Randolph coming for her, she heard a vehicle approach the bin, and a siren power down. Help had arrived. She heard voices and shuffling around the front of the bin.

"Anyone in there?" Deep, male voice. She prayed again that it was from a man in uniform.

"Yes. Please help me out!" Rhetta sobbed with relief.

"Are you all right?"

"I'm freezing. Please, hurry." Her voice cracked and her teeth chattered. She clutched the phone, Randolph still on the line.

His inquiry was followed quickly by a sawing noise.

Rhetta chattered into the phone, "They're here and must have a hacksaw. I hear them sawing through the lock."

"All right, I'll skip looking for a hacksaw. I'm on my way."

The Dumpster lid flew upward and a light beam wobbled over the rim to her. "Ma'am, are you all right?" an officer asked.

"No. No, I'm not. I got walloped on the head and tossed in here. My head hurts."

To Randolph, still on the phone she added, "I'm going to hang up now. The police are here. I want out."

They pushed the lid open all the way, and shone the flashlight in as best they could. "Is there anything in there for you to stand on?" an officer asked. He played the light beam around the interior. He snugged up close to the Dumpster and reached up as high as he could, trying to direct the beam back toward Rhetta. "God, this stinks," he muttered.

Rhetta ignored his comment. "I'm already standing on it. This pile of garbage."

She couldn't scramble out over the top. When she tried clambering up, she was too short to get any purchase. Plus, she wasn't sure she had the strength to pull herself up to the edge. Her head throbbed.

"If we can get a ladder in there to her, we won't have to get into the Dumpster," the cop said to someone Rhetta couldn't see. "Is there a ladder nearby?" The officer then aimed his light beam around the outside of the Dumpster.

Oh gee, don't inconvenience yourselves on my account. Rhetta forced herself to keep her retort locked up in her mouth. "There's probably one in my building, but I don't have my keys. They were with my purse. My husband is on his way, and he's bringing a ladder." She began shivering harder now. The wind had picked up and the temperature had dropped considerably.

"Hold on, Ma'am, I have a blanket in the patrol car." She didn't hear the trunk open, but heard it slam shut. "Ma'am, I'm going to throw a blanket in to you." He tossed it over the side and she caught it.

"Thanks," she said, truly grateful, and began tugging the blanket around her. Her teeth chattered at high speed while her shivers kept time to the chattering.

Just as she wrapped herself up, the sky lit up with headlights. Randolph had arrived. He drove straight to the Dumpster, and was out of the truck almost before he had time to put it in park, leaving the motor running.

"Officers, I have a ladder. I'll climb up there," he said as he went to the truck bed and grabbed the ladder. He flattened it against the bin, then began climbing calling out to Rhetta. "I'm here, and I'm coming in there to get you."

When he reached the top, he leapt into the Dumpster unhesitatingly, and landed on the garbage. "Help me get the ladder inside here," he shouted down to the cops. They pushed the ladder over the side. Randolph set it against the bin's interior wall. Rhetta hugged his neck as he scooped her up. "Are you all right?" he whispered as he hugged her fiercely. She nodded and hugged him back as hard as she could between shivers. "All right, then, let's get you out of here." He steadied the ladder and helped his shaky wife up the ladder and out of her Dumpster prison.

An officer shouted as Rhetta reached the top. "Can you ease yourself over?" She shook her head.

"I'll help her over," Randolph said, climbing up behind her, and steadying her as she slid her legs over the top of the bin, and sat on the narrow wall.

"I'm going to toss the ladder over again, so she can climb down," Randolph shouted.

Rhetta gripped the side as hard as she could while Randolph turned her loose for a moment to hoist the ladder back up and over. After he did, she half slid, half stumbled down the ladder where the officers caught her. They held her arm as she regained her balance. Not waiting for the cops to slide the ladder back over, Randolph hoisted himself up and over the side of the Dumpster, and scurried down the ladder.

"Do you feel up to giving us a statement, ma'am?" one officer asked Rhetta. "If not, we can follow up with you at the hospital, or at home. The sooner we know what we're dealing with, the sooner we can apprehend this guy."

"I want to get her right to the hospital," Randolph answered before Rhetta could.

"I understand." The officer, said.

"It's okay, let's get this over with now, Randolph," Rhetta said. The officer nodded and guided her toward the patrol car. He fished his notepad out of his pocket.

Randolph hugged Rhetta's shoulders and held her close in the backseat of the warm patrol car while she gave her statement. In a few minutes, the officers were done.

Rhetta pointed to her SUV. "Streak is still here. Can you make sure it's locked?"

As Randolph checked the Trailblazer and found the doors locked, the officers jogged to the front door of Rhetta's office to search out any clues. The door was secure, with no sign of Rhetta's purse anywhere around, and no sign that whoever had attacked her had tried to get into her office. The outside light near the door was still out.

Randolph tucked Rhetta into the front seat of the Artmobile where she melted into the warmth of the truck's interior. The officers tapped at the driver's door window, and asked if Rhetta would please come to the station as soon as she felt up to it. She agreed, and handed Randolph the blanket to give back to them. They went to their car, then pulled out of the parking lot. Randolph followed.

Rhetta lay back against the soft seat back and closed her eyes, savoring the tiny whiff of her husband's aftershave, a distinct improvement over the rank smell of her clothing. Eyes closed, soaking up the warmth from the electric seat heater, she said, "You know, Sweets, I feel better. Let's just go home."

"Sure," Randolph said, and turned on to Kingshighway. Then he barreled straight for Saint Mark's Hospital. Rhetta closed her eyes and sighed, but didn't protest. Her head still throbbed. She opened one eye and glanced at the truck clock. The LED read 10:35. She'd been locked in the Dumpster for more than four hours—some of that time, unconscious. She shivered.

Someone had tried to kill her.

Chapter 19

Saturday morning, December 22

RANDOLPH EASED INTO THE BEDROOM, balancing a small tray with fresh coffee and wheat toast. He set it down carefully on Rhetta's nightstand just as she woke up.

"How're you feeling?" he asked, fluffing the pillows behind her so she could sit up.

"Kinda like I got hit with a baseball bat." Rhetta fingered the small bandage on the back of her head that covered the stitches and the shaved spot around them as she scooted upright, balancing against the pillows.

After arriving at the hospital, they spent over three hours in the emergency room getting X-rays and a CAT scan, and then waiting for a radiologist to read them, and a staff physician to clean and stitch the wound. They hadn't made it home until after two.

"What time is it?" Rhetta twisted to peer at the clock.

Randolph caressed his wife's cheek. "It's nine-thirty, but don't worry about what time it is. It's Saturday and you don't have to go anywhere."

Relieved, Rhetta lay back against the pillow.

"Oh, great." Rhetta squeezed her eyes shut. "It's the Saturday before Christmas. Yikes. I had shopping left to do, and stuff to get ready for the open house," Rhetta lamented. She began to sit up.

"Let's cancel the open house. I don't know what other shopping you need to do, but whatever it is, it can wait until after Christmas. Besides, everything will be on sale the day after Christmas." He kissed her gently. "Don't worry about it. Our friends will certainly understand."

She reached for her coffee. "I really don't feel all that bad, Randolph. Can't we at least have the open house? I was so looking forward to seeing everyone. That's three days away. I'll be up to it." She set her coffee down, and slid the covers back. She searched the floor with her feet until she found her slippers. "That coffee went right through me, so look out, I'm heading for the bathroom." With that, Randolph helped her to her feet. She listed to the left, but managed the rest of the way unassisted.

As she made her way back, Randolph said, "If you feel better and still want to do this, I bet Mrs. Koblyk would probably love to help hostess the open house. She planned to bring some of her famous baked goods anyway. If you're better tomorrow, I'll talk to her." He kissed Rhetta, then helped her back into bed. "But not until tomorrow, when we see how you're getting along. If you're still walking like a drunken sailor, then I'll cancel." He picked up the coffee cup. "You want a refill?"

"Please," she said, smiling. "Mrs. Koblyk would be perfect."

Rhetta began practicing walking straight as soon as Randolph left the room.

The phone startled her, but she ignored its insistent ring. She knew better than to hurry to answer it. She didn't need to fall. Randolph could answer it. It stopped, but a minute later, it began again and continued belligerently until she finally reached it. When she picked it up, she heard only the steady hum of a dial tone.

Randolph returned just as she set the phone down. "Who was that?" He handed her an oversized mug of steaming coffee, which she accepted gratefully.

"There was no one on the line. Probably a sales call or, worse, a political call." She made a face as she reached for her toast.

Randolph said, "By the way, Woody and Jenn brought Streak home last night, so you don't have to worry about that."

Crap. She had forgotten all about her vehicle!

He went on. "I'm going to feed the cats, then head to the studio. I have my cell," Randolph said, as he waved it at her. "Call me if you need me. That way you can practice walking and I won't disturb you." He grinned, but his smile faded. "Your pistol is in your nightstand. I may have to run to Albertson's Supplies for some odorless paint thinner, but I won't be over ten minutes. Make sure you can get to your pistol. I'm locking the house when I leave."

Rhetta stretched across the bed to the drawer in the nightstand and verified her weapon was at the ready.

Chapter 20

Saturday morning, December 22

AFTER HOOFING IT AROUND THE bedroom until she could navigate without listing, falling or getting dizzy, Rhetta headed for the shower.

After rummaging through her travel bag, she produced a shower cap that she had scored from a hotel room when they were on vacation a couple of years ago. She normally washed her hair with every shower, and as short as her hair was, it was usually dry by the time she finished dressing. A little gel and a blow dryer was all she ever needed.

She eased the plastic cap gently over her head. The doctor had warned her not to get the stitched area wet. Turning the water on as hot as she dared, she pointed the nozzle away from raining directly down on her, and then stepped cautiously into the shower. Now would not be a good time to fall.

After showering long enough to deplete the hot water, Rhetta stepped out feeling almost human again. She picked her favorite giant white towel to dry off with, then donned a dark blue jogging suit. She returned to the bathroom mirror to study the skid marks on her face, and apply some antibiotic ointment. The phone began to ring. She ignored it, hoping that Randolph would hear it in the studio and answer. After six rings, it quit. Within seconds, it began again. She padded out of the bathroom and to the desk in the corner of the bedroom, the closest phone to the bathroom.

"Yes?" she said abruptly, unable to keep the annoyance out of her voice. If it turned out to be a sales call, she'd give someone a giant piece of what little was left of her mind. None of her friends or business contacts ever called her on her home number. She preferred using her cell, so she was sure this was not a call she should have even answered. Their home number was on the "No Call List." She looked forward to blasting whoever it was.

"Rhetta, I need you to meet me. Today." His voice still sounded like it was gurgling through a barrel of water. Her immediate urge was to hang up. Instead, she said simply, "No."

A raspy cough finally broke the silence. "You must. This is critical. I'll explain everything."

"Then let's hear it."

"Not on the phone. Meet me behind the Tri-County Impound Yard on Highway 177. Can you be there in two hours?"

"Not just no, but hell no! I was attacked and robbed last night, my skull took a pretty good smack and I was thrown into a Dumpster the size of a Burlington Northern rail car. I'm not driving anywhere today, especially not to meet you."

The line went quiet except for a few gurgling sounds. Getting angry, Rhetta spouted, "Did you hear me?" When she didn't hear an answer, she reached over to slam the phone down. Frank began speaking again before she disconnected.

"My God, Rhetta. That was no robbery. Someone's after you. Someone who thinks you know what I'm going to tell you, and for that he'll kill you. You have to be very careful. You can't come alone. Bring your husband with you. And a gun. I'm sure you have one."

Icicles of fear tickled her spine. "Why can't you tell me on the phone? I had our lines checked, and they aren't tapped."

"I don't trust conventional methods of checking lines, Rhetta. There's so much you don't understand. Meet me and I'll explain it all to you. You deserve to know all of it. The impound yard sits on high open bluffs. You have to find a way to get there. I'll be waiting. If anyone follows you, I'll be able to spot them, and I won't show myself. Please be very, very careful. And don't forget. Bring your weapon." He disconnected.

Rhetta flung the phone across the room.

Chapter 21

Saturday morning, December 22

HER HEART THUDDED AGAINST HER ribs in fear, while at the same time anger sliced through her like a meat cleaver through butter. She couldn't believe she'd just tossed her new phone-cum-clock radio across the room.

Damn him anyway! What does he mean that someone tried to kill me? It was a snatch and grab, according to the police. What the hell is so mysterious? I don't want to meet him. I won't go!

She retrieved the phone and slapped away a tear. *Stop it. Put the phone back and think about what you're going to do. You know you want to go if for no other reason than to get to the bottom of this.*

She plopped down on the side of the bed and ran her fingers through her hair. "Ow," she yelped. She'd unthinkingly run her hand over her tender spot.

She went to the bathroom, peered at her reflection and checked out her head. *Au naturel* would have to be her *coiffure du jour*. She wasn't going to blow dry or spike her hair today. She still bore skid marks that were now bruising a nice purple shade where she'd greeted the concrete face-down. She splashed cool water on her face, toweled it gently, and then applied a light dab of makeup.

She thought about what her father had said as she donned a pair of freshly-ironed jeans and a tan sweater. What exactly did he have to tell her that was so critical that she had to meet him in person? Did she dare meet him? She pulled a few strands of hair this way and that to cover the circle of stitches, but her hair was too short. She gave up and pulled a loose sock hat on her head instead. She decided she had to go. She'd persuade Randolph to take her.

Downstairs, she called out to Randolph. He didn't answer. He was probably in his studio. She spied her iPhone in its charger on the kitchen counter and called him. The call went to voice mail. Tossing her phone into her purse, she decided she could drive down to the barn, find him, and persuade him in person. As she began backing Streak out of the garage, a blue, seventies-model Chevy C-10 pickup truck roared up behind her, blocking her exit. A petite figure in green coveralls wearing a Camaro cap bounced out and jogged to her. Ricky clasped Rhetta fiercely.

Ricky's cap tipped back and several tendrils of red hair escaped, curling down the side of her small oval face. Her green eyes glittered. "I was so upset when I heard. Are you all right?" She released her hug and held Rhetta out at arm's length, scrutinizing her up and down.

"Just a little smack on the head," Rhetta said, turning around, and pulling up the sock hat to display the results of her misadventure.

"Ow, that looks painful," Ricky said as Rhetta carefully repositioned the sock hat.

"Randolph called and told me what happened. I was under a car, but I showered and came right over. Can I do anything for you?" She narrowed her eyes as she took in the open garage door and Streak idling. "Wait a second, just exactly what were you doing? Were you going somewhere?" She put a hand on her hip and tapped her foot.

"I was only going down to the barn to get Randolph to see if he would drive me to the Tri-County Impound lot."

"To the impound lot? What for?"

"It's a long story. Back your truck up over there." Rhetta pointed to the circular turn around. "Come with me. I'll explain."

Ricky bounded over to her truck and backed it to the designated spot. She scurried into the passenger seat of the Trailblazer. "Are you supposed to be driving?" Rhetta shook her head. "Then I'll drive." Rhetta put Streak in park and the two women traded places. Rhetta reached over and turned down the oldies she had blaring out of the Bose sound system.

Ricky wheeled Streak out of the garage and veered toward the barn and Randolph's studio while Rhetta filled her in about the most recent phone call as well as the robbery and attack.

"I can't believe you got tossed into a nasty Dumpster." Ricky made a face. "I'm sure glad you're okay." A smile teased her lips. "I have to ask, Miss Fashionista, what did you do with the clothes you had on?"

Rhetta wrinkled her nose. "The slacks are toast. There's a hole in the knee from where I must have fallen because I have a bruise on my knee that matches the location of the hole." Rhetta touched her knee gingerly. "I tossed the pants into the trash. I'll take the blazer to Lenderman's Cleaners. I hate to throw it away. It's one of my favorites." She sighed, and shook her head sadly. "I'm not sure anyone can ever get the smell out, but if anyone can, it would be Lenderman's."

Ricky nodded. "Your face is pretty messed up too."

Rhetta touched her bruises. "Yeah, where I face-skidded on the sidewalk." She peered in the mirror on her visor. "I guess I don't have on enough makeup. I remember having my purse, and I think it broke the fall, or I might look worse. Of course my purse was gone by the time I woke up in the Dumpster."

"I knew you carried that ginormous purse for some reason! It finally got put to good use." Ricky smiled as they reached the barn. Pointing to the purse Rhetta now carried, she added, "I figure you wouldn't miss one purse anyway. You have several more."

"True, but it's my wallet that I'm upset about. Randolph said he would notify all the credit card companies to stop the accounts. What a pain."

They pulled around to the studio. Randolph's truck was gone.

Rhetta fished in her purse for her cell phone. Before she could dial, she spotted a voice mail from his number. "I didn't even hear this thing ring," she groused, tapping on the message. "Our service out here is horrible."

A tinny version of Randolph's voice said, "Since you're not answering, I guess you're taking a nap. I'm out of thinner, so I'm going to get some. Be right back. Keep the doors locked. Call me if you need me, okay? Love you. And, Rhetta? Get some rest."

Rhetta dialed his cell number. The call went to voice mail. "Sweets, Ricky is here and is taking me to Tri-County Impound. Call me and I'll explain."

Ricky threw up her hands. "I guess this means I'm taking you to Tri-County Impound."

Chapter 22

RICKY PROPELLED STREAK AROUND THE final curve on Highway 177 before the road snaked to the top of the hill overlooking the Mississippi River. The city of Cape Girardeau, originally settled by French-Canadian immigrants, sits in a large bend in the Mississippi, framed by massive limestone bluffs overlooking the wide river. Ricky stole a glance at Rhetta. "Do you think your father really will be at the impound yard?"

Rhetta shrugged. "I presume so. If all of this is so unbelievably important, I figure he'll stay at least long enough to make sure I'm going to show up. Or not." She pulled her .38 from her purse.

"Dear God, Rhetta, don't be waving that thing around." Ricky nearly drove off the side of the road when she spotted Rhetta's gun. "Why do you need that? Who are you going to shoot?"

"I don't plan on shooting anyone. He said to come armed just in case. So I grabbed my .38."

"Oh, God, Rhetta, now what are we getting into?" Ricky immediately began chewing her fingernails. They were already as short as humanly possible, so she began gnawing on her cuticles. "Dang, now I'm bleeding." She had gnawed too close.

"I seriously doubt everything he tells me. I have a conceal-and-carry permit. I know how to shoot. I didn't want to take any chances."

"I know you're a good shot, but you know I don't like it when we go somewhere and need a gun. That's never good."

Ricky rolled to a stop in front of the locked gates of the impound yard. Inside, all was quiet, no one moving about. No sign of Eddie Wellston, the owner. The lot contained several vehicles, some wrecked, some waiting to go to auction. Eddie picked up repossessed cars as well as wrecks. An eight-foot tall chain link fence topped by razor wire extended from the back of the rectangular metal shop building-cum-garage with a small wood-sided addition, which served as the office, enclosing the lot and yard. Eddie owned a large private junk yard behind the impound lot that was also fully enclosed.

"Stay here, and keep the motor running. We may have to leave in a hurry." Rhetta tucked the gun into her purse, swung open the passenger door and strode toward the gates. A black and tan German shepherd the size of a pony lunged at the fence when she approached. He slammed into the chain link, growling and barking, biting at the chain link, sending spittle flying in a five-foot arc around his swinging head. Rhetta's heart felt like it could explode until she realized the dog was also enclosed. She nearly let loose her bladder. She jumped back from the fence. The shepherd crouched at her retreat, but continued growling, curling his lip and baring very long teeth.

Rhetta returned to the safety of the Trailblazer and tried to get her hyperventilating under control. "Crap. That dog nearly scared the pee out of me. I think we need to get the blazes out of here and go home. I don't see any sign of Frank." She had a hard time calling him her father.

Rhetta buckled in and studied the side mirror as Ricky threw Streak into reverse and began backing away. "When in God's name did Eddie get a killer dog?" She tried to resume breathing normally. She clutched her hand to her chest, praying her heart would slow down before she had a heart attack.

From the corner of her eye, she caught a slight movement off to the side of the lot. She shouted, "Stop!" Ricky slammed on the brakes.

"I just saw him." Rhetta twisted around and stared out the back windows, but there was no one there. "I swear I just saw him."

Ricky followed her gaze. "You did. There he is." She pointed to a man standing at the edge of the lot, camouflaged by scrub trees and brush.

"Drive over there." Ricky made a Y-turn and drove across the parking lot, stopping at the edge, near the woods that surrounded the property.

A figure stepped out from the camouflage of the trees and approached Rhetta's side of Streak. She powered down the window.

Frank swiveled his head, apparently scoping out the area, then reached in to the interior pocket of his worn leather coat and pulled out a thick brown envelope tied with heavy string. He handed it to Rhetta. She felt something cylindrical shaped inside the envelope. Could it be the cylinder she saw in the video? She turned the envelope over in her hands before settling it on the seat next to her.

"What is this?"

Frank straightened up and peered around before answering. Then he leaned in close, pointing to the package. "There's information in there about what you saw on the video. About the trust. What's important to realize now is that I'm the last one, Rhetta. I guess I was supposed to already be dead." He coughed so deeply Rhetta wondered if he would ever take another breath. Finally, he did, and continued, wheezing loudly. "In fact, the bank sent me notice that someone claiming to be George Erickson tried to claim it already." He coughed hard, and struggled to breathe. When he managed to catch his breath, he continued. "Not sure, but I think it was just after he was killed. I believe his murderer is after the trust money. He must've thought I was already dead. There have been lots of rumors about my death, but they were greatly exaggerated." A quick smile crossed his face. "Once I'm gone, it's all yours, Rhetta. You're my only child, and as my survivor, you get it all." He pulled an inhaler from a coat pocket and tried taking a deep puff of the medicine. The effort only produced more coughing.

"Get all of what? What is this?"

He cleared his throat. "Read it carefully. It's all in there. And remember the name Garibaldi. G-A-R-I-B-A-L-D-I. Repeat that back to me."

He's not making any sense. What car? Who or what, is this Garibaldi? They called themselves that on the video. Is it a club?

"Repeat that back to me, Rhetta." He said again. "It's vital. You will need Garibaldi as a password, a verbal ID. The rest of what you need is in the envelope. And you'll need to get the car." He wheezed harder.

"I don't follow you. What car are you talking about?" She swiveled her head to locate the vehicle he was referring to. She saw none. "And what's a Garibaldi?"

"The car's not here, Rhetta. Write the name Garibaldi down, if you have to, but remember it. Now, listen carefully." He wheezed, coughed so violently again, that Rhetta wasn't sure he could go on. He sucked in air and continued. As he spoke, the air he expelled from his lungs made a whistling noise. "You have to go to Kansas City to get the car. The address is in the papers." He pointed to those beside Rhetta. "It's a cave storage facility. The unit is under my name and your name." He coughed and spasmed again, but this time he didn't hide his handkerchief quickly enough. She saw the blood. He stuffed the handkerchief into a pocket.

"What's wrong with you?" she asked, pointing to his pocket.

"I told you. I'm dying." He said it so simply he might have been announcing the weather. "That's not important. Listen carefully." He paused, getting his breathing under control enough to continue. "Someone killed George Erickson. We were the last two. Now that he's gone, I'm the last person left in the trust. When I'm gone, it's all yours. Whoever killed George is after you now. I don't know who it is. There's an imposter out there trying to steal the trust. I'm sure that's why George was killed, and why you were attacked. Someone who knows about the trust is trying to convince the bank he's the last one." His wheezing was so loud, it made Rhetta wince. "I know everyone else is dead. I have proof. It's in the pouch, inside there." His chin jutted toward the large envelope on the seat. "You need George's death certificate, and mine after I'm gone. I'll be dead soon, so it's up to you to go and claim the trust."

He rolled up the sleeves on his right arm and showed it to Rhetta. "See this? It's the mark. It was in the video and it's all explained in the papers. George had the mark, too."

Rhetta remembered seeing a tattoo on the video. She stared at his arm. It bore the same tattoo, a triangle with a bar, and looked to be about two inches square. Exactly like the ones she saw in the video.

"Where did the money come from? Is it stolen from the Vietnamese?" Randolph had thought there was something very suspicious about the men in the trust acquiring a large sum of money. He was sure it was stolen. Rhetta thought so, too.

He shook his head. "That money came from Uncle Sam. And we earned every penny. You just need to read what's inside there." He gestured toward the envelope.

His death certificate. That there was a death certificate for her father and George Erickson could only mean something military, classified. "Were you Black Ops?" She stared at him. He didn't flinch.

He wheezed so heavily that Rhetta thought she might have to take him to a hospital. When he finally caught his breath, he said softly, "We were darker than Black Ops. That's all you need to know. The important thing is, we had an agreement, and now I'm the last one. What's left is mine."

"If you're the last, and it's all yours, why don't you go and get this money?"

"I wouldn't survive the trip. It will be up to you."

"What if I go with you?" *What the heck did I just say?* She mentally slapped herself.

He stared at her a moment, another tiny trace of a smile teasing one corner of his wrinkled lips. He shook his head. "The money won't do me any good. Besides, I won't live through the trip. Then you'd just have to deal with an old dead man." He coughed long and hard again. In spite of herself, Rhetta began to feel sorry for him. She wondered if he was going to keel over here, and she'd have to deal with him now.

"When you do go, how will I know, and who's supposed to handle your funeral?" *Oh God, did I really just ask him that?*

He waved his hand. "Don't worry about that. I've made arrangements. When I leave this place today," he waved around the lot, "I'm going to be with someone who will contact you when I'm gone. Someone I trust. I don't want you to have to deal with my death. You didn't have to deal with my life."

Rhetta nodded slowly. "Did you tell the police all this?"

"No, I want you to do that. I can't go to the police. I'm already dead." He took another labored breath. "Don't lose these papers, whatever you do." He laid a thin hand on her arm. She felt a current shoot through her. In that moment, she knew without a doubt that this man was her father.

His voice cracked again, and he began another coughing fit. As unreal as all of this seemed, Rhetta was now convinced that someone was after him and now her, for a mysterious trust with an unknown sum of money. The cops were dead wrong about her attack. That was no "snatch and grab," as they put it.

She needed to look through those papers.

"After you go through these papers, go to Kansas City, then go to the cave and get the car." He coughed again. His hand returned the tissues to his coat pocket. More blood. Rhetta's head began to spin. He shifted gears so quickly Rhetta had trouble keeping up.

"Okay, dammit. What cave? What car?" Her head was reeling. Maybe it was from the bump, or maybe it was because she was having a conversation with a man she now believed was her long dead father about Black Ops, trusts, caves and cars. She felt a massive headache crowding her stitches and worming its way around to her forehead.

He raised his head slowly, piercing green eyes identical to hers boring through her. Even though he wheezed heavily, his breathing labored, she heard his answer clearly enough.

"My 1967 Camaro."

Chapter 23

Before Rhetta could answer, her father turned abruptly and melted into the woods. For a sick man, he moved like a cat, a quick and dangerous one. She sat, stunned, staring at the envelope. Ricky, who'd been listening to all of this, was the first to speak.

"Did he say he has a 1967 Camaro in a cave in Kansas City? I bet I know that place. It's called The Cave Storage, and it's fantastic. All underground natural storage. Like having stuff in climate-controlled units. How silly. It is climate controlled. It's a cave." Ricky slapped her head. "Sorry. I'm babbling. I think I'm stressed."

Rhetta closed her eyes and sank against the backrest. "What the heck is going on?" She sat up and turned to Ricky.

Ricky placed both of her hands on the steering wheel. Her expression turned serious as she faced Rhetta. "Somebody attacked you and tossed you into the Dumpster. The cops told you it was a robbery, but how many robbery victims are thrown into a Dumpster? Let's get out of here in case he's right and someone is after you." She swiveled her head in both directions apparently scoping out for any intruders, then put Streak into gear and aimed for the entrance onto Highway 177, about fifty feet from where they'd parked. She stopped, checking the traffic in each direction. Even though it bore a fancy name like State

Route 177, it was only a two-lane blacktop road, not unlike a lot of county roads in the area. The impound yard sat on a large curve in the road, which made getting out of the yard dangerous.

Rhetta lay back against the seat, eyes closed, pondering everything Frank had told her. Did she dare believe he had a 1967 First Generation Camaro? And that it had been in storage all this time in Kansas City? Why was he telling her about this? To prove he was really her father and wasn't dead? Was it because, as he said, he was close to death? If his racking coughs were any indication of his health, she believed that to be true. How much longer did he have? A month? Two? Six? A week? She had no idea. She believed now he really was her father. Yet it was hard to have any feelings for him, except sympathy for his struggle for breath. Maybe he'd been a lifelong smoker and was paying the price now. She remembered seeing him with a cigarette in the video.

Ricky's voice jolted her back from her musings. "I can't believe it. When are we going to go and get it?" Ricky always had a way of bringing everything to a bottom line. "I wonder what kind of shape the Camaro is in." Turning to Rhetta, she continued. "You know, those caves stay very dry. The car could be in perfect condition. I'll hook up the aluminum car hauler. Maybe Randolph will let us use his Artmobile."

Rhetta just shook her head. Her father, who was supposed to be dead, who claimed he was going to die soon, just gave her a mysterious bundle. He declared it was associated with some form of Tontine Trust, and told her to go to Kansas City to the Cave Storage to get a Camaro that had to have been there for more than forty years. And that she should remember the name Garibaldi? She began to think she'd gone to sleep and awakened inside a Woody Allen spy movie. Did Woody Allen ever make a spy movie? Maybe he just did, and she was the star. She groaned.

How did he come to have the car? When did he buy it?

"Don't get too hopeful, Ricky. It's probably a hunk of junk. Let's hope at least that he's paid the storage fees current or I'll probably have to pay a whopper of a bill to get it." Rhetta sat forward. "I'll call the place and see if I owe anything before I think about going. I won't do anything until I read through these papers." She patted the bundle alongside her. "And I sure want Randolph to go through this package, too."

"I wonder what color…" Before Ricky could finish, an explosion ripped the still, cold air. Rhetta pivoted toward the sound in time to spot a ball of fire as it rocketed to the tops of the trees.

Right where her father had walked into the woods.

Chapter 24

"OH, MY GOD! WHAT JUST happened?" Rhetta shouted as she reached for the door handle. Before she could turn it to get out of Streak and investigate, she spotted a man running from the woods, away from them toward the other end of the impound lot. His unbuttoned sheepskin jacket flapped as he fled.

She threw open the door, jumped out and shouted, "Stop. You there, stop!" The running man ignored her and bolted to his ride, a pickup partially concealed behind a towing trailer at the end of the lot. She hadn't seen any truck when they got there. Had he arrived while she was talking with Frank? Frank! Where was he? Did he go up in that inferno? In spite of her mixed feelings about Frank, tears threatened to spill out of the corners of her eyes. She batted them away. The departing truck's engine had roared to life and gravel spun as it flew through the back gate. Why was that gate unlocked?

"What kind of truck was that?" Rhetta shouted to Ricky, who had followed her out of Streak.

"Looks like a 1999 Ford F-100 extended cab," Ricky answered. If Ricky saw it and identified it, you could take it to the bank.

The trees and underbrush were now blazing. Rhetta ran back to Streak in search of her phone. When she reached for her purse, Ricky was already calling it in on her cell.

"I'll call Eddie. I hope his whole place doesn't go up." Rhetta groped around her purse until she found her phone. His number was in her contacts list.

After reaching Eddie, she hung up and stared at the orange sky and billowing black smoke. In a few short minutes, the piercing wail of sirens signaled the arrival of the fire trucks. This inferno could be disastrous given the drought and the dry underbrush. Even though they'd had some snow, everything was still dry. She was relieved the fire department responded so quickly.

"What on earth was that explosion?" Rhetta asked Ricky as they sat in Streak, watching for the fire trucks. "Was that the direction where Frank went?"

Did Frank cause that explosion? Or did someone just try to kill Frank, just like he had worried about? Who was the man who spun away in the truck? What on earth was happening? She cradled her head in her hands. She thought her head might explode, too.

Three fire trucks roared into the lot followed closely by the Cape Girardeau Sheriff, Talbot Reasoner. Rhetta knew immediately it was Reasoner from the license plate bearing *Cape Girardeau County Sheriff* and the number one. She groaned. That's all she needed to top the day—an encounter with Sheriff Unreasonable.

Back when Randolph was still judge, Talbot Reasoner had asked for Randolph's support in the election. Randolph explained that as a judge, he had to remain non-political and couldn't endorse anyone, but pledged that Rhetta would give generously to his campaign. Which she did. Later, when Randolph had a bad accident and was arrested for driving while intoxicated, Reasoner bailed on their friendship, and did nothing to investigate the accident. Rhetta was forced to solve the mystery herself. She couldn't stomach the law officer after his treason to their friendship.

She joined with the many defense lawyers and prosecutors who called him Sheriff Unreasonable. The name suited him perfectly.

She'd called him that to his face once when she was selling him tickets to the Humane Society gala. His face had reddened and he'd stammered. Rhetta had merely smiled.

Rhetta wasn't smiling now as she leaned back against the seat and watched Reasoner amble over to the Trailblazer.

"Well, well, if it isn't Rhetta McCarter. Again. And Miss Lane. What a surprise." Reasoner beamed his phony politician megawatt smile, showing off a mouthful of dazzling white teeth. She decided he must have them whitened regularly or had caps. No one over thirty-five could possibly have natural teeth that looked like Chiclets gum—perfect little squares. He removed a wide brimmed Stetson that perched squarely on his head, and then finger-combed his thick black hair. He replaced the hat carefully, and smoothed the brim. "What are you two involved in now that brings you out here?"

Rhetta didn't bother with a courteous response. Instead, she coated her answer in aspartame. "Oh, nothing, Sheriff. We thought it might be a good afternoon for a ride up the bluffs to see the Mississippi." She cut a glance at Ricky, whose head bobbed in silent agreement.

"Uh, huh." Reasoner stared at her. She said nothing else, just smiled her best phony smile at him.

"And while you were sightseeing, you happened to pull in here where there just happened to be an explosion." He stared at her but she didn't answer. She didn't see the need since he hadn't asked a question. Then he sighed, and she swore she saw him roll his eyes.

"I don't suppose you can tell me anything about what happened here?" He continued, while waving a gloved hand toward the brush where the fire trucks had pulled up and firefighters were tugging hoses and shouting instructions.

She peered up at him and hoisted her shoulders. She twisted around the seat to gaze back at the fire. "Have no idea, Sheriff. We just pulled in here to turn around, and spotted the fire. That's when Ricky called the fire department and I called Eddie Wellston." She pointed to a late model Dodge extended cab four by four that spit gravel as it swerved to a stop. "There's Eddie now." She batted her eyes, and gave Reasoner a smile that she hoped matched his in its lack of genuineness. "I guess it was lucky we were here, or who knows what might have happened if the fire had raged unreported."

"It sure was bad luck or coincidence that you were here, Mrs. McCarter. I don't like coincidences. I know how trouble seems to follow you around." She didn't find a question there either, so she said nothing. She smiled on the outside, but inside her stomach was churning and she thought she might vomit. Reasoner had better stand back.

He added, "I'll have an officer over here shortly to take your statements. Don't leave." He actually waggled an index finger at her, as though scolding a five-year-old. She wanted to bite it off.

"Of course not, Sheriff. Wouldn't dream of it."

He gave her another long stare then tipped his hat again and spun around, heading for the fire trucks.

"He is such a turd," Ricky said. "I can't stand him."

"I bet he's just tickled to death to find us here." Rhetta sucked in mouthfuls of air to settle her stomach. She opened the door to meet Eddie, who was trotting over to her.

"Oh my God, Eddie, this is terrible. Is your place okay?" Rhetta jutted her chin toward the shop building, which did not seem to be anywhere close to the fire. As far as she could tell, the fire had been contained in the woods.

"No problems with anything here, thank goodness," Eddie said, his arm making a sweeping motion. "But I can't say the same for the poor guy out there." He jerked his thumb over his shoulder toward the burning thicket. "The firefighters said it looks like he got burned up in the car."

Chapter 25

EDDIE'S WORDS HIT RHETTA LIKE a mule kick to the belly. She blinked as she stared at the scene, mesmerized by the firefighters' teamwork. They worked in sync, like a well-oiled machine, every member knowing exactly what to do without any wasted motion. The chief used a small megaphone to amplify his orders so he didn't have to shout over the noise of the fire. Rhetta was surprised at how loud the fire's burning and crackling sounded. Did Frank burn up in the explosion? Her hands began to tremble. She clutched the package he gave her.

She stared at the ever-shrinking black plume of smoke that the firefighters were dousing with foam. Didn't he tell her he was the last one, and whatever it was, was now hers? What was hers? If Frank died in that burning mess, she would certainly step forward and claim him, and take care of a burial. He hadn't revealed who his confidant had been. She decided she couldn't turn her back on giving him a decent burial. He was a soldier, and as a soldier, like his friend George Erickson, he deserved a funeral. In fact, Rhetta decided to call the same funeral director if she needed to arrange for Frank's funeral.

Sheriff Reasoner rapped loudly on her window. She was so lost in her thoughts that she hadn't seen him walk up. She jumped at the sound, then powered down her window.

"Mrs. McCarter, I see you're still here."

Rhetta tried not to glare at him. She also forced her eyeballs not to roll. "You told me to stay here, and that an officer would take our statement, Sheriff. I'm doing as you asked. No one has taken any statement, yet, by the way. Unless, of course, that's why you're here."

"I may as well. My officers are pretty busy."

Doing what? Rhetta watched two officers off to the side, chatting with each other. Unlike the firefighters who were laboring intensely, the two cops weren't doing anything that she could tell. They did string yellow tape up across the entrance. That was the extent of their hard work so far.

"Yes, I can see that." Rhetta stole a glance at Ricky who stared straight ahead. Rhetta caught the corners of her mouth twitching.

Unreasonable unbuttoned a shirt pocket and removed a small notebook and a pen. He clicked the ballpoint annoyingly as he waited for her to begin. *Click,* on, *click,* off, *click* on, *click* off. Rhetta stared at the pen. She fought the urge to reach out and snatch the damn thing away from him, and fling it as hard as she could. Instead, she sucked in a deep breath, and said, "What would you like to know, Sheriff?"

Click, click. "So tell me again, Mrs. McCarter, what you and Miss Lane there," he bobbed his hat brim toward Ricky, "were doing up here?"

"I already told you. We were out driving around. I got attacked last night, and just wanted to get out and relax. The view up here is spectacular, you know. Anyway, we decided to turn in here to go back, and that's when we spotted the blaze."

"Just driving around. Right. I see." He scribbled a line into his notebook. "I read the report about your being tossed into a Dumpster. That had to be, uh, rather unpleasant." The edges of his mouth began curling. She anticipated a snarl was imminent. He cleared his throat, and waved a hand in a circular motion toward the impound lot. "Did you see anything?" He held the pen poised over the page, ready to write down her words of wisdom.

Rhetta nodded to Ricky, who answered. "As a matter of fact we did. We saw a man run out of the woods, get into a pickup and squeal his tires getting out of here." Ricky pointed to the back gate. "Over there."

Reasoner whipped his head around and peered toward the gate. "Why didn't you tell me this earlier?" Reasoner slapped at the radio on his shoulder. "Michaels, get a car over here by this Trailblazer," he snapped, then clicked off when he heard an acknowledgement.

"You didn't ask," Ricky said.

"Ask what?" Reasoner ducked to look in at Ricky, behind the wheel.

"You didn't ask us if we saw anything," she said. "So now that you asked, I'm telling. I didn't know if you needed to know that. It might just be a Looky-Lou."

Are cops supposed to roll their eyes? Reasoner just did so, magnificently. "I don't suppose you happened to notice what type of truck, Miss Lane?" He let himself sigh, an obvious indication that he didn't expect much from her.

"Let's see." Ricky placed her index finger along the side of her cheek and looked skyward as though searching her memory. She paused a few seconds for effect. Then she leaned across Rhetta as far as she could, and stared into Reasoner's square face. She spoke very softly, but rapidly. "It was a blue 1999 extended cab, F-100 Ford pickup. No plates on the back. Probably pulls a trailer. If he's licensed over twenty-four thousand pounds, he doesn't need a rear plate. There was a trailer hitch on the back that I suspect came from U-Haul."

Reasoner scribbled furiously. "Why do you think the hitch came from U-Haul?"

"Because it had an orange and white sticker with black lettering that said, U-Haul."

Reasoner spun on his heel to jog over to the deputy. After a minute, the deputy squealed out of the parking lot through the back gate.

Chapter 26

Saturday afternoon, December 22

THE *FIRST NEWS* VAN ROLLED in as Ricky steered the Trailblazer out of the lot and onto the highway. The newspaper had already arrived in the form of one college student intern driving an older lime green four-door Honda. The young man driving it wore a lanyard bearing a laminated press card. He had ambled toward the yellow tape blocking entry to the fire area, and began chatting with one of the cops.

Rhetta's phone bellowed a foghorn ringtone, startling her. She had turned off the radio, finding the joy of the oldies music inappropriate after the horrific explosion, and the realization that her father might have been incinerated. She and Ricky had fallen into silence. Rhetta slid her finger along the screen to answer the familiar tone.

"Hi, Sweets."

"Where are you? When I came home, I found both you and the Trailblazer gone. You're not supposed to be driving." By Randolph's tone, Rhetta felt his concern.

"I'm not driving. Ricky came by and drove me out to meet Frank at the impound lot on 177. I left you a voice mail."

A pause. "The service out here is so bad. I don't have any voice mail," he muttered. "Did you say you went to meet Frank at Eddie's lot?

Would that meeting have anything to do with the big fire there? The one that's all over *First News*?"

"Yes, but he didn't start it."

"That's comforting."

"No, Sweets, it's not. I think he burned up in that fire, and that somebody murdered him."

"Hold on. Murder? There has to be a lot more to this story. Come home and tell me what's happened."

"We're on our way. Love you."

"Love you, too. Please, Rhetta, be careful."

Ricky had started asking Rhetta about her father as soon as they rolled onto 177, but Rhetta was so tired and upset she could barely hold a conversation. Finally, Ricky grew still, allowing Rhetta to lay her head back against the soft interior and close her eyes.

As they wound their way up the long McCarter driveway, Rhetta peered through half open eyes and marveled again at the hundreds of glittering white Christmas lights that adorned the house, the garage, even the barn. The tranquility of the scene calmed Rhetta. She still couldn't believe they had just witnessed a fire that very likely had claimed her father.

She basked in the warm Christmas glow that enveloped the house and yard. As the Trailblazer came to a stop and the garage door creaked upward, Rhetta tugged the sock hat off, giving her head a chance to breathe. The knit hat had made her head almost too warm. Her short hair lay damp and matted against her scalp.

Ricky clicked the remote to lock the Trailblazer, then handed Rhetta the keys. "There's never a dull moment with you." She hugged Rhetta, then pointed her toward the door leading into the house from inside the garage. "Are you all right?"

Rhetta nodded.

"Then go on in and lie down. You shouldn't have been out today. Randolph's right."

"Of course, he's right. But after that call from Frank, I had to go."

"Did I really hear you say I'm right, for once?" Randolph stood at the doorway, and had obviously overheard the last of their exchange.

Rhetta hugged her friend. "I'm fine. I'll call you soon."

Ricky trotted to her truck. After the truck had warmed a minute, she backed down the driveway, turned and chugged away.

Randolph led the way to the kitchen.

Rhetta turned back to the door. "Hang on, Sweets. I need to get the envelope out of the Trailblazer." She scooted toward the garage.

"I'll get it. You stay here." Randolph slipped out to the garage before Rhetta could give him the keys.

He stuck his head back around the doorway, and she tossed him the keys.

In a minute, he was back, clutching the envelope her father had given her. He set it down on the granite countertop, where they heard a soft metallic *clang*.

"I need to use the facilities." Rhetta tossed her purse on the counter. She tugged off her jacket as she sprinted to the bathroom.

By the time she'd returned to the kitchen, Randolph had a steaming mug of hot chocolate waiting for each of them on the counter. She hugged him fiercely. "I love you so much. How did you know I needed hot chocolate?"

"Chocolate always soothes the soul." He found a bruise-free zone on her cheek and kissed it.

Rhetta hoisted herself on to a kitchen stool, then began sipping around the floating marshmallows.

Randolph stood next to her and carefully opened the envelope. Inside was a bundle wrapped in a cotton cloth that resembled a frayed section of a man's white T-shirt. The first item they spotted was a typed letter. It appeared to have been printed recently on a computer. He handed it to Rhetta.

Dear Rhetta,

Please read this before you open the rest of the bundle.

If you are reading this, it probably means that I'm gone. That's ok. It's time you know. The first thing I want to make clear is how much I loved you and your mother. In looking back, I should have realized the secret operation I agreed to would rob me of my family. At the time, the money seemed so important.

In 1973, the war was pretty much over. I was ready to come home to my family. Instead, I agreed to continue working for Uncle Sam in a "private" capacity. You'd probably call it Black Ops. In exchange for getting very well paid, we had to agree that we "died." There were 12 of us in the beginning. We lost a few guys on the first few missions. That's when we formed The Trust. We knew if we were injured, because we no longer existed in any records, we were on our own, so we wanted to be taken care of and to take care of our families. When we agreed to work privately for the government, we each received one million dollars as a sign-on bonus. Laurent, Marcel, Cooper, William, Alejandro, George and I each invested our million in a Tontine trust. Over the years, after we could no longer work, we received a decent annual stipend from the trust. Every time one of us passed away, his share stayed in the trust. According to the way we set it up, the last person living is the final owner and can claim all of it. I believe that I am now the last. Until recently, there were three of us, Cooper, George and myself. Cooper was electrocuted in a freak accident in Maine last year. And you know what happened to George. He believed Cooper was murdered. Before we could put anything together, George was murdered. I gave him your card because I knew you would help. Now that I'm gone, the money is yours, Rhetta. You must go and get the car. You'll need it to get the money. I know and trust you will use the money wisely.

I spent the rest of my life working for a country I loved. I just didn't realize that I had made a choice to love it more than my family.

Rhetta stared at the letter. It wasn't signed.

Was her father now dead? How much money was there?

Where was it?

Chapter 27

Saturday afternoon, December 22

FRANK'S BUNDLE HAD BEEN WRAPPED in tattered cloth, with drawstrings that looked like worn shoelaces. Slowly Randolph untied it and spread the flaps, displaying the contents. A steel cylinder about the size of a lunch-sized Thermos bottle rolled to the side. Next to it, held together by a wide rubber band, lay a sheaf of very old papers, if the brown stains and yellowing were any indication.

Tucked under all of it was a four by six inch faded black and white photograph of the same men they had seen in the video. Randolph carefully picked it up, and turned it over. On the back were their names. And the date: August 6, 1973.

Next, he picked up the metal cylinder. It had a screw-on top that had rusted closed. Randolph turned it over in his hands, looking for a way to open it. He tried unscrewing the top, but the rust had guaranteed it stayed sealed. He went to the garage and returned a moment later with a spray can of Bolt Buster. He carried the cylinder to the sink, wrapped it in paper towels, and gently sprayed the grooves around the top. He twisted again, and the top came loose.

He carried the cylinder and the contents back to the counter.

"Looks like they used an old Thermos-type vacuum bottle." Rhetta nodded and peered at the rolled up document inside. Randolph presented the metal clad bottle to her. "Here, see if you can get this out. Your hands are much smaller than mine." She reached for it. "Slowly. That parchment looks old. We don't want to tear it."

Rhetta reached in and carefully withdrew a scroll. Using both hands, she unfurled it and read it.

"I can't make much sense out of this." She let it curl back up as she handed it to Randolph.

He carefully laid it flat, then studied it. "I think it's in Portuguese or Spanish. Let me put the words into a Google translator and see if we can generate a translation.

Randolph carried the parchment to the computer and booted up. As soon as it chimed, he opened a browser and a Google translator page. After trying French, Italian, Spanish and Portuguese, he finally had a translation. "I have it," he said and turned toward Rhetta who had come up behind him to watch. "This document is the charter of the Garibaldi Tontine Trust. And it's written in Catalán." Randolph opened a new translation window. "Here is the top line." From the print on the document he typed, *Garibaldi tontine establert pel Banc Real de Santo Domingo a Vera Mardola*. "I believe it means our Garibaldi trust is at The Royal Bank of Santo Domingo in Vera Mardola." Randolph Googled it. He turned to Rhetta. "Vera Mardola is an obscure island in the Mediterranean."

He read aloud, "Wikipedia says that the tiny island of Vera Mardola's chief source of income is money. It rivals Switzerland and Monaco as a financial center. It claims to be independent, being neither French nor Spanish. Depending upon the political climate, it may align itself with either France or Spain for currency. The official language is Catalán." He looked up from the screen. "The only way you can get there is by ferry from the northeast part of Spain or the southwest of France."

He picked up the thin parchment. After studying it again, he typed the remaining text into the translator. Randolph shook his head. "There isn't much more here. It says that anyone claiming the trust has to do so in person, have the account number and the proof, and be the last survivor. It doesn't say what the proof is, or what the account number is. The only real information is that there is no information other than location. The rest of the information is stored within the institution, and whoever brings in the claim has to match what's on file." He found a plastic folder in the desk drawer and carefully placed the delicate page inside.

"Did your father tell you anything, like maybe what the account number is? Or if there's any money left in the trust? Is it even worth going after?"

"On the phone he was adamant that I remember the name Garibaldi. He even spelled it for me."

Rhetta and Randolph returned to the kitchen where Rhetta finished her chocolate and chewed on the sticky marshmallows. "There must be a significant amount of money for someone to have killed three people for it. But if all of them are gone, who is the killer?"

Now that she'd said the "K" word out loud, she shuddered. She was positive that whoever had tossed her into the Dumpster meant to kill her.

Randolph picked up the cups, took them to the sink, and began rinsing them. "There has to be another heir, a son or daughter of one of the seven original members. That must be who is after this. The question is, how do we find out who the surviving family members are?"

Rhetta shook her head. "That shouldn't matter. Frank said that he had proof of everyone's deaths, and according to the trust agreement, only the heirs of the final survivor can get what's left." She exhaled deeply. "I'm not sure that's fair, but that's what it says. We'll have proof of Frank's death, so who else would be trying to get the money?"

Randolph dried the cups, then put them away. "I can't imagine who. Plus, don't forget, according to the charter, even if we can get to this bank, if it's still around, we need the account number. And I don't see an account number anywhere in this stuff."

Rhetta jumped down, her eyes blazing. "I know exactly where it is."

Chapter 28

Sunday morning, December 23

THE LONG SHOWER DIDN'T HELP clear the horrific images out of her mind. She padded around the bedroom, careful not to disturb Randolph who was still sleeping peacefully.

At 5:14, Rhetta's eyes had flown open, her heart jackhammering against her ribs. She had to lie back against the pillows until her heart quit racing. She dreamt she was inside the Dumpster and Randolph wouldn't get her out when he got there. "You're way too much trouble," he'd lamented. "I'm going to leave you here. That should teach you a lesson." Then he slammed the lid down.

Rhetta guessed she was feeling guilty and that's what brought on the dream. *I didn't do anything to bring my father into my life. Why would Randolph blame me for this? No, he's not blaming me. I need to get a grip.* Her thoughts ricocheted between the fire, her father, and what she'd told Randolph about feeling that the VIN on her father's Camaro was the trust account number. That was why the Camaro and the title were so important to Frank. "We'll wait until after the holidays before thinking about heading out to get it," Randolph had said. "For one thing, the weather is supposed to turn bad tomorrow, with snow and ice possible right before Christmas. We may have to cancel the open house after all."

"You're right. We'll wait for better weather. After all, the car isn't going anywhere." Rhetta knew Ricky wanted to take off as soon as possible to get the car, but Randolph made sense. Best to wait. She didn't look forward to the four hundred mile trip on wintry roads, even though Ricky was an excellent driver. Even knowing it possibly held the bank account information, the money wasn't going anywhere either. If there was any money. Also, she would need to properly bury her father, once the coroner released his body. That had to come first.

Her head wound felt better, although it still hurt when she touched it. She decided coffee and ibuprofen would fix her right up. She prayed they could still hold the open house. She loved Christmas. Randolph had decorated the outside of the house, transforming it into a magical light show, while she spent hours dragging boxes of Christmas decorations from room to room. She wanted a tree in every room, and this year she had purchased a two-foot high fiber optic tree at the Dollar Store that was perfect for the kitchen. With its tips changing color all the time it was cheerful and colorful in any light.

Sitting at the counter in the kitchen, she turned the television to the Sunday morning news, located her cat mug, and made a pot of coffee. Just inhaling the heavenly aroma jump-started the soothing around her injury. If not her injury then, at least, her soul.

As she watched a report on Christmas shoppers, she decided to beg Randolph to take her to the mall to finish her shopping. He hated shopping, but he would take her, she was sure. That way she could drop hints about what she wanted, in case he hadn't yet bought her an iPad. She smiled, and took a sip of her brew. She began reaching for her iPhone to catch up with her email when she spotted a news item scrolling across the bottom of the television screen. *Scorched remains found in the burning car at yesterday's impound lot fire on Highway 177 will be sent to St. Louis for autopsy. Police hope dental records will help identify the female victim.*

Rhetta spit out her coffee. Holy crap!

Female?

Chapter 29

"M ERRY CHRISTMAS!" RICKY HUGGED RHETTA and handed her a gaily-wrapped box about the size of an eight by ten picture.

"I thought we said no gifts this year," Rhetta chastised her friend, but only mildly. She had gotten Ricky a gift, too. When she was at Macy's she found a beautiful silver pin of a silhouette of two dogs that looked remarkably like Ricky's two little dogs, Taffy and Tater. She pointed to Ricky's present lying on top of the sofa table. "I see you listened like I did. There's yours, girlfriend." Ricky grinned broadly.

Ricky and Billy Dan handed their coats to Randolph who carried them back to the guest room, adding them to the heap on the bed. While Randolph busied himself arranging the coats so they wouldn't slide to the floor, Ricky and Billy Dan mingled with the other guests. The day had dawned clear and bright, and because all the snow had melted, no one had worn winter boots. Meaning no one had tracked slop into the house. Rhetta smiled. She wouldn't have minded cleaning up, but not cleaning up was better.

Ricky was stunning in an emerald green short dress cut low in front, matching leggings, and knee high boots that wouldn't have been any use in ice or snow. Billy Dan's blue-gray velour shirt enhanced his gray eyes. Rhetta smiled as she watched Billy Dan's arm encircle Ricky's waist.

The house was bursting with the aroma and good cheer of Christmas. All the decorated trees were glowing with colored lights, while all around, scented candles treated the olfactory senses with sweet vanilla and pine.

Woody and Jenn were wrapped in each other's arms in the living room slow dancing to "I'll Be Home for Christmas," while LuEllen and her husband, Manny, maneuvered through the buffet line balancing plates laden with veggies, deviled eggs, and meat. There were plenty of yummies for dessert, including some gluten-free for LuEllen. At the end of the line, which snaked around the overflowing dining room table that had required inserting the two extra leaves, Mrs. Koblyk stood triumphantly, silver serving triangle in hand, ready to attend to her homemade desserts. Her merry laughter could be heard above the chattering.

Rhetta had set up several sturdy wooden TV tables near the chairs and couches in the living room, family room and even the closed-in porch, so that there would be plenty of spots for everyone to sit and eat. The open floor plan of the house made it feel cozy, even though many folks were scattered in different rooms. More people sat in front of the fireplace where split oak logs glowed red, radiating warmth where Randolph had banked the fire.

When the music changed tracks, Jenn and Woody strolled over to the wine cart and served themselves a fresh glass. After refilling, Jenn went to chat with LuEllen while Woody ambled over to Ricky and Rhetta who were standing near the closed-in sunroom.

"I read the online wire services yesterday. It appears the woman's remains were tentatively identified," Woody whispered, looking around furtively, as though not wanting anyone else to overhear. "It hasn't made the news here yet." Woody, the newsaholic, constantly scoured numerous news sites on the computer, especially the Associated Press. Doing that had earned him the nickname AskWoodydotcom.

Rhetta glanced around and whispered, "You must be right. I haven't seen anything. Why are we whispering?"

"I don't want anyone else to hear me." He stretched his neck as though searching for someone. Rhetta followed his gaze. He was watching Jenn.

"Okay."

Rhetta waited for Woody to go on. When he didn't she prodded him. "Well, are you going to tell me who she is? Jenn is way over there." She pointed toward Mrs. Koblyk who was talking animatedly with Jenn. Mrs. Koblyk's grey curls danced around her pixie face as she smiled and laughed at something Jenn said.

"Jenn said not to talk about all of this during the open house."

"Okay, but since we're not talking about it, who did they identify? Is it someone we know?"

Woody shook his head. "Not anyone from here. Authorities were able to match the VIN to a car registered in Kansas City. The police matched dental records from a woman in New York by the name of Rushia Coughenour."

Rhetta and Ricky glanced at each other. Rhetta shrugged.

He whispered, "She was also known by another name."

Rhetta waited.

Woody leaned forward. They inclined toward him as he whispered, "Rushia Caldwell. She had been married to Alexander Franklin Caldwell."

Chapter 30

Tuesday afternoon, December 25

RHETTA'S GUT CLENCHED AS THOUGH she'd been swift-kicked by a mule. In a way, she had—at least a metaphorical one. She sucked in a sharp mouthful of air. The room started spinning around her like a Tilt-A-Whirl.

Spotting Rhetta's distress, Ricky grabbed onto her by one arm while Woody seized the other and together they propelled her to a chair.

Rhetta lowered her head between her knees until the wave of dizziness passed. A vivid replay of the fire rolled across her brain. Anger and confusion coursed through her like floodwater surging through a canal in New Orleans. If he wasn't dead, then he had some serious explaining to do. A wife? If that were true, shouldn't she have inherited the trust? Of course, now she was dead. Burned to a crisp. By whom? Her father? Did he kill his wife? Or was she an ex? Rhetta's heart pounded again. Did they have any children? Did Rhetta have any half siblings out there? No, she remembered her father telling her that she was his only child.

Was that woman, then, the confidant he'd referred to?

Randolph edged his way to the sunroom where he found Rhetta slumped in a wicker chair. Woody hovered while Ricky had headed to the kitchen for water.

"Are you okay?" he asked as Ricky arrived with a glass of water and handed it to Rhetta. Randolph hugged Rhetta to him. "Are you sick? What's wrong?"

Woody filled Randolph in about what they'd just learned about the woman's identity.

"That does it, Rhetta. It's time to stop any further escapades involving Frank Caldwell. Enough is enough." Randolph gripped his wife's hand.

Rhetta nodded. "I agree. I'm through, Sweets. I don't want any more to do with this charade. I don't know what's going on, but as far as I'm concerned, I don't care. Let Frank figure it out and go to the police. They can catch the hit and run driver. And now all this…" She gestured vaguely. "I don't know why he's dragging me into it."

Rhetta swallowed the last of the water. She stood, declaring. "I'm fine now. It was just the shock of hearing that he had another wife, I guess, that knocked me sideways." She spotted the McEwens from the country feed store where she and Randolph bought organic cat food in bulk, as they edged toward the door. She nodded at Randolph, who released her hand, and set out to find their coats. He returned several minutes later after they had hugged Merry Christmas and said goodbye.

Their leaving cued the other guests. One by one, they filtered to the hallway toward the front door. Randolph grabbed an armload of coats and laughed with everyone as they good naturedly fished though the stack for their own coats. Rhetta waved at everyone as they left. After thirty minutes, only Woody and Jenn, and Ricky and Billy Dan remained. Mrs. Koblyk promised to come back in a few days for empty plates. Which meant there were plenty of desserts left over. For the moment, the prospect of hoofing it on the treadmill was enough to discourage Rhetta from any extra sweet treats.

"Let's have coffee," Rhetta suggested. "I need an extra charge of caffeine." They trooped into the kitchen and hopped up on the stools around the counter. Randolph plugged in the coffee maker and began brewing coffee.

The heavenly aroma soothed Rhetta, and she began feeling better. She hopped down and went to get the gift she wrapped for Ricky, along with two envelopes loaded with red bows for Woody and Jenn. She had given Randolph his gift—a custom-made wood folding easel—that morning. His gift to her was a new buttery smooth leather wallet, stuffed with a shopping card to Macy's. It wasn't exactly an iPad, but she loved the wallet, which she needed after losing hers. And she would splurge on a new pair of boots at Macy's.

Jenn and Woody were thrilled at their gift cards to the bookstore and sporting goods store respectively. Ricky squealed in delight at her silver dog pin.

Rhetta opened Ricky's gift to her and smiled at the white iPad cover. Ricky's eyes welled at seeing what Randolph's gift was to Rhetta. "You can return it, Rhetta. Best Buy will exchange it."

Before Rhetta could answer, Randolph spoke up. "No need," he said, and ducked out of the room a moment. He returned with a package in his hands, kissed Rhetta on the cheek and handed it to her. "It will go perfectly with this."

Rhetta tore open the package and grinned at the white iPad box. "You're awesome, Sweets. How did you know?" Randolph executed an exaggerated eye roll to everyone's laughter.

They waited for the coffee, chatting amiably. Then Randolph cupped Rhetta's chin. "I think you need to call Unreasonable first thing in the morning and tell him what Woody found out. Even though Woody managed to find out before *First News*, the sheriff probably knows by now. Calling him will show good faith."

"I read it on the wire service feeds," Woody said. "I doubt if *First News* has run it yet. There's no other exciting news, like Butler County cows having triplets, so they might run it."

"Hmpf," Rhetta muttered. "I don't care a whit about what Unreasonable thinks of my faith—good, bad or otherwise."

"I get that," Randolph said. "However, by showing said good faith, you can convince him you are not involved except accidentally. Also, while you talk to him, ask if he has any updates on whoever slugged you and stole your purse. Even though it's a city police issue, he may know something. If you're nice to him, maybe he'll be nice to you."

Rhetta said, "I think it's too late for that. But I'll still ask him anyway." She reflexively touched the back of her head. It was healing nicely, and she'd managed to pull at least twenty hairs over the shaved spot. Ricky said the orange hue on her scalp matched the deep orange sweater she wore.

Ricky piped up. "If you don't want us involved in this, does that mean we can't go on a road trip to get the Camaro?"

"If that car is really my father's, then I would love to have it." Rhetta fingered her spoon. "Especially if it's truly an early First Generation."

"First Generation Camaros are those from 1967 to 1969," Ricky explained to Billy Dan. "Chevrolet changed the body style in 1970 and kept that basic style through model year 1981. Those are second generations, like Cami, which is a 1979 model."

"Yes, ma'am," Billy Dan said and saluted. Everyone laughed. Ricky was a fountain of information on muscle cars.

Randolph passed out coffee mugs to everyone. Rhetta smiled as he handed her the cat mug. He knew it was her favorite. He poured and everyone watched him, waiting for his answer.

He stared back at the expectant faces, then slowly shook his head. "I don't know, Rhetta. Do you think the car is really there?"

"I'll certainly find out. I'll call them tomorrow, and try to get all the information. Then we can decide." Rhetta massaged her coffee cup. The cup was warm and comforting in her hands.

Billy Dan cleared his throat. "Randolph, if the car is there, Ricky and I can go and get it."

Ricky squeezed Billy Dan's hand.

"Not on your life," Randolph said. They all stared at him. Rhetta started to protest.

He held up his hand. "Do you think for a minute Rhetta would let anyone go without her along to pick up that car?" He raised his mug in salute. "Here's to a road trip."

Chapter 31

THE MCB MORTGAGE AND INSURANCE branch office was closed on Boxing Day, the day after Christmas. Although the other businesses in the area didn't recognize the British and Canadian holiday, Rhetta was very glad when the owner of the bank had decided to close the mortgage offices, making for a long holiday weekend. For whatever reason. Maybe he was a closet Canadian.

After two cups of coffee, and with Randolph's help, she began tidying up from the open house. She was still a bit stiff from her adventure in the Dumpster, but happy that the attacker hadn't stolen Christmas from her, in addition to her purse.

"I'm so glad we had the open house, Sweets," she said as she dumped stale crackers and chips into a trash bag. "I'm actually feeling pretty good and I think everyone had a grand time."

"Especially the cats," he answered, and pointed to the deck where the four were snarfing hungrily on leftover meat scraps. He massaged her shoulders. "Why don't you call the Cave Storage in Kansas City? I think you need to know right off if the Camaro is there. Then we can plan accordingly."

"You're right." Rhetta slid her phone in front of her and Googled the storage unit. The number came up on the first window.

She had awakened before dawn that morning worrying about the car, and wanting to call, but hadn't wanted to appear too anxious. She wasn't sure why, other than she didn't want Randolph thinking she was willing to stay involved with her father. She took a deep breath and tapped the number.

On the sixth ring, a gruff voice answered, "Cave Storage."

"Uh, yes, I need to check on a storage item of mine."

A long pause. "What do you mean? What is there to check?"

"I want to make sure it's still there."

Another pause. Rhetta said, "Hello, are you still there?"

"Why wouldn't it be here? Are you saying someone may have removed your item?"

"I'm sorry. No, I don't think anyone removed it. Let me start over. My father said he has a car in storage there and that the unit is in both our names. I just want to make certain the car is still there before I come to get it."

A long sigh. "We have a lot of vehicles here ma'am. What's the name on the unit?"

"Frank Caldwell and or Rhetta McCarter."

"Just a sec. She heard a thud as he laid the phone down. Then paper shuffling noises. A pause. More shuffling, then he returned to the line. "I found the information."

Rhetta cringed. "How much is the bill? We want to come in the next few weeks to pick it up."

"Do you know what day?"

"No, sir, let's say around the first of February." Rhetta calculated that the weather would be cooperative by then.

She heard the chatter of a calculator. Her forehead popped sweat beads. She really wanted the car, but was apprehensive about how many thousands of dollars it might cost to get it. She could imagine a ten thousand dollar rental bill. *Don't be silly. The storage company would have sold it off before it could have accumulated that much of a bill.* She grabbed a tissue and wiped her brow.

"Thirty-three hundred dollars. Sixty months at fifty-five dollars a month."

Dear God, how did he let it get so far behind? She scribbled the amount onto a slip of paper and handed it to Randolph. His eyebrow shot up.

"Uh, okay. Thanks." Her forehead was soaked.

"Call me and let me know what day you'll be here, so I can cut you a check. I won't have that much cash around."

"Excuse me?" *What did he say?*

"I'll have to get you a refund. That unit was paid ahead a long time ago, and there's still five years left."

Three thousand, three hundred dollars? Who pays that much in advance?

Chapter 32

Thursday morning, January 10

FOR OVER A WEEK, SNOWSTORMS had raged across the plains from Kansas to Illinois, blanketing mid-Missouri with its heaviest snowfall in twenty-six years, according to *First News*. The outlook for a trip to Kansas City in the near future was bleak. Rhetta reconciled herself to the bad weather mid-state, while dealing with ice storms and freezing rain at home in southeast Missouri. Her father's car would have to stay tucked away in the cave for a while longer.

Rhetta parked Streak at the rear of her office, not wanting to walk across the frozen parking lot and take any chances on the sidewalk out front. Evan hadn't kept up with salting down the sidewalks and Rhetta decided to call Jeff today and mention it. She spotted Woody pulling in and waited as he parked his Jeep next to her.

"I'm going to call Jeff today about the parking lot out front," Rhetta said, juggling her large coffee and her purse as she dug for her keys. "He needs to keep it cleaned off. It gets downright dangerous out there. I thought Evan was supposed to salt down the sidewalks in front of the building, too. Where the heck is Evan anyway?"

"I'm surprised no one else has fallen out there," Woody said.

"Who fell?" Rhetta produced her key and started up the steps, which, miraculously were not iced over.

"Nobody, why?" Woody said.

"You just said you were surprised that no one else has fallen out there," Rhetta said, inserting the key into the lock, and pushing the door open with her hip.

"Because it's so icy," Woody answered.

Rhetta turned to stare at him. She decided not to pursue the disjointed conversation. She stomped her booted feet on the rug at the back door, while Woody sailed on past her into the main office area. He continued out the side door that opened into the hall, and disappeared around the corner.

"Where's Woody going?" LuEllen asked as she met Rhetta.

Rhetta shrugged. "Couldn't tell you. Maybe he's going to see the accountant about his taxes." She hadn't seen the resident greasy accountant, Philip Corini in a while. That was a good thing.

"Or, maybe he's going to the new chiropractor," LuEllen said, taking Rhetta's coat and hanging it for her. They walked side by side into the main office.

"There's a new chiropractor in our building?"

LuEllen nodded, then picked up a card from her desk and handed it to Rhetta. "Doctor Panwar Rashad. He moved in over New Year's. He's just starting up. Woody has been complaining about his back, so maybe that's where he went."

Rhetta examined the card. "Sure will be handy for us. Especially if the sidewalks don't get any salt. By the way, who salted our back steps?" She sat in her chair, adjusted it up, and then tugged off her snow boots. She pulled open the bottom drawer and withdrew a pair of dress shoes, and dropped her purse in.

"I decided I didn't want a broken neck so I salted them earlier. I picked up some salt on the way in," LuEllen answered.

"You're a doll. I should have thought of getting a bag of salt, but honestly, Jeff told me Evan was taking care of that. By the way, have you seen Evan lately? Or Jeff, for that matter?" She got busy. She had a stack of applications on her desk that she had to log into the loan origination system for processing. Refinance requests had shot up after rates had dropped again.

"Hm, now that you mention it, I haven't seen either one of them. You know this weather is a bit hard on some older folks. Maybe Evan can't get out much. As for Jeff, I heard that he is travelling abroad. Europe, I think."

"How nice for Jeff. I hope the weather there is better than here. Where in Europe did he go?"

"He took his wife on a second honeymoon. To the Mediterranean— Spain, I think, and Italy. Not sure where else."

Rhetta got up, and walked to the back room and peered out the window. "You're probably right about Evan. I don't see his van. Oh well, maybe Jeff assigned some other work for him at one of the other buildings. By the way, LuEllen, did Woody fall in the parking lot?"

"Not that he told me about. Why?"

Rhetta told LuEllen what Woody had said.

LuEllen shook her head and smiled. "Sometimes Woody leaves out parts of sentences."

"You mean the parts that make sense?"

"Yes," LuEllen said. "Those parts."

"That reminds me. I have to call Jeff. Or, at least his office about the parking lot." Rhetta trotted back to her desk.

Before she could punch the numbers, the phone rang.

"MCB Mortgage and Insurance," Rhetta said.

"May I speak with Mrs. McCarter?"

"This is Rhetta McCarter, how can I help you? Rhetta had her pen ready to jot notes.

"This is Sergeant Delmonti of the Cape Girardeau police department. We have a suspect in custody that may be your assailant. We have evidence that we would like you to identify. How soon can you get down to the police department to identify those items?"

"That's great news, Sergeant. I'll come right away."

She disconnected and turned to LuEllen. "Sergeant Delmonti thinks they may have captured my assailant. I'm going to go down to the station. They want me to identify some stuff, but I didn't ask what they had."

Just then, Woody returned, headed straight to Rhetta's desk and leaned over it. "I went to see that new chiropractor," he said. *Score one for LuEllen.* "When I left just now, I went past Corini's office, and his door was open, but nobody was at the front desk."

"I heard he hasn't got a secretary or receptionist," Rhetta answered, reaching into the bottom drawer for her purse.

Woody nodded. "I know that. It's what I saw that bothered me. A woman's purse on the floor, near the corner of the desk."

Rhetta couldn't understand why that concerned Woody. She kicked off her shoes and tugged on her boots. "Maybe he hired a receptionist."

"No," Woody shook his head. "There wasn't anyone else in there. I heard him on the phone, so he was alone."

"Okay, so he didn't hire a receptionist. Maybe he carries a man-bag. He is from Saint Louis, you know."

"If it's his man-bag, it looks exactly like the purse you had when you were mugged."

Chapter 33

Thursday mid-morning, January 10

RHETTA SPRANG FROM HER CHAIR and swept across the room in two strides on her way to the hall door. She totally understood Woody that time.

He snatched her arm as she flew by. "Hold on, where are you going?" he asked, when her feet finally stopped. He held her fast.

She tried to wrestle free. "I want to see that purse for myself. If that no good, little slime bucket is the one who attacked me, I have a few words for him."

LuEllen caught up to her and edged herself between Rhetta and the doorway. "Just a minute, Rhetta, you just said that the police called you to go down there and identify stuff that may have been stolen by whoever knocked you over the head. Don't you think you should go down there first? Besides, if Mr. Corini did conk you on the head and steal your purse, why would he leave it in plain sight?"

Rhetta simmered down enough that both of her colleagues stepped away from the door.

She sucked in a lungful of air, and let it out slowly. "I suppose you're both right. Woody, come with me, I'll just casually ask Mr. Corini where he got his new purse." They turned right, and trooped down the hall toward Philip Corini's office.

"Exactly how do you intend to phrase that question?" Woody asked.

"I'll think of something."

"That's what I'm afraid of." Woody laid a hand on Rhetta's arm and slowed her down. "Don't be accusing him of anything, Rhetta. Let's hear his explanation first."

Corini's door was still open. Rhetta stepped into his cramped entryway, and let her gaze follow Woody's index finger, which pointed to a purse lying against the corner of the desk.

She stage-whispered, "That's my purse! You were right, Woody." She sucked in hard enough to empty the air out of the small room.

Corini came out of the back office in time to hear Rhetta suck in the air. "Well, howdy there neighbor," he said, smiling broadly at Rhetta. *Did people say howdy neighbor in St. Louis? I doubt it. That's probably his way of trying to get down to our country bumpkin level.*

Rhetta arched her eyebrows and pointed to the purse on the floor. "Excuse me for saying so, Mr. Corini, but your man-bag looks like the purse that was stolen from me the night I was mugged."

Corini's head whipped back and forth, finally stopping when his eyes lined up with the purse. He pointed to it. "You mean this purse? That's not my man-bag. I don't carry a man-bag." He marched over to it, bent, and picked it up. "I found this behind my office a couple of days ago." He dumped it over, and shook it a little. "It's completely empty so I didn't think it was important enough to call the police. I guess I just forgot about it."

"May I see it?" Rhetta asked.

He handed it to her. "Sure. Do you recognize it?"

She narrowed her eyes at him. If he was lying, he was doing a really good job. He sounded sincere. "You know a thief stole mine the night I was mugged here?'

He stepped back, hand flying to his mouth. "You were mugged? Here? I thought I left all that behind in Saint Louis." His face paled. His shock appeared genuine.

"Yes, it happened a few days before Christmas." As a reflex, her hand went up and touched the spot on the back of her head. "I got hit on the head, and my purse was stolen." She walked over toward the little man, who took a step back at her approach. "I don't suppose you know anything about that?" She deliberately left out the Dumpster part.

"No, I didn't know. That's just terrible. Are you all right?" He wrung his hands. *I can't believe he's wringing his hands. Is that a sign of stress, like Woody's head rubbing? Why is he so stressed? Maybe I should've called the cops.* Just then, a movement at her side caught her eye. Woody was rubbing his head. *Looks like they're both stressed.*

Rhetta inspected the handbag. "I believe this is my purse, Mr. Corini. I'd like to take this to the police station. I have to go down there in a little while. I'm going to inform them that my purse showed up here. They may want to talk to you about that."

"Of course, of course." He pulled a handkerchief out and rubbed his forehead. "But, honestly, I found it in the back, near my steps. I only picked it up because I thought there might be some ID in it. When I didn't find anything, I just set it down. I guess I forgot about it."

From the looks of the disarray in his office, Rhetta figured Corini didn't know where anything was, and almost believed that he did forget he had a woman's purse lying on the floor in his reception area. Looks like no one had done any cleaning in there in a while, either.

"By the way, I use Taylormaid Cleaning Service. If you like, I'll bring you Wendy's card." Rhetta grasped one handle of the purse in two fingers, turned abruptly, and headed back down the hall to her office.

"Were you insinuating that his office was a mess?" Woody trotted alongside her.

"That was no insinuation. Did you see that place?" She wrinkled her nose.

"Did you notice the comb-over is gone? I think he got hair transplants. They look like somebody row cropped his head."

"You mean corn rows?"

"No, I mean row cropped in bad soil during a drought. Jenn said if I ever did that, I could move out." Woody rubbed his own smooth pate. "Do you know what part of the body they get the hair from for transplants? From—"

Rhetta put her hands over her ears. "Stop! I don't want to know any more. Now I'll be studying his hair to see if some is curly and some is straight. I wish you hadn't told me that!"

Back at her office, Rhetta rummaged through the cabinets and came up with a plastic bag bearing a Walmart logo. She tucked the purse in it and tied the end closed. "I doubt if the cops will get any prints off this, but I'm going to take it to them anyway. If they do find prints, I bet the only ones on it are mine and Corini's. Did you notice how guilty he was acting?"

"He admitted to picking it up, so it's a given that his prints are on it. That won't prove he did anything." Woody sat at his desk and grasped the computer mouse. His screen sprang to life. "I think he's intimidated by you. After all, you are a judge's wife, and I think he regrets being in an office in such close proximity to a member of the court." He tapped a few keys on his keyboard.

"Why should that bother him unless he has something to hide?"

"There may be more to Mr. Corini than meets our eyes. Look at this." Woody swiveled so that Rhetta could see the monitor. "I found this on the Saint Louis Post-Dispatch website when I did a Google search of his name."

Rhetta squinted to read the screen but failed to decipher anything. She glanced around for her glasses. She finally located them on her head, then transferred them to her nose. She scrambled over to Woody's desk and peered over his shoulder at the monitor. After reading it, Rhetta whistled.

Rhetta read the two-year old news column aloud. "Local accountant arrested for assault." *Seems like our own Philip Corini was once arrested in St. Louis!*

Chapter 34

Thursday mid-morning, January 10

"PRINT THAT, WOODY. I'M TAKING it to Sergeant Delmonti."
Woody was ahead of her. He'd already sent the document to the printer. He retrieved it and handed it to her as she threw her new purse on her shoulder and stomped toward the back of the office.

"That little slime ball. I knew there was something about that little weasel I didn't like. So help me, if he turns out to be the one who robbed me, I… I… Damn." She jerked her coat from the rack. It snagged on a hook. "Crap," she said, freeing it and threading her arms into it. She turned to Woody as she snatched her sock hat, gloves, and scarf, and practically ran for the back door. "I can't wait to discuss this with Sergeant Delmonti." She tucked the plastic bag containing the old purse under her arm and fished in her new purse for her keys.

"Uh, Rhetta, your hat…it's…"

Rhetta interrupted him. "I have my hat, Woody. I'll see you in a while." She flew out the back door, slipped down the steps and nearly fell, then recovered her balance enough to make it to her car. *I really hate winter!* She couldn't wait for summer, driving Cami with the sunroof open to the warm blue skies and singing her head off with the Oldies.

Finally settled in her SUV, she tugged the hat down over her ears. The hat felt scratchy, but she ignored it. She'd rather go bare-headed, but it was too cold. She didn't keep her hair long enough to keep her head warm.

That damn Corini. She knew she didn't like him. It wasn't just a vague sensation of dislike. She was convinced that he was up to no good. She now had the evidence in a Walmart bag.

She didn't turn the radio on. For once, she didn't want to sing along and be cheered up. She wanted to stay plenty upset with Corini. She found a parking space in front of the main door to the police station after having to circle the block only four times. She locked Streak and jogged as quickly as her boots on the slushy sidewalk would allow. She was grateful that the city had cleared the sidewalk, but there was enough slush left to cause her to fall if she didn't watch her steps.

The cop shop was located in the city's administration building, a renovated two-story structure built in the 1930's through WPA, or Works Project Administration. Originally an elementary school, it now served to house the local city government offices, including the police station. The rock sided outside looked much like it did after it was built, thus keeping the original look and pleasing the historically-minded citizens who had wanted to preserve it. Inside, however, all the space was divided into office cubbies that comprised a warren any rabbit would envy.

Finally finding the correct corridor to the Police Department, Rhetta strolled into the waiting area. A young duty officer sat behind a wire cage and glass enclosure, protecting him from any unpleasantries from the masses. She assumed the glass was bulletproof. She turned and glanced around. She was the only person in the waiting area. Maybe she wouldn't have to wait long to see Delmonti.

"Can I help you?" the officer asked. He cocked his head, and eyed her. A smile began to work the corners of his mouth.

She bent to speak through the opening. "I need to see Sergeant Delmonti, please. My name is Rhetta McCarter."

The officer stifled a laugh by clearing his throat. "I'll see if he's in, please have a seat." He turned sideways and tapped on a phone console. His shoulders began shaking and he appeared to be suppressing his laughter. He cleared his throat.

Rhetta again gazed around the room, searching for the source of his mirth. Finding nothing or no one there, she dismissed his actions as an inside joke to which she wasn't privy, and picked up a magazine. She hadn't yet scanned it when Sergeant Delmonti appeared at a door at the opposite side of the room. She'd thought about a stop in the restroom, but his presence pre-empted the visit.

"Mrs. McCarter. Thanks for coming." He stepped aside to allow her to pass ahead of him through the doorway. He walked alongside of her in silence for a few steps until they came to the first office on the left. He motioned her inside, then followed her, closing the door. She sat in the single guest chair in front of the desk while he lowered his slender frame into a roll-around office chair behind his desk, facing her.

She handed him the plastic bag containing her evidence. "Sergeant, this is my purse. One of the tenants in my building, Philip Corini, a CPA, said he found it near the Dumpster in back. He claimed it was empty, so he didn't call anyone, especially the police. He told me he didn't know that I had been mugged." She sat back, waiting for Delmonti's reaction.

He opened the bag, then glanced inside. "Are you sure this is yours?"

"Positive. It's a Harvé Michel bag. I bought it in Saint Louis at a boutique in Clayton. I'm sure you're thinking that there are plenty of purses, and how can I be positive it's mine? Well, Harvé Michels are all numbered. This one is 0707, and if you check with Alexander's in Clayton, they will have a record of me as purchaser."

Delmonti jotted on a note pad. "Thank you. We'll check that." He set the bag down, and folded his hands on top of the desk. His perfectly creased dark grey shirt couldn't conceal the bulk of the bulletproof vest under it.

"We recovered a wallet containing credit cards with your name on them and your operator's license and checkbook when we busted a crack house on Good Hope Street. We arrested Jamal Browning, who was the one who actually had your stuff. We think he broke into several homes in the area. We also believe a second party got the cash and anything else of value that may have been in the bag, because this is all we recovered." He pressed a button and spoke into his phone console. "Corporal Neysmith, please bring the Browning evidence bag to my office."

He continued speaking to Rhetta. "I don't know why your credit cards and ID were found, but I suspect that the two perps had a deal whereby one took the cash and anything else of value while the other got to keep checkbooks and credit cards. They'd need ID to cash checks or use the credit cards." Delmonti shook his head and muttered, "Not that anyone in that place remotely resembled you."

He went on. "I'd like you to look through the contents to see if you recognize anything else. We're pretty sure he's the one who robbed you. He's been identified by several folks who were victims of his snatch and run. Although none of those folks were attacked." Delmonti frowned, as though pondering something. He didn't share it with Rhetta. "I know you said you didn't see your assailant, so I won't ask you to identify him. But would you mind looking at a picture of him to see if you know him?"

The door opened and a female officer brought the bag of evidence into the office and stood there with it while Delmonti slid it and a picture of a young male over to Rhetta to inspect. The female officer's badge read, *Neysmith, G.*

Rhetta examined the contents and nodded. She pointed, and announced, "That's my wallet. It's hand-tooled calf leather. Randolph bought it for me when we were in Mexico." She also spotted her driver license. That really was a terrible picture of her. She hadn't realized her eyes were almost closed. Sheesh. Maybe it was a good thing she had to get a replacement. Spotting a pair of earrings, she added, "Those are my garnet earrings. I forgot they were in my purse. I wondered what I had done with them." She remembered then, with perfect clarity the last time she wore them. They dangled into her sweater, where one caught and pulled out of her ear. She found it on the floor and removed the mate, and slipped them into the zipper compartment in her wallet. "You'll find one with a broken back on it. It got caught in my sweater and nearly ripped through my ear. I put them into my wallet." A Kohl's and a J C Penney credit card lay amidst the rest of the evidence. "There are still two cards missing, a Visa and a Master Card."

"Did you notify the credit card companies?" Delmonti asked as he nodded to the officer who cleared her throat and stifled a smile as she picked up the evidence bag.

"Absolutely." *What did Neysmith, G find so funny?*

"Good. We'll bag and tag this purse and enter it as part of the evidence report of your mugging. I'm sure we'll be able to verify your purchase at," he glanced at his notes, "Alexander's in Clayton." He handed the purse to the officer.

Rhetta stood. "Do you know when I might get my property back?"

"I'm sorry, no. We'll have to keep this until we go to trial. It may be a while. Browning has denied attacking you and stealing your purse. Claims he found it." Delmonti shrugged. "He confessed to several snatch and grabs but is vehemently denying this, even in the face of finding your wallet and other items on him. He's adamant he found them. Of course, you are the only victim he assaulted, so he's going to fight the assault charge." He picked up the picture. "Does he look familiar to you?"

Rhetta shook her head. "Nope. I don't believe I've ever seen him before."

The warmth inside the station had made Rhetta's head itch under the sock hat. She hated to remove it because she knew her hair would stand straight up from the static electricity. She slipped her index finger under the edge of the hat and scratched her scalp.

Rhetta turned to leave, but stopped. She turned around. "Sergeant, do you have any more leads on the hit and run accident I witnessed?"

Delmonti shrugged. "We haven't found the truck you said you saw, nor have we had any other witnesses come forward. This one will stay on the books for a while longer, but I fear we may never know what happened."

"I think the poor man was deliberately run down. For who he was." Rhetta said, staring straight at Delmonti.

Delmonti fixed her with an equally hard gaze. "Do you know something you're not sharing with me, Mrs. McCarter?" He tapped the desktop with his pen.

His tone rankled Rhetta. She wasn't in the mood to get another big fat rejection or an eye roll. And truly, she didn't know anything. She hadn't had any conversation with Delmonti about her father. What was the point? Her father wasn't a murderer. Of that, she was positive. "No, I sure don't. Just what I read in the papers, that he was identified as someone who had died in 1973. Don't you find that odd?"

He tilted his head. He ignored her question. "Thanks for coming in, Mrs. McCarter. And if you do see that truck you identified, you will let us know, right?"

She nodded. Her head really itched. She couldn't wait to jerk the hat off and scratch her head. "Of course."

Delmonti pointed to her hat. "By the way, I have to ask, are sock monkey hats the new fashion trend?"

Crap. Her hand flew to her head and she snatched it off and glared at the red-lipped monkey that had adorned the back of the hat. She swore it was mocking her. She had grabbed Woody's hat instead of her own. As soon as the hat cleared her head, her hair stood at attention. She tried to smooth it down. And failed.

No wonder everyone was snickering. The fashionista wore a sock monkey hat to the police station. She felt her face redden. That would probably make *First News* tonight.

Chapter 35

Thursday afternoon, January 10

"I HOPE YOU'RE HAPPY. I made a fool of myself at the police station wearing your stupid sock monkey hat." Rhetta clomped back to her desk. She didn't bother taking off her boots. She tossed the hat at Woody.

He reached up and caught it. "I tried telling you. But you were too irritated to listen." He continued gazing at his computer. She did, however glimpse an upturn at the corners of his mouth. He tugged at his beard and cleared his throat.

Rhetta pulled out her chair and sat heavily. She glanced at her computer displaying the *Weather Now* radar. The long-range forecast called for cold weather for another four days. On the bright side, the forecast also predicted clearing and warming by the following weekend and lasting for at least a week. That was typical for southeast Missouri. *January Thaw is what the old timers around here always called it. Might be a good time to think about going to Kansas City.*

She hadn't yet called Ricky about planning the road trip, and when her friend called her earlier that afternoon and suggested they meet for lunch, Rhetta begged off. Although she really wanted to lay eyes on her father's '67 Camaro and bring it home, she couldn't shake the sense of foreboding that blanketed her when she thought about it. She still had no word from Frank. Was he still alive? Had he married again? Was the woman who died a stepmother she'd never gotten to know? She felt an unexplainable sense of loss at the thought.

Who was trying to kill him if he was the last member of the Tontine? She had no answers and felt frustrated.

"Let's get together Monday, instead, if that's okay. I have a pile of work to catch up on today," Rhetta had countered. She wanted to check Randolph's schedule before planning the trip. By waiting until Monday to get together with Ricky, she'd be able to go over Randolph's calendar this weekend. A road trip with Ricky and Billy Dan might be fun after all.

"Sounds great. Meet you at Dockside?"

"Sure. Dockside it is. I've been craving one of their burgers. Eleven-thirty?"

Ricky agreed, and Rhetta added it to her iPhone calendar.

"Did I hear you mention Dockside?" Woody asked as he ambled around the corner from the kitchen. "I love their hamburgers. In fact, I think I'll take Jenn there tonight. Thanks for the suggestion." He sauntered to his desk and went back to work.

Rhetta pulled open her middle drawer and stared again at the familiar manila envelope. She fingered it, then decided not to open it. She knew the contents by heart. Instead, she closed the drawer, then headed for the wall safe. She wanted to check out the roll of paperwork, pictures and the cylinder that her father had given her. Randolph had suggested she place it in their office safe for better safekeeping. She had everything still in it except the car title. That was at home.

She rounded the corner to the safe, dialed the combination and opened the door. She went straight to the shelf where she had placed the package from her father. The shelf was empty.

She backed out of the safe and called out to Woody. "Woody, did you get anything out of the safe since yesterday?" She distinctly remembered locking the safe when she closed up last night. Woody must have gone in and removed it.

"Nope. Why?"

"Would you mind coming here a minute?" Her heart thudded so loud she swore she could hear it. Along with the ringing in her ears she noticed when she got upset.

"What is it?" He hurried over, went in and glanced around the safe. When he came out, he said, "What's wrong? You look awful. Have we been robbed?"

"The package my father gave me is gone."

Chapter 36

Thursday night, January 10

"WHO HAS ACCESS TO YOUR safe besides you, Woody and LuEllen?" Randolph asked as he set the table while Rhetta tossed the salad.

"That's just it, Sweets. Nobody. Not even the main office in Saint Louis has the combination. So how in the world did the package leave? Did it grow feet and trot out when we weren't looking?"

"When did you see it last?"

Rhetta paused her tossing. "Let me think. It would have been the first day I went back to work after the holiday. That would have been, let's see, Wednesday the second, the day after New Year's. I was the only one in the office when I put it in the safe." She placed the salad on the table and went to get small bowls from the cabinet.

After she finished helping set the table, Rhetta sat at the counter and cradled her head in her hands. "I'm not very hungry. I'm too upset. There are some very weird things going on around that office."

"Could someone have used your stolen keys and gotten in?"

She shook her head. "I had all the locks changed. Besides, the safe is a combination lock. It doesn't have any keys."

Randolph folded Rhetta into his arms. "Who could have done this?"

Rhetta shook her head. "I can't think of anyone. Besides us, no one but Jeff has keys to our office. Absolutely no one besides us has the combination to the safe. It doesn't make any sense. Of course, the culprit could be a safecracker. But how did he know what was in the safe? I have to think it's related to the trust. "

"Did you report it to the police?"

"Yes. I called and they said they made a note of it, but because there was no tangible value to what was stolen, they didn't even send an officer to the office." She returned to the salad bowl and carried it to the table. "What good is that roll of stuff to anyone?"

"Come and sit down and let's talk this through." Randolph pulled out a chair for her. "Let's see what we have. The cops found the thief who attacked and robbed you. I don't believe the attack on you had anything to do with your father, or the hit and run. So let's leave that element out of this.

"I think the hit and run, your father, this stolen package and the fire at the impound yard are all connected. Frank told us about the Tontine Trust. He believes that someone killed his friend, and is trying to kill him. Therefore I think, like Frank told you, you are a target for someone who feels threatened by you and it concerns the trust. There must be a lot of money at stake. Somebody wants you out of the way so they can claim the trust for themselves."

"But Frank said he's definitely the last one alive. He has all the proof of the others' deaths. He can collect the money now. Maybe he's gone to get it after all, and that's why we haven't heard from him." She nodded. That sounded credible to her. "That would leave me out of the picture. If Frank is dead, and he was the last to die, and hasn't claimed the money, who else could have a claim besides me?" She stood and began pacing.

"That, my love, is what we don't know. I can't figure out who or what, either. But, here's what I think: someone your father doesn't know about has figured out the Tontine Trust, knew your father gave you a package and figured that package included the account number.

Whoever it is knew he needed the stuff Frank gave you in order to get the number. Someone thinks they can get the money."

Rhetta whirled around. "Then they're still going to be looking. The car title is what he needs, since the VIN is the account number. Frank didn't write it down anywhere." She hugged her husband and shivered. "The car title wasn't with that stuff. It's still here at the house."

Randolph held her. "And, if he knows where we live…"

Chapter 37

RHETTA FED THE CATS AS she waited for Randolph. He appeared shortly after she started, and waited for her at the patio door, ready to go, fully decked out in his running clothes. After collecting her purse, phone and keys, she locked all the doors and set the alarm. Randolph pressed the automatic door opener and they piled into Streak. A run would be just what they needed this morning—a good way to shake off the winter blahs.

After Thursday night's conversation, the next morning Randolph drove to the mall and purchased a fire safe. He told her he didn't want to take any chances on leaving any important paperwork lying around. He had it delivered to his studio, since it was too heavy to risk placing on the wood floor joists in the house. Once the two delivery men wrestled it into the corner he had chosen, he placed the car title, along with some other important papers like their insurance policies inside. The model he got was too large and heavy for one person to carry off.

A whiff of spring teased them as the sun gleamed overhead. Randolph backed out of the garage, and Rhetta pointed to the flowerbeds off to the side. "Look, I see some daffodils nearly blooming. Their little yellow heads are just about to pop open. We may get an early spring after all." She captured the image on her iPhone, intending to post it to Facebook. Randolph twisted in the seat and looked behind them as he backed up. The garage door stopped and began rising as though one of the cats had dashed inside. Randolph clicked on the opener again, and the door continued its descent and closed snugly. He parked Streak.

"One of the cats must've sneaked into the garage. I'll go get him out."

While waiting, Rhetta scanned her picture to post. Randolph climbed back in and put Streak into gear and continued backing. He put the SUV in drive and headed down the lane to the county road.

"There weren't any cats in the garage, and the storage unit door was shut, so they couldn't have run in there. Maybe the garage door is sticking on the track. I'll check it when we get back. Do you want to do Dockside for brunch after our run?"

Rhetta grinned. "Sounds great. I'm meeting Ricky there on Monday for lunch, and we're going to plan our trip to Kansas. City. What's your schedule like? Are there any days that you can't go?"

"Not really. I'm flexible. We should try to leave on a Friday, so we can get back on Saturday and you can inspect the car all day Sunday."

She dug in her purse for her iPhone and ear buds. "Let's go to Capaha Park and run around the lake."

"Can you keep up with me? You've gotten slack since your noggin got conked."

"It's you who'll have to keep up with me. You haven't run since my noggin conking either. And I've been running on the treadmill and pedaling my butt off on the bike. So we'll see who's out of shape."

She reached over and cranked up the oldies, and began singing along. The sun was brilliant, the temperature at fifty degrees already, and the prospect of a delicious brunch awaited. What a perfect day!

―――――――

"I can't believe I let you talk me into running errands after lunch," Rhetta groaned. "I think I saw everyone we knew when we were at Lowe's."

Randolph had pleaded for a quick trip to the home improvement store to pick up some wire and framing materials. "I think you look cute in your sweatshirt, tights and sneakers." He grinned. And ducked as Rhetta slapped the air where his head had just been.

"You are a brat, husband. Just because I wasn't all dressed up was no reason for Kelly Davenport to snicker when she saw me."

"She didn't have her camera crew, so you won't be on *First News* tonight. Or maybe she heard about the sock monkey hat." That earned a full-blown glare.

Rhetta paid for their purchases. As they left the store, she said, "As long as I'm making a public appearance in my running clothes, I guess we should stop at the grocery store, too. I need a few things. And we'll definitely have to stop at *Primo Vino!* I need some good white wine tonight."

"Hello missus," Mrs. Koblyk called out and waved from her porch as Rhetta and Randolph stopped at the end of their lane to collect the mail. The stubborn mailbox was stuck again, so Rhetta hopped out to manhandle it. Sitting in the SUV and reaching out the window, she couldn't quite get a grasp on it. Rhetta returned her neighbor's wave.

Mrs. Koblyk disappeared for a minute and reappeared clutching a bag. "I have some of the bread for your husband that he likes." She waved a plastic bag as proof.

Rhetta loped to the porch and climbed her neighbor's steps. Mrs. Koblyk beamed as she handed Rhetta a foil package snugged into a plastic bag that felt warm. Mrs. Koblyk must have just pulled the bread from the oven. "Thanks so much. Randolph loves this bread. Me, too," she added, glad that she'd run this morning. She imagined breaking off a chunky bit of the delicious poppy seed bread and sipping white wine.

"Your visitor, missus, he drives too fast," Mrs. Koblyk said, and clucked her disapproval as Rhetta descended the steps.

Rhetta stopped and stared up at her neighbor. "Pardon? What visitor?"

"This morning after you leave, your visitor he leaves, oh, about an hour after you." She glanced at her watch as though to confirm the time.

"I'm not sure we had a visitor, Mrs. Koblyk. Did you see what he was driving?"

Mrs. Koblyk's grey curls bounced with her head bob. "Yes, of course, I see. Like what the Mister Randolph drives. A truck." More bobbing.

Rhetta felt bile rise. "Thanks, Mrs. Koblyk. I'll speak to Randolph about this." The old lady nodded and waved again before disappearing into her house.

Rhetta bolted for the SUV, and clambered in. She tossed the bread into the back seat. "Mrs. Koblyk says we had a visitor who left our place after we did this morning." Randolph grunted, threw Streak into gear and churned up gravel as he sped up the lane.

Chapter 38

Saturday afternoon, January 12

"D EAR GOD!" RHETTA CRIED AS she opened the door from the garage into the house.

If she hadn't known better, she'd have sworn that Super Storm Sandy had barreled through. Every kitchen cabinet door gaped open, as did the pantry. Boxes and cans of food lay tossed to the floor and all over the counters. Smashed jars spilled out colorful contents amidst shards of broken glass, while indistinguishable foodstuff splattered along the walls and the cabinet fronts. Piles of dishes lay smashed, while the silverware, cooking utensils and the remaining contents of the drawers lay atop the heap.

The living room furniture was upended. Two lamps lay on their sides, their shades smashed. The fireplace screen lay in the middle of the floor while ashes from the fireplace covered everything.

The dining room chairs lay on their sides. One had a leg dangling.

Rhetta ran upstairs only to stop at the top and let out a wail. "Oh, God! Everything has been ransacked. The entire house!" She ran back downstairs, outside and to the Garage Mahal. "What did they do to Cami? Oh, no, please, no."

Randolph stopped her at the door to the garage, and enveloped her in his arms. "Wait here, let me look first." Rhetta choked back a sob. He kissed her forehead. She started to follow him. "No, honey," he insisted. "Stay here. Let me check the garage."

In a minute, he was back, a faint smile on his lips. "Nothing out of place. Cami is fine."

Rhetta buried her head in his shoulder. "Thank God. I couldn't stand it if they tore up Cami."

Randolph pulled out his phone and dialed 9-1-1.

Sheriff Reasoner had donned plastic booties and gloves before entering the house. Rhetta and Randolph waited outside and repeated their story to the young deputy while the sheriff inspected inside. The deputy had just finished taking their statements when Reasoner ambled up.

"I hope you called your insurance agent," he said. Rhetta nodded. That would be herself. She had called her adjuster, since she was her own agent. She had worked with Carlton, her adjuster for several years, and considered him a friend. He promised to drive out right away.

"What do you think they were looking for?" Reasoner asked as he slipped off the gloves, and smoothed his hat brim.

Randolph motioned for the sheriff to join him on the patio. Reasoner settled onto a wood bench, and Rhetta sat next to her husband on the double platform swing.

"It's a rather long story, but here goes. It started with Rhetta's father." Randolph and Rhetta then told Reasoner everything they knew about Frank, the Tontine Trust and her recent attack.

Reasoner said, "I spoke to Sergeant Delmonti after you went down there to identify your things. He's pretty confident they have your assailant. So obviously this," he waved toward the house, "isn't connected. Their suspect is still in custody."

Rhetta glanced at Randolph before commenting. "You're right, Talbot. This looks like someone breaking into our home looking for something specific. Can we go in now and see if we can tell if anything is missing? I only just glanced at my bedroom, so I don't know if any of my jewelry has been stolen. Although, how I'll tell if anything's missing, I don't know." She stood and wiped her hands on her jacket.

Reasoner motioned for the deputy to come forward. "Deputy, since you're done taking pictures, please accompany Judge and Mrs. McCarter and let them look through their things." They headed for the door. "Wait," Reasoner called, "Suit them up first. We're waiting on the fingerprint team."

Rhetta and Randolph "suited up" in shoe coverings and latex gloves and trudged up the stairs. The deputy followed. The bedroom was as chaotic as the rest of the house. Although her jewelry armoire lay on its side, after a quick examination, she felt that all her costume jewelry was there. As she riffled through it some more, so was all her good jewelry, including several valuable rings. She examined the rest of the room. Her walk-in closet had barely been touched, except that the drawers at the end of the closet were pulled out and dumped over, as had been all the dresser drawers in the room. The mattress had been pulled off the bed, too.

Randolph's computer and her laptop, plus her new iPad were still on the desk. The intruder had, however, pulled open and tossed the drawers of the desk. Now that she was calming down, Rhetta could see a pattern.

It was clear that the home invasion was all about finding something specific. She knew what it was. The car title.

After they trooped back downstairs, and out onto the porch, Rhetta told the sheriff, "I'm pretty sure they were only looking for one thing." Rhetta and Randolph exchanged glances.

After Randolph and Rhetta removed their protective coverings, Randolph spoke up, "Talbot, we need to check my studio. I installed a safe there yesterday. I believe a car title is what he's looking for, and we put that in the safe."

"My office safe was broken into and a cylinder with some papers was taken," Rhetta said, breaking into a trot. "I reported it to the Cape police. If the same guy did this, he may have gotten the title."

Reasoner examined the lock to the studio door. "This doesn't appear tampered with," he said. "Do you have your key?"

Randolph inserted his key, and pushed the door open. Nothing inside was disturbed. "Evidently, whoever broke into the house didn't know I have a studio here, or didn't think what he wanted was in the studio." He walked to the safe, spun the combination and when the door opened, he examined the contents. "Still here," he said, closing the safe and locking it again.

Reasoner walked around the studio. "Nothing's out of place?"

"Everything looks fine," Randolph answered, sidling up to his shivering wife and placing his arms around her shoulders. "Someone is on to the trust," Randolph said. "It can't be George Erickson, but whoever it is has figured out he needs the VIN from your father's car. He obviously didn't know about the safe."

Chapter 39

Monday morning, January 14

"THE NEW LAMPLIGHTER SUITES IS really nice, Woody," Rhetta said.

She and Randolph had spent the night in the new motel near the cancer hospital. The police had strung yellow crime scene tape around the house and had informed them it might be a few days before they got finished sifting through the debris and collecting evidence.

"I heard that. I think they built it to accommodate the cancer hospital next door to it. Lots of folks probably stay long term. How long will you stay there?" her assistant asked as he swiveled his office chair around to talk to her.

"I think we're going back home tomorrow, so just one more night. They should be through sifting around today or tomorrow at the latest. Sherriff Reasoner is supposed to call and tell me when we can go back."

"I bet they won't find anything. I'm sure your intruder wore protective clothing, et cetera. He seems pretty smart to me." The way Woody said it, made it sound like he almost admired him, or them.

"Why do you say that?" She took her coffee cup back to the kitchen then returned to her desk. "He, or they have obviously been following me, and I haven't been aware of it. So I guess I agree with you." She opened her middle drawer and fumbled through the envelope with her father's death certificate, hoping to find anything that would enlighten her about who might be following her. She folded it back and replaced it into the drawer. Nothing there. A chill passed over her. The thought that somebody knew to break into her safe for something that would have key information meant that whoever did it had probably looked at the envelope in her desk drawer, too.

Woody rolled his chair up to her desk, held up his hand, and began raising a finger each time he spoke, ticking off each item. First finger, "Whoever broke in here knew how to get in, how to get into the safe, knew we were going to be at the airport before we got there, knew about your meeting with Frank at Tri-County Impound." He waggled four fingers at her. "I think he's been stalking you. He knows you're Frank's daughter, that's a given. Therefore, he knows all about the trust, and now knows that the VIN on Frank's car is the code for the bank account. By the way, I sure hope you put that title in a safe place."

Rhetta picked up a pen and began drumming on a notepad. "Somebody must know all about the trust, but what I can't get past, is how does whoever that is figure he's going to collect on the trust, even with me out of the picture? Frank was the keeper, and he's provided evidence to the bank that he was or is, the last of the members." She shook her head and tossed the pen down. "Dang it, Woody, I can't make a connection. Does somebody want me dead, or does he think he can get the money without me? Is Frank dead? Dammit, I wish I knew what was going on!" She stood and began pacing.

"Well, did you?" Woody asked.

"Did I what?" She stopped in front of Woody.

"Put the title in a safe place?"

"Yes, I…" She clamped a hand over her mouth and dashed to her desk. Grabbing a pen and paper, she scribbled, *I put it in my bank safety deposit box this morning.* She showed it to Woody.

"In your…" Rhetta shushed him by putting her index finger up against her lips.

She continued writing. *I think someone is listening in on our office. That's how they know everything!*

Woody nodded and scribbled furiously, *I thought you had Billy Dan sweep the office?*

Rhetta motioned for Woody to follow her outside. She strode to the middle of the parking lot. Woody trotted behind her.

"I did, and Billy Dan didn't find anything. Somehow, somebody is listening to our conversations. That's the only way I can figure that he or they know what's going on in here, and also know when we aren't here. We keep erratic hours. Well, at least you do. You meet people down here by appointment, so somebody has to be listening to know when you're here." Rhetta ran her hands though her hair and winced as she fingered her almost-healed wound.

"That makes sense," Woody said, rubbing his head. One hand, not two.

"All right, if there is no listening device, how do they hear?"

Rhetta paced, then turned to Woody. "I know how."

Woody stared at her. "How?"

"Someone in our building can hear through the walls, or vents, or something. You know whose office is right behind us? Philip Corini. I knew I didn't trust that guy! I bet he's behind this!"

Chapter 40

Monday lunchtime, January 14

"I'M ON MY WAY TO Dockside to meet Ricky for lunch," Rhetta told LuEllen as she headed to the door. Ellen waved at her in acknowledgement. She never looked up from her monitor.

The January thaw made the day temperature hover around sixty, so Rhetta left her coat at the office. While her music blasted from the car radio, she thought about when a trip to Kansas City might be in order. As she pondered that, she began checking her rear view and side mirrors to see if anyone was following her. *Good God, now I'm paranoid.*

No, I'm not, she chided herself. *Someone who knows how to crack a combination on a safe broke into our office and got Frank's stuff. That's not being paranoid. That's a fact. Yet, he didn't touch our safe at the studio. It had to be because he didn't know we have a safe there. That was just lucky.*

She insisted on meeting Ricky in person to plan the trip, regardless of whether or not lunch was involved. Combining discussing the plans with eating at Dockside was the best idea. She no longer trusted saying anything at the office. Besides, Dockside served the best lunch in town.

As she made a left turn onto Spanish Street, a thought bounced into her head. If someone was listening in at her office, her customers' privacy may be compromised. Thinking about that made a headache start. Before it could explode into a full-fledged head crusher, she reached into her purse to confirm that she had a bottle of headache medicine. She lucked into a spot on the street near the front door at Dockside, and thanked the parking gods and goddesses that she didn't have to park at the public lot and hoof it four blocks. She needed to take a pill right away. If she didn't, she knew from past experience that the headache could send her to bed.

Once inside, the clamor of voices and the clattering of dishes reverberated inside her skull. While waiting for the hostess, Rhetta groped in her bag for the medicine, then flagged a waitress down to beg for water. She clutched the pill bottle to her chest.

"Sure thing, hon." The tall, gum-chewing waitress clucked sympathetically and disappeared around a partition and returned almost instantly with a glass of ice water. Rhetta swallowed three pills quickly. She prayed the headache would dissolve quickly.

Ricky bounced in, waving across the lobby. She scurried over and hugged her friend, then held her at arms' length. "What's up, Rhetta? You don't look so hot."

"Just trying to get a headache. I'll be fine," Rhetta answered and looped her arm through her friend's. "Let's get a seat. I'm hungry," she lied.

Fifteen minutes later, the same waitress brought them their salads and warm cheese biscuits. Amazingly, the medicine had prevailed and had pushed the headache away. Rhetta felt much better.

Ricky had her appointment calendar up on her phone. "How about we go this weekend? The weather is supposed to stay nice until the following Monday or Tuesday." She scrolled to her weather app, then nodded. "Yep, says here a front may move in late Sunday night or early Monday morning with the possibility of snow flurries." She tucked an errant strand of hair behind her ear. "This crazy Missouri weather. You know what the old saying is, 'if you don't like the weather here in Missouri, just wait a minute. It'll change.'"

"Can we go Friday, then come back Saturday? That way we will miss the weather. And, as Randolph said, by coming home Saturday we'll have all day Sunday to check out the car." Rhetta said and grinned at Ricky.

"With all of us driving, this should be a walk in the park. No problem. Can we use Randolph's new truck? We'll use my new aluminum car hauler. I don't trust my farm truck to drive that far."

"Absolutely. The hitch and hookup should be the same and work just fine for your trailer."

"I'll stop by and look at the truck and make sure. But I think it's all good." Ricky rubbed her hands in glee. "I have to tell you, I can't wait to see it. Do you remember what color it is?"

Rhetta shook her head. "No, I don't think he said anything about the color. Don't get your hopes up. It may be a rust bucket."

Ricky sighed. "You're right, but if it's been in storage all this time, you may be pleasantly surprised. I watched a segment on Speed Channel where the owner of a storage facility sold the contents of a delinquent unit to the Speed Channel guys. The facility owner knew there was an old beater car inside and had called them. Turned out the car under the cover was a 1971 Oldsmobile 4-4-2. The storage guy didn't even bother to lift up the tarp and see what was there. The Speed Channel guys bought it for a thousand dollars and it was absolutely beautiful. Probably would bring at least twenty grand at a car auction." Ricky paused long enough to chomp a mouthful of salad. "Do you know what the 4-4-2 stands for?" She smeared a blob of butter across a cheese biscuit, then plopped it into her mouth.

Rhetta said, "Nope, I don't think I ever knew that." She slid the nearly untouched salad bowl aside, and selected a cheese biscuit. No butter. It melted in her mouth.

"It means four-barrel carburetor, four-on-the-floor and two bucket seats." Ricky grinned. "Would I ever love to have one. In red, of course. With a white interior." She sighed dramatically.

The waitress brought their ticket then, and Rhetta grabbed it. "Are you feeling better, hon?" she asked Rhetta as she began stacking the dirty dishes.

Although being called "hon" rankled Rhetta about as much as someone saying "no problem" instead of "you're welcome," Rhetta just smiled. "I'm feeling a lot better, thanks. That glass of water did the trick."

"No problem," the woman said, as she whisked away the dirty dishes.

Rhetta closed her eyes and shook her head.

As they walked together out the door into the sunshine, Rhetta said, "Let's leave Friday morning about seven, and we can have brunch on the road."

"Sounds good. I'll come by Thursday and pick up Randolph's truck, and leave mine. That way, I'll get the trailer hooked up. Billy Dan and I can pick you and Randolph up early Friday and we'll be ready to go."

As they stood talking beside Streak, a dark pickup truck cruised slowly by. When Rhetta glanced at it, she swore it picked up speed and careened around the corner.

"Did you see that truck?" she asked Ricky.

Ricky's head swiveled, but the truck was long gone.

More paranoia.

Chapter 41

RANDOLPH LOADED THE LAST OF their bags and a cooler under the hinged lid on his pickup truck's bed cover next to two very small bags belonging to Billy Dan and Ricky. "Good grief, we're only going to be gone a couple of days. Did you pack for a week?" Rhetta blessed him with a look. Randolph continued, "Look at Billy Dan and Ricky's bags. They could have put all their stuff into half of one of your suitcases. Why do you need two?" She narrowed her eyes and hoped she looked suitably irritated. Randolph seemed to have decided to push her buttons this morning.

"We have two, because there's one for each of us. They aren't full," Rhetta said, clenching her jaw. "I figured we'd need our laptop and my iPad, too, so I packed them. Besides I needed room for boots."

"Uh-huh," Randolph said. The corners of his mouth were tugging upward into a smile. "Why do you need boots?"

"In case it snows."

Randolph grinned. Rhetta knew that grin. He was pulling her chain. The weather forecast called for mild but overcast skies. She was sure he was thinking that it was too warm to snow, but this time, he was apparently smart enough not to comment further.

Randolph climbed into the back seat with Billy Dan while Rhetta joined Ricky up front. Everyone had their coffee in travel mugs.

"This truck is awesome," Ricky said, after negotiating the truck and aluminum flatbed car hauler down the lane to the road, stopping near the mailbox. "I barely know the trailer is behind us."

Randolph beamed like a proud parent who just got told his child won the spelling bee. "It pulls really well. At least it does when I pull the fully loaded art trailer. We'll be able to judge better on the trip home after the car is loaded."

As they made the turn onto the county road, Rhetta waved to Mrs. Koblyk. It was barely seven o'clock.

"Are we still stopping at Mabel's Cuisine in Sainte Genevieve for breakfast?" Billy Dan asked. Rhetta thought she heard someone's stomach growl. She did. Hers.

"This coffee will barely last me to Sainte Gen, so absolutely," she answered. "I snacked on a piece of poppy seed bread, but that's beginning to disappear, too."

"My stomach is growling," Billy Dan said. "My stale donut is long gone. We got up at five."

"If Mabel's isn't too packed this morning, we should make Kansas City by this afternoon," Randolph said, laying out a Missouri map. "You know how packed the place can get." The locals loved the place, famous for "hubcaps," or very large cinnamon rolls. Getting a meal there during tourist season was almost out of the question without a very long wait. Today's breakfast would be a special treat. Rhetta groaned thinking about how those hubcaps turned into spare tires around her middle.

"Can you park this rig in that cramped downtown?" Randolph asked. Rhetta cringed and stole a glance at her friend. Now it was Ricky's turn to bless Randolph with a look.

Rhetta jumped in before the sparks could fly. "So, do you think you can find the Cave Storage place on Google maps?" she twisted around to ask Randolph.

"I'll use your iPad. Should be a good test for the Google map application."

In her best "told you so" tone Rhetta said, "See, I knew we'd need it. That's why I made sure to pack it. I'll get it out when we stop." Rhetta glanced out the side window as they pulled on to the interstate just north of Cape Girardeau. She sat up as a dark pickup truck merged into traffic behind them. She craned her neck to see past the air dam, the large vertical spoiler in front of the aluminum trailer. The air dam acted like a shield, designed to keep rocks and road gravel that spewed from the truck tires from reaching whatever was on the trailer. It also blocked her view of the side lanes. She couldn't quite make out the make and model of the truck. The truck pulled out into the passing lane and breezed past them. Rhetta leaned back against the seat and closed her eyes. *I'm definitely being paranoid. I'm seeing bad guys in pickup trucks everywhere*. The once-suspicious truck gobbled up the miles as it disappeared ahead of them.

By the time they reached Kansas City and Randolph guided Ricky to the Cave's address, it was 3:35 in the afternoon. The sign at the entrance indicated the business was open until six. They had plenty of time to get to the car and push it out, if they needed to, and load it. Ricky's flatbed trailer was equipped with a winch, which they would use if they needed help to load.

They had stopped twice on the way for fuel and bathroom breaks. They had all decided to skip lunch and eat at the Holiday Home Restaurant adjacent to the Holiday Inn where they would spend the night before leaving early in the morning. They had planned on parking the trailer in front of their rooms, within earshot if anyone happened to mess around with the trailer or the car. Ricky had brought along a car cover, too, to conceal the car and quash any bystander curiosity. Old Camaros had a way of attracting people, not all of them interested in only looking.

Ricky had handed over the piloting to Randolph one time at a break, but took her turn again to navigate up the winding county road to the Cave. Rhetta could tell that her friend was high on excitement and couldn't sit still. Driving made her focus and stay calm.

The weather had been mild when they left Southeast Missouri, but the temperature had dropped thirty degrees by the time they got to Kansas City. The wind had also picked up. A definite change was in the air. "Sure hope it doesn't snow," Billy Dan said, as he stepped away from the truck to smoke. He pulled out a pack from his flannel shirt pocket, and cupped his hands around the cigarette as he lighted it. Rhetta caught a whiff of the newly lit cigarette and inhaled sharply. She pivoted around to catch Randolph watching her. He walked over to her and put his arms around her.

"I know it's hard. But you're doing great," he said. Rhetta felt ashamed, remembering the times she'd cheated lately. *I'm going to conquer this. I know I can.* "Thanks, Sweets," she said and slipped over to the truck to retrieve her purse. She slung it onto her shoulder. It weighed a little more than usual.

Inside, lying next to the title tucked away in the bottom of her purse was her pearl-handled .38 Smith & Wesson.

Chapter 42

Aᴄᴛᴇʀ Rɪᴄᴋʏ ᴅᴇꜰᴛʟʏ ᴍᴀɴᴇᴜᴠᴇʀᴇᴅ ᴛʜᴇ truck and trailer into a nearby parking slot, everyone got out and jogged to the entrance. The temperature had dropped even more and although they had brought sweatshirts and lightweight jackets, in their rush to see the car, everyone had left theirs in the truck.

Rhetta stopped so suddenly to stare at the imposing cliffs that Ricky nearly slammed into her. Alongside the bricked addition that jutted out from the hill were four oversized garage doors built into the stone wall. Other than the twelve-foot-tall sign atop the hill proclaiming, "Cave Storage. Over 200 units. Climate Controlled," which was clearly visible from the interstate below, an observer would never guess what the hill contained.

Rhetta reached for her husband's hand. He gave hers a little squeeze, and then smiled. She took a deep breath and then marched through the door to the office.

She stepped through the doorway and back into time. The front part of the office couldn't have been more than twelve by twelve, but behind the counter was the opening into the cave, with a concave ceiling soaring at least twenty feet upward. Three of the walls were lined with filing cabinets of black, grey, green, tan or whatever color may have been on sale at the time of purchase—soldiers of time, guarding information and secrets of the storage units within.

Rows of Rolodexes and a manual cash register sat atop the front service counter. Next to the cash register, a sheaf of papers was impaled on a lethal-looking chrome pick sticker. Perpendicular to the end of the counter was a walnut wood desk and wooden swivel chair. The chair creaked as a white-haired gentleman began to stand as soon as they entered, finishing the effort by the time they all stood in front of the counter.

"Yes? Can I help you?" he asked as he stroked his Santa beard. His matching thick hair glimmered silvery gold under the glow of three incandescent bulbs overhead. Rhetta recognized his gravelly voice.

"I called you about picking up a car. My name is Rhetta McCarter."

The old man reached for the stack of kebobbed papers on the giant chrome needle, pulled off a handful, took one out, then replaced the rest.

"I have you right here. I suppose you have some identification for me?" His clear blue eyes peered at her over his wire framed reading glasses.

"Yes, of course." Rhetta reached into her purse and after only a minute of digging, located her wallet. She fished through it for her driver license, and pulled it out. She handed it to him. He reached into a drawer and withdrew a manila filing card crisscrossed with lines and boxes containing numbers and dates.

He painstakingly wrote down all the information, adding it to a Rolodex card that was paper-clipped to the filing card.

"Why don't you just make a copy of my license?" she asked. Randolph, Ricky and Billy Dan all turned to stare at her. "Oh, right. Never mind."

The proprietor smiled. "Never found the need to get one of those copy machine things." He pulled a check off the bottom side of the file card, and handed it to her. "Thirty-three hundred dollars. I don't split up a month. The unit is paid until the end of the month, so you picking up early doesn't warrant a refund. This here's a refund for the rest of the months that were paid ahead, like I told you on the phone."

Just as he said, "phone," a bell that could both wake the dead and bring the fire department rang out. The old man's gnarled fingers punched a button on the black desk phone. The instrument was probably fifty years old, earning its place in the office as the newest appliance from the twentieth century.

As he chatted, Rhetta glanced around, wondering where the restroom was located. She decided she found the doorway to it, against the east wall in a gap between the filing cabinets. She remembered seeing similar old wood doors with frosted glass on the bathroom doors at the Scott County, Missouri Courthouse.

The old man finished his call, hung up, then continued providing her with items that went with the car. He handed her a brass key with the number 147 stamped on it along with a small wooden box the size of a matchbox.

"The unit you want is one forty-seven. Go through the next room, and into the big room, and veer left. It's against the back wall."

Ricky leaned over Rhetta's shoulder and peered at the little box. Rhetta couldn't stop trembling as she opened it. Inside were two sets of keys attached to a small fob that said, "Caldwell, 1967 Camaro."

Was there truly a car here that was a part of her father's life? A life that didn't include her.

She trembled at the thought. She needed to find a restroom.

Chapter 43

Friday afternoon, January 18

RHETTA LURCHED THROUGH THE DOORS and out of the restroom. The cool air of the storage unit greeted her, helping her overcome the mixed feelings that were a cross between anger and anxiety. The bathroom wasn't the one in the manager's office. When she asked about a restroom, the manager directed her through the doorway that led to the main storage area. She didn't have time to take in the gaping vast interior rock walls of the hill. She pushed through the glass windowed door similar to the door to the bathroom in the manager's office and headed right to the sink. She splashed cold water on her face and gulped in several deep breaths. The nausea passed. She dried her face with gritty paper towels that probably survived from the Korean War era, then joined her husband and Ricky and Billy Dan who stood outside the door.

"Are you okay?" Randolph asked. He slid his hand into hers.

"I'm fine. Just felt dizzy for a minute there." She opened her other palm and gazed at the locker number on the fob. "It should be down this way," she said, grasping Randolph's hand and leading the way down a long corridor between rows of giant cages.

The cages were the storage units themselves. The entire interior of the hill was hollow. In this room with elevated rock ceilings, wire cages framed with wood lined the walls and interior, with separations between them that made rows. Those were the corridors. Each cage had a door equipped with padlocks and chains. At the back of the giant cage area, they stepped through another doorway into an even larger hollow room with walled in cubicles. These larger units afforded total privacy as the boxes and stored items couldn't be seen from the outside. She found unit one forty-seven.

All four of them stopped in front of the door. Rhetta handed the key to Randolph. "Would you open it, Sweets?" He nodded solemnly, and walked to the padlock, inserted the key and turned. To Rhetta, the soft "click" sounded as loud as a cymbal in a marching band. She winced.

She turned to Ricky, whose hand was entwined with Billy Dan's. Both Billy Dan and Ricky nodded to her. Everyone was solemn, as though participating in a religious ceremony. Randolph pulled open the door and stepped back. Rhetta hadn't realized that as soon as Randolph opened the door, she squeezed her eyes shut. When she heard a muffled yelp from Ricky, her eyes flew open.

There sat the most beautiful deep red 1967 Camaro coupe that Rhetta had ever seen.

"Bolero," Ricky said.

"What?" Rhetta asked.

"Bolero red. That's the color. The only year for this particular red." Ricky touched a front fender reverently. She walked around the car, which glimmered from the overhead fluorescent lighting. "This is amazing," she muttered. "This cave storage unit is like having it stored inside your house." She dropped down and wiggled under the car. She scooted back out, stood, and brushed off her coveralls. "This car doesn't look like it's ever been driven," she exclaimed. "What's the mileage?"

Rhetta opened the driver's door, and sat gingerly. The seat was pushed all the way back. Her feet didn't reach the pedals. She grasped the shifter and rubbed her palm over the shiny ball handle.

She peered at the odometer, and blinked. She couldn't read the numbers. They all looked like zeros to her. She reached into her purse and located her reading glasses in an internal pocket. She put them on and tried again. The odometer numbers were indeed all zeros except the last three, which read 7-8-1. *Holy Cow. Seven hundred and eighty-one miles? Or was it one hundred thousand seven hundred eighty-one miles?* She read the numbers off to Ricky. Around the other side, Billy Dan had also crawled underneath. He shimmied out and joined Ricky at the front of the car.

"Even though the tires look good, they'll have to be replaced. They dry rot with time, and might blow out under any stress, like road driving," Billy Dan said.

Ricky dusted herself off and came to stand at the driver's open door. "Let me take a look at the VIN. Do you have the title with you? We can match it to the VIN tag on the door frame." While Rhetta reached inside her purse for the title, Ricky squatted down and began jotting down the numbers from a metal tag that was attached to the body between the door hinges.

"The tag's still attached with rosette-style rivets. That means it's never been removed," she remarked. Rhetta nodded as though she understood.

Ricky stood and read the numbers off to Rhetta. After reading the numbers, Ricky unfolded a couple of sheets of paper and perused them, mumbling, "Oh. Oh, no. This can't be right. Holy smokes! According to this," she tapped her paper, "it's one of the very first production cars ever built. I went online and did some research." She raced to the front of the car, reached through the grille, pulled the hood release and quickly popped open the hood. She and Billy Dan disappeared under it.

Billy Dan peered around the hood. "Rhetta, this engine compartment is so clean. Everything still looks new. I bet the odometer is accurate." Billy Dan said, and disappeared back under it. Ricky agreed.

Rhetta heard Ricky add information. "Looks like the only thing here to worry about are the belts and probably the battery, if they're the originals."

Ricky stuck her head out and shouted at Rhetta. "I've just verified the numbers on the plate to the partial numbers on the firewall. This car was one of the very first Camaros ever built. It's a 1967, with a 302. In fact, not only is it one of the first ever off the line, there were fewer than six hundred of these Camaros built. Be still my racing heart!" She disappeared back under the hood.

Rhetta heard her friend, but couldn't grasp all the technical jargon right away. From the sounds Ricky was making, this car was a unique model. Of that she was sure. She gazed around the spotless, white interior. She caressed the dash and then the passenger seat. She twisted around to look into the back seat area. The seat itself looked as though no one had ever sat in it. The car was immaculate.

She reached over and tugged the glove box open. A neat package of window pricing stickers along with the owner's manual held together with a thick rubber band sat wedged in the glove compartment atop a white mailing envelope that was tied together with brown cords, like shoelaces, similarly wrapped like the package Frank had given Rhetta. As she picked up the package containing the owner's manual, the rubber band broke. She set everything down on the passenger seat and reached for the mailing envelope, which had started out white, and had, with time, discolored to a pale beige.

She removed the thick envelope and opened the flap. Then she gasped, stuffing her fist in her mouth

There was so much cash stuffed into the envelope that she couldn't begin to pull any out.

Chapter 44

RHETTA STARED AT THE ENVELOPE in her hands. She heard Ricky's continued exclamations, but couldn't understand what she was saying. She had tuned everything out except the thumping of her heart.

Her head swirled. Where was her father? What was the story behind this car? Had he gone to collect on the trust and then left the cash in the car in a storage unit? Had he robbed a bank? He said he'd done some not-so-savory things in his past. *Good Lord, had he killed someone and was this the blood money?* That thought made her drop the envelope as though it had heated up and scorched her fingers. It fell to the floor in front of the passenger seat just as Randolph opened that door and poked his head in. He whistled.

"This car looks like it was frozen in time. Like the day he bought it." He shook his head in obvious admiration.

"Look what else comes with the car," Rhetta said, reaching to the floor and gathering up the envelope. "A bonus." She handed it to him.

He took it and opened it, his eyes growing large. "Good grief, I wonder what this is for?" He turned the envelope over and studied it. He peered inside. "Was there any kind of note?"

Rhetta shook her head. She ran her hands through her hair, then spied a snippet of paper on the floor where the envelope had fallen. It was folded over. She reached down, retrieved it, then opened it up. "Hold on, I think this fell out."

She read aloud. "*Rhetta, this is for you. I couldn't save any money in any bank. This is my savings. It's yours.*" No signature.

She handed the scrap to Randolph who studied it, then slid it inside the envelope.

"I'll hang on to this," he said, clutching the envelope to his chest." At least 'til we get back to the truck and can put it in one of your suitcases."

"Now aren't you glad I brought those two bags?" She grinned at him. She wasn't sure why, but emotions rolled over her in waves, and tears rolled down her cheeks. Must have been all the memories of her mother, and everything she missed with her father. Randolph reached in and kissed his wife, and thumbed the tears away. She snuffled then smiled. "I love you, Sweets. I'm fine now."

Ricky and Billy Dan were oblivious to what had just transpired. They were still head to head studying the motor. They were holding a discussion about the condition and appearance of everything in the engine compartment. Ricky's excited exclamations reached Rhetta. She grinned. *Ricky will be in Classic Car Heaven with this one!*

After closing the hood carefully, Ricky bounded over to Rhetta, who still sat behind the wheel, staring out. "Oh my God, Rhetta, this is unbelievable! This car is totally unmolested, and I think, barely driven. Your father must have parked it here shortly after he bought it, and never drove it again. I don't get it. I wish I knew what had happened. Why would someone do this? It's absolutely beautiful and worth a small fortune. It's…" She didn't finish. "What's wrong?" she asked Rhetta.

Rhetta got out slowly, and eased the door shut. "Nothing, nothing at all. Other than I found an envelope stuffed with cash inside the glove box."

Ricky spun toward Randolph. "Cash? How much?"

Randolph said, "I don't know 'til we count it, but it looks like a heck of a lot."

An hour and a half later, the Camaro was loaded securely onto the trailer and covered with Ricky's car cover.

They had been pushing the car to the front of the Cave, when the manager had stopped them.

"Why don't you just drive it? Mr. Frank came regularly to start it up and drive it around the parking lot. He took real good care of that little car, and did the maintenance on it as though he drove it somewhere besides around our lots. It runs good."

Ricky had shaken her head and whispered to Rhetta. "Let's not take any chances. We can load it on the trailer, and I can check it out from top to bottom when I get it to the shop. I want to make sure the oil is good and the fluids are right before we crank it over."

"You're the boss on this," Rhetta said. "We'll load it."

After easily pushing the car outside to the waiting trailer, Ricky and Billy Dan hooked up the winch. Randolph hopped up on the trailer to monitor the winch, while Ricky and Billy Dan guided the car up the ramps. Rhetta sat behind the wheel and steered. Once the car was on the trailer, Ricky and Billy Dan secured it with tie-down straps and tucked the cover over it. Once she was satisfied, Ricky announced they were ready to leave.

As they eased down the long winding driveway from the Cave Storage to the service road, Rhetta pulled out her iPhone and started the maps application. "The Holiday Inn is just over here a short ways. We don't even have to get onto the Interstate." She pointed eastward.

The temperature had continued to drop and they all shivered as the truck warmed up.

"I just checked the weather. A winter storm is coming through." Rhetta said.

"Sure am glad I brought a jacket," Billy Dan said.

"Are we supposed to get much snow?" Ricky asked, as she steered into the motel parking lot.

"About six to ten inches," Rhetta said after checking her weather app. Everybody groaned.

"That'll make our trip tomorrow a very long one," Ricky added.

"Let's see what happens tonight, and if we have to stay an extra day here, we will." Randolph said. "I sure don't want anything to happen to that car. Besides, I want to call our insurance agent and add this to the policy before we get very far."

"I can call Mrs. Koblyk to feed the cats," Rhetta said. She glanced again at her phone. "We're not supposed to get anything but rain at home."

"I'm glad we live in southeast Missouri. We usually miss all the nasty winter weather the rest of the state gets, especially like here in Kansas City," Billy Dan said.

They pulled into the motel, and Rhetta jumped out to go inside to register.

Chapter 45

FINDING A CONVENIENT PLACE TO park the truck where they could see it from their first floor rooms as well as from the adjacent restaurant took a few minutes. Ricky parked it lengthways at the edge of the parking lot where no one could park alongside them. They walked around the trailer to check everything before trooping in to enjoy a relaxing supper. Rhetta and Randolph faced the window to keep an eye on the trailer. They had secured adjoining rooms down from the dining room that also faced the parking lot.

After settling in at the table and giving the waitress their orders, Ricky said, "I doubt if I'll get any sleep at all, as wound up as I am about this car. But boy, am I hungry!" She stabbed a chunk of salad with her fork.

"I think we should take turns watching," Billy Dan said. "That way all four of us won't have to stay up all night."

"That's a great idea," Rhetta said, finishing the last of her salad just as the waitress returned with their steaks. She carried all the meals on a round tray. Oval metal plates sizzled with hot steaks. "We should check in with each other as we change shifts."

The waitress set the tray down on an adjacent table and placed everyone's steak dinners in front of them.

"These smell delicious," Randolph said. "I can't believe I'm so hungry again after eating that huge breakfast at Mabel's."

Rhetta glanced at her watch. "Sweets, that was ten hours ago, and we didn't have lunch. Except for the Snickers bars we had in Columbia when we stopped for gas."

Ricky sliced her steak. "I'll take the first shift." She signaled the waitress. "Can you bring me some extra-caffeine coffee?"

"Sure thing," she said. "Coming right up." She turned over the white cups and began pouring from a silver carafe.

"How did you know I wanted extra-caffeine coffee?" Ricky asked. She pointed to the carafe. "You had it at the ready."

The waitress grinned, then leaned in. "All our coffee is extra caffeine. Unless you want decaffeinated." She smiled and winked at Billy Dan, then sashayed over to the next table with four men in business suits. Ricky threw Billy Dan a look, at which he just shrugged.

Billy Dan glanced at his watch. "All right, here's my suggestion: Ricky and I will take the first shift together. We'll watch until midnight. Then Rhetta and Randolph can take the second and call us around four." Nodding at Rhetta and Randolph, he added, "You can get a couple more hours of sleep before we get on the road. After a good breakfast, of course."

"After this giant steak, I doubt if I'll be hungry." Rhetta trimmed all the fat off her meat before slicing it. She popped a forkful into her mouth.

"I'm sure I'll be hungry by morning. Marsha said they serve a mean stack of blueberry pancakes," Billy Dan said.

"Who's Marsha?" Ricky asked, dabbing her chin with her napkin.

"Our waitress." Billy Dan tilted his head toward the silver-haired server, and smiled. The waitress smoothed her black skirt and smiled back.

"Are you flirting with her?" Ricky swiveled around to give the woman another look. "She's old enough to be your mother."

Rhetta interrupted, hoping to head Ricky off and distract her from Marsha. "That's fine with me, but I doubt if I can fall asleep very quickly, either. I'm pretty keyed up."

They had all finished their meals and coffee when Randolph checked his watch. "I guess we should call it a night and try to get as much rest as we can." He glanced outside, where snow was falling in large flakes. "If we get a lot of snow, we may want to reconsider leaving tomorrow. I'd hate to slide off the road with that car on the trailer."

They all murmured their agreement.

Rhetta followed Ricky outside to inspect the trailer and check the car's protective cover, making sure all was still snug while Randolph settled the tab. Billy Dan ducked outside the door to wait for Randolph, capitalizing on the opportunity to light up a cigarette.

Ricky and Rhetta jogged carefully across the parking lot to the trailer where over an inch of snow had already accumulated. Fat snowflakes were still falling. The orange glow from the parking lot lamps made the snow appear to be coming down diagonally.

Rhetta pulled her jacket around her. It didn't offer much protection from the cold. The wind had picked up and carried the cold through her denim jeans to her skin. Ricky wore only a hooded sweatshirt over her coveralls. Both shivered.

Ricky walked along the far side of the trailer, which because of where they had parked it, was away from their line of vision from the restaurant. They could only see along the driver's side. Ricky stopped and tugged at the cords holding the cover in place. "These are a little loose." She pulled the cords tighter. She re-inspected the trailer.

Rhetta pointed to the ground. "Ricky, look at this. Are these footprints?"

The evidence of someone's recent visit was not yet completely covered with snow. Rhetta gazed around the parking lot. No one but the four of them was out in the worsening weather. Rhetta showed Randolph the footprints. "Sweets, look at these. Somebody must have been checking out the car."

Ricky said, "Probably somebody wanting to peek at it. It's almost obvious what it is by the shape. Anyone who knows old cars could identify the silhouette right away."

Rhetta's stomach tightened. "Sure, you're probably right. I'm glad I locked the doors. I guess I'm just nervous about the car."

Ricky nodded. "As well you should be. This car is worth a fortune."

Randolph and Billy Dan stooped to inspect the tracks. They stood, then scoped out the whole parking lot. "I don't see anyone," Randolph said.

"Me neither," said Billy Dan.

"On that encouraging word, let's all hit the rooms, and start our lookout," Ricky said.

They turned and stomped their way across the parking lot. The snowflakes got heavier and the wind began whistling. A full-out snowstorm had begun.

Chapter 46

RHETTA LAY WIDE-AWAKE AND fully dressed across one of the double beds in the room. Randolph didn't suffer any insomnia. Removing only his shoes, he had slid under the covers of the other bed and had fallen instantly asleep. She listened to his soft rhythmical snoring. Her head kept spinning with everything that had happened. Not the least of which was the huge amount of cash that her father had socked away in the Camaro's glove box.

As soon as she and Randolph locked the door behind them in their room, they pulled out the envelope stuffed with money and began counting. There were four hundred and twenty-five bills, all thousand-dollar denomination—four hundred twenty-five thousand dollars.

"Rhetta, I can't believe these thousand dollar bills. That denomination hasn't been in circulation since the late sixties. I wonder where Frank got these."

"Holy smokes. Are they any good? Did they recall them and now they're worthless?"

"Heavens no. In fact, they may be worth even more than their face value because of their rarity. Some collector may pay more than face value for every one of these."

Rhetta had stared at the bills. *Dear God. How on earth are we going to report this money to the IRS? That's going to mess up our taxes for sure.* Maybe they could just sell the bills and give most of the cash away. She would check with her accountant.

Her mind flew into high gear. If she gave the money away, who should be the recipient? The animal shelter in Cape was dear to her heart, so some of it would have to go there. And what about the PTSD support group? Didn't Woody say that the government wasn't helping some of the guys with their medicine? Definitely, she would help some of Woody's buddies. And for sure she wanted some to go to Saint Jude's Children's Hospital in Memphis. A friend of hers had a granddaughter currently getting treatment there, and Rhetta had helped with a fundraiser last fall. She sighed and couldn't believe that she was worrying about places to spend money.

She got up from the bed and tiptoed to the sink for a drink of water. As she passed the window, she glanced out at the truck and trailer. The snow had stopped, and a full moon bathed the snow-covered lot in an eerie silver glow. Although she wished it hadn't snowed, the scene outside looked like it was taken right from a Currier and Ives Christmas card.

Except for the tiny white light that flitted around the far side of the trailer. It flickered once more, then disappeared.

Rhetta's heart sped up. She stared harder at the trailer, but couldn't see any more light. Were her eyes playing tricks on her? She slipped over to the door and eased on her boots. She pulled on her sweatshirt and jacket and returned to the window to peer out again. Nothing stirred. She sat in the armchair by the window and continued staring out at the truck and trailer. Her heart slowed, and she resumed breathing normally.

She had stared so long that she had almost dozed off when the flicker reappeared. Adrenaline pumping, she bolted up from the chair and snatched her purse, rummaging inside for her .38. She withdrew it, and slipped out the door, closing it quietly so as not to wake Randolph. No sense in him losing sleep if she was imagining things. She flattened herself against the wall of the motel, and eased over to a post. She stayed behind it while she studied the trailer again. If there was something there, why hadn't Billy Dan and Ricky seen it? Didn't they have the first watch?

Her heart began racing again. They probably hadn't seen the light because it was a very small beam and had disappeared quickly. She only glimpsed it because she had been staring at the trailer. She didn't see it now. What if it was nothing? No, those footprints in the snow earlier weren't her imagination. They had all seen them. Heart hammering, she crouched behind some tall holly bushes and checked her weapon. She shivered from cold and anxiety. Her hand shook. Nothing moved for a minute. Then she saw a faint glow from under the car cover. Someone was messing with the car. She bolted upright, gun drawn and began sprinting across the snow-covered parking lot.

"Hold it right there, buster, or I'll shoot!" Rhetta yelled. She'd only managed to run about ten yards when her feet flew out from under her and she landed hard on her butt. The gun went airborne, then skidded across the parking lot ahead of her. Billy Dan and Ricky burst from their room and gave chase to a man running thirty feet ahead of them. A pickup truck beeped and the figure opened the door and leapt into the driver's seat, and started the truck. In the cab light that stayed on only for a second before he slammed the door shut, she caught a glimpse of the driver. Definitely a man, and wearing a jacket or coat with the collar pulled up around his neck. That was all she could see.

The truck skidded as it flew out of the parking lot and onto the street. Still slipping sideways, it throttled down the outer road and disappeared.

Billy Dan and Ricky ran to Rhetta, who was sitting up. Billy Dan reached out and helped her to her feet. Billy Dan found her gun, brushed it off and handed it to her.

"Ow, that hurt," she said, slapping the snow off her backside and limping toward the trailer. She pointed toward where the truck had screamed out of the parking lot. "I found someone messing with the car. I bet that was him tearing out of here."

Ricky was already at the trailer, and clambering up. She cussed loudly and jumped down. "Somebody just got into the Camaro." By now, Rhetta and Billy Dan had joined her. "Look, the car cover is cut." Then she lifted the cover like a tent flap. She turned to Rhetta, her eyes moist. "Damn him. He cut the top, too and got into the car."

Chapter 47

Very early Saturday morning, January 19

THE FOUR OF THEM SAT at a table in the darkened restaurant. Although it was still closed, the night desk clerk had come over and made them a fresh pot of coffee. Rhetta had gone back to the room and awakened Randolph, who wasn't happy to learn that she'd taken off across the parking lot wielding her .38.

"You should have come and got me," he admonished.

"I didn't have time. I was afraid he'd get away. I didn't plan on falling on my backside. I think I could've stopped him." She squirmed to sit on the cheek that didn't hurt as much.

Ricky had gone from angry shock, to full-out tears of outrage. "What did he want?" She poured coffee and distractedly added several packets of sugar, until Billy Dan touched her arm gently.

"That's five packets of sugar," Billy Dan said, his grey eyes twinkling.

"Oh blazes! I won't be able to drink it like that."

He grabbed another clean cup from a nearby table and poured half of her coffee into it. Then he topped off her cup from the carafe, and handed it to her.

"Thanks." She smiled at him, and he patted her hand. "It's such a shame that he cut through that gorgeous top. That was all original. But it's okay, don't worry, we can get it fixed. I know people." She stirred her coffee noisily.

Rhetta said, "I bet it's someone who overheard us at the storage unit when we found the money in the glove box." She set her own spoon down, and slid her cup away. "Do you remember if there was anyone nearby when we were all talking about that money?" She glanced at each of them, and they all shook their heads.

"There was nobody anywhere around us," Randolph said. "I'm positive."

"I was too excited looking at the car. I didn't really pay attention," Ricky said.

Billy Dan agreed with Randolph. "I didn't see anyone else on the place except for the manager."

"Just how much money was there?" Ricky asked. When Rhetta told her, all the color drained from her face. "No wonder somebody tried to steal it."

They sat silently for a moment. Ricky scooted her chair back, and stood. "I'm going to look at something." She downed the last of the coffee in the first cup.

"You shouldn't touch anything else. There may be evidence there," Randolph said.

"I think I remember seeing that the driver side door wasn't shut all the way. The light stayed on. He got in the passenger side, so why was the driver's door not closed all the way? He had to have opened it from the inside. I want to go and look again. I won't touch anything." Ricky tied the string on her hoodie and flipped the hood over her head.

Rhetta said, "I saw the flicker of light, too. I'll go with you." Rhetta snugged her jacket around her and they hustled out the door.

At the trailer, Ricky pulled back the cover enough to see the driver door. Just as she'd said, the door wasn't fully closed. And the interior light was on. That meant the battery was still charged. The manager at the Cave Storage had told them Frank drove the car routinely. Rhetta believed him now.

"These doors are really heavy, so when the thief closed it, it didn't shut completely." Ricky slid the cover back into place. Turning to Rhetta, she continued, "You locked the doors after you got out when the car was loaded, right?" When Rhetta nodded, she said, "I'm going to show this to the cops. I won't close that door tightly until they get here and see it."

"If he was already inside the car, why would he have opened the driver side?" Rhetta asked as they walked back to the dining room. "If he was looking for the money, he would have ransacked the car."

"There's no reason to open the driver door and risk the light coming on. Maybe he didn't know that the battery is good and the interior light would work. Probably why he closed it so fast it didn't catch." She shook her head. "It doesn't make any sense."

Ricky scrunched her face as she thought. "There's nothing in the door except the hinges, and…wait a minute! On a '67 Camaro, the VIN is on a plate on the door pillar between the hinges. Could that be what he wanted to see?"

Rhetta's blood ran as cold as the snow.

"Of course," she said. "That's it." She was certain now that the break-in had nothing to do with the money. *Somebody knows about needing the VIN for the trust.* She was sure of it.

But, who?

Chapter 48

Saturday morning, January 19

TO EVERYONE'S EXASPERATION, THE POLICE didn't arrive until after eight o'clock and several pots of coffee. By that time, the restaurant had opened and several of the motel guests had assembled for breakfast. The smells of bacon and sausage cooking mingled with the aroma of coffee. The quiet chatter of conversation replaced the silence of a few hours earlier.

The good news about the police delay was that the snow had quit falling and the temperature had already climbed above freezing. It appeared the front had passed through and warmer air had slipped in, allowing the snow to melt. In spite of having to wait longer than they would have preferred to make the police report, it meant that the roads would be in better shape than they had first thought. The trip home wouldn't be so bad.

While they waited, Rhetta and Randolph had filled in Billy Dan and Ricky on everything that they knew about the Tontine Trust.

"That would definitely explain why he needed to get inside the car," Ricky said. "He had to read the VIN. I wonder if he was able to get to it."

After all the excitement, they had all gone back to their respective rooms, where Rhetta showered and changed her clothes. She packed the money from the glove box carefully into a small foldable fabric suitcase and nestled the car's paperwork next to it.

"I want to be sure that the bag with the money rides up in the cab with us on the way home," she told Randolph as he came out of the shower. "I stashed the cash in it along with all the papers. Whoever broke into the car is after the VIN, but he may be after this money, too. We don't know. If he didn't get the VIN last night, he may still try to hijack us for the title, or the car, or the money or whatever." She held the small bag aloft. "We have to hide this."

Randolph had slipped into his clothes and fired up the hair dryer, its hum drowning out Rhetta. "I hate to go out in the cold with my hair wet," he said as he noticed Rhetta studying him in the mirror. His dark hair grazed his collar. He had never worn his hair long when he was on the bench. Rhetta liked the new look.

Holding the bag, which measured about sixteen by twenty-four inches, she asked, "Will this fit behind the back seat?"

He shut the dryer off. "If I move some of the stuff around, it should. Why?"

"If someone is really after us, or me, and wants the VIN and the money, he may follow us and try to get it. I'm keeping my .38 close and ready." She patted her purse. "We have to be very careful and super alert. We need to hide this bag as best we can."

"Are you sure you're not just being paranoid?"

She blessed him with a look.

"Okay, right. What was I thinking? I'll stow it behind the truck seat before we leave, so that nobody can spot it, unless he knows to look there. We want to make sure no one sees us do that when we leave."

"You're right. Let's just toss both these other suitcases into the truck as though they don't contain anything very important, in case someone is watching us. I can't shake the feeling that someone is watching everything that we're doing. I'll hide this one in my purse, then once we're on the road, we'll do it when we're in the truck. For once, you should be glad I carry a very large purse."

"All right, but I'll need to take some stuff out from behind the seat before I can even squeeze that little bag in there."

"No, don't do that. If he's watching, he'll get suspicious."

Randolph shook his head. "Okay, we'll see what we can do." He finished drying his hair.

She ran her fingers through her own spiky do and applied some spray. "I'm glad my hair is so short. It's always dry by the time I get dressed."

Randolph settled the bill with the hotel, then carried their two larger bags out to the back of the truck and tossed them in before returning to the lobby to wait with the others. Rhetta, clutching her purse with the small bag squeezed into it, had already met up with Ricky and Billy Dan.

An officer pulled up next to the trailer. As Randolph headed toward the door, Rhetta stopped him. "I don't know if we should tell this cop too much about how I happened to come by the car. It's such a strange story that we may be here all day."

"Let me do the talking. You all stay here, unless he specifically needs to asks one of us a direct question," Randolph said. Rhetta agreed, and Ricky and Billy Dan nodded.

Randolph strode out to the cruiser and met the young officer as he was getting out. The officer shook hands with Randolph, and then produced a notebook from his shirt pocket. He began writing as Randolph led him around the car. After a cursory inspection, the officer nodded, shook hands again with Randolph, added a few more notes, then returned to his patrol car.

It all took less than five minutes.

As the officer rolled out of the parking lot, Randolph joined the others

"Wow, that didn't take very long," Rhetta said.

"I minimized the whole episode. Told him the car was broken into, but nothing was damaged or stolen. I definitely got the impression that he was mainly humoring me because I'm a retired judge. Otherwise, I doubt if he would have even looked at the car. Said he'd let me know if they find out anything. I thanked him for his time." Randolph strode back to the coffee shop. "Is anyone hungry for breakfast?" When everybody shook their heads, he said, "Let's get our coffee for the road and get on our way. We can stop somewhere, maybe in Columbia, for breakfast."

Rhetta clutched her purse tightly. Ricky and Billy Dan disappeared inside their room, and returned in minutes with their things. They tossed them into the rear of the truck with the other suitcases.

Everyone circled the trailer making sure that the Camaro was securely fastened. Then, after a few minutes of arguing about who would drive, Ricky proclaimed herself the winner, and crawled in behind the wheel, with Billy Dan riding shotgun next to her, and Rhetta and Randolph in the back seat.

They eased out onto the service road, stopping at the Conoco next door to fuel up, and get more coffee. The temperature had improved and the road was clear.

Fifteen minutes later, they were on Interstate 70 heading east, toward Columbia, and home.

Chapter 49

Saturday afternoon, January 19

TWO HOURS LATER, RICKY BEGAN to squirm as they approached the western edge of Columbia, on Highway 70.

"I need a bathroom break, does anyone else?"

Rhetta sat up, and stretched. "I do."

She had laid her head on Randolph's shoulder and although not asleep, was keeping quiet. Randolph was snoring lightly. Billy Dan and Ricky were chatting quietly.

After some creative maneuvering, some of which involved Rhetta's backside being in the air a time or two, Randolph had managed to get stuff moved around behind the back seat to allow enough room to squeeze in the small bag. He piled the truck jack and some rags and a small tool box on top of it, and once he'd satisfied Rhetta that he'd stashed the little suitcase well enough, finally sat back against the seat.

"I know you think I'm being paranoid," Rhetta said. "But honestly, I can't shake the feeling that someone's watching or following us. I think either someone is after the money or the paperwork. Or both. I tucked everything into that bag." That's when she cuddled next to Randolph. She really had to since a toolbox shared the seat with them along with her notoriously oversized purse. It was nice having someone else drive, and cuddling in the back seat. Even if her husband did fall asleep.

Ricky exited the highway and pulled into a truck stop. She parked in the back at the end of the rows where the tractor-trailers parked. Everyone but Rhetta got out.

"I'll wait here until you get back," she said. "I don't want to leave the bag, even if we do lock up the truck."

Randolph said, "Let me stay, you go on and I'll run in when you get back."

She agreed, and hurried in. She was back to the truck in no time. Ricky went into the restaurant, and Billy Dan stood near the restaurant door, firing up a cigarette.

Randolph left to take his turn. While waiting for everyone to return, Rhetta got out, locked the truck doors, leaving her purse with the toolbox, and checked the trailer again making sure the car was still secure. When she reached the far side, she checked the tire pressure on the right rear tire of the trailer. It appeared low to her. Before she could straighten, she felt a sharp prod in her back.

"Real quiet. Stand up. Make any noise at all and you're dead. Unlock the truck."

Rhetta's heart slammed against her ribs. Good thing she had just gone to the bathroom. She nodded and slowly straightened. She started to turn around.

"Don't turn around. Or it will get ugly." He said ugly like he meant it.

She nodded, kept her back to him and inched her way to the truck. She pointed the key fob at it and the door locks shot upward. She tried surreptitiously to glance around, hoping that Billy Dan or Randolph would appear. "Quit stalling. Get out of the way. Turn toward to the restaurant. Do not turn toward me, or I will have to kill you."

She obeyed. She heard him snatch the toolbox. Then in that ugly voice again, he said, his words like measured venom, "Do not turn around. I will definitely kill. Do you understand?" She vigorously nodded her complete understanding. She believed with all her heart that he would do as he threatened. She had her head turned just enough to catch a glimpse of him in her peripheral vision. He was clutching the toolbox. Not her purse, just the plastic toolbox, which had several of Randolph's truck tools inside. He obviously wasn't a run-of-the-mill bandit. He was after something specific and believed it to be in the toolbox. She knew that what he wanted wasn't in the toolbox, but he hadn't yet discovered that. She hoped he would be far away by the time he did. Still trying her best to size him up with her peripheral vision, she couldn't shake the feeling that he seemed familiar. Had she seen him before?

Then she knew. That's who was at the impound yard the day her father met her there and the car burned up. He was the one who escaped in the truck. She was sure of it. Had he caused the explosion?

He darted sideways, ducked between the trucks, and because she didn't dare turn her head, she quickly lost sight of him. She stood very still. When she believed he was truly gone, she locked the truck and bolted for the restaurant. As she rounded the corner, she collided with Randolph.

"We just got robbed! And I think I know who it was."

Chapter 50

"DEAR GOD, RHETTA, WHAT HAPPENED?" Randolph came to her, and put his arms around her. She was trembling. "It's going to be all right," he said soothing her.

His tone indicated to her that he misunderstood why she was trembling. "I've had it with someone attacking me!" She stomped her foot and pulled away, turned, and looked into Randolph's face. "I'm so mad I could just shoot him! I wish I'd had my gun. I would have."

"Lord, Rhetta, think of all the paperwork that would cause." Randolph's lips twitched in a grin. She knew he was trying to make her feel better.

"I mean it, Sweets, next time—"

"You said you thought you knew him. Who was it?"

"The same guy that was out at the impound yard. I'm sure of it. That truck we saw was his, too. I recognize it now."

"Did he get your purse?" Randolph asked before he peered inside the truck. When he did, her purse was still on the seat. "What did he get?"

"He took the tool box. He'll be disappointed when all he finds inside are your tools."

"He probably thought since you had it with your purse that the money and paperwork were in it." Randolph checked behind the seat. "The other bag is still here. Wonder why he didn't take your purse?"

"If he knew there was a lot of money, he would have realized it wouldn't have fit in my purse." She held her hand up. "Don't say it. Even though you think it's as big as a suitcase, it really isn't."

Billy Dan and Ricky strolled up. Billy Dan dropped his cigarette to the pavement and ground it out with his shoe.

"I'll drive for a while," Randolph said, slipping behind the wheel. Rhetta took the front passenger seat next to him. Billy Dan and Ricky opened the back doors to the truck, and began climbing in.

"Where's the tool box?" Ricky asked, glancing about.

"I just got robbed. Again," Rhetta said, as she fastened her seat belt.

"Are you serious?" Ricky gaped at Rhetta.

Rhetta nodded.

Randolph had his cell phone out. "I'm not sure where the 9-1-1 calls from here go, but we'll find out."

Once everyone was buckled in and they were underway again, Rhetta spoke up. "That officer was a lot nicer than the ones at home. I doubt if Unreasonable would have assigned a patrol car to follow us." She turned around and spotted the highway patrol car about three car lengths behind.

Rhetta had given the officer as much of a description as she could, considering that she didn't see much of her attacker. "I feel sure that it's the same man we saw at the impound lot. If so, I can describe him, and his truck." Together she and Ricky provided the patrol officer with a description of the truck and the driver. The officer had radioed in the description.

"I wonder if he and his truck are still on the interstate. If he's smart he would have gotten off."

Ricky swiveled around to look out the back window. "Hey, our officer back there just threw his blue lights on."

Rhetta's head snapped around. The patrol car zoomed around them in the outside lane.

Randolph leaned forward. "Looks like another patrol car has a blue truck pulled over up ahead." As he spoke, Rhetta spotted a dark blue truck stopped on the shoulder. The officer had the driver spread over the hood of the truck. Rhetta's heart began pounding. Randolph eased the rig over onto the shoulder and joined the two patrol cars.

As they stopped, Rhetta's heart sank. The driver, a young man was turned facing the officer. He looked like he was scared enough to pass out.

It wasn't the right truck.

Chapter 51

Saturday afternoon, January 19

AFTER RHETTA HAD TOLD THE officers that she was sure this wasn't the truck, and that she was also sure the young man wasn't the perp, the officers released the truck and its driver.

The officer had flipped his notebook closed. "I hate to say it, ma'am, but your assailant is probably long gone by now. We will keep the BOLO active and see if anything turns up." He tipped his hat at them before he left.

"Be on the lookout, right?" Ricky asked when Rhetta returned to their truck. "That's a BOLO?"

"It is. Not exactly a bonafide police term these days, but most officers still use it. Most folks know what it means from cop shows," Randolph said as he eased himself in behind the wheel.

"I guess it was hoping for too much to think they got this guy caught that easily," Randolph said. "We need to be especially watchful. I think our bad guy is looking for the paperwork for the car. Maybe he didn't get the VIN off the car after all."

"I don't know what's going on with the business with your dad, Rhetta, but I do know I don't want anyone damaging this precious Camaro. I still can't believe somebody cut the top." Ricky shook her head. "I'm afraid for you, too. Please, please be very careful."

"I haven't heard any more from my father. I don't know anything since the fire at the impound lot. I don't know if he's dead or alive. Since that letter I got from him was supposed to come to me after his death, I wonder about him."

Randolph glanced sideways at Rhetta, and added, "Your father is probably dead."

Rhetta nodded. "I should feel worse, I guess, but I feel ambivalent about him. I'm angry he has me involved in all of this. Yet part of me feels sorry for him. I just don't know what I should feel."

Randolph reached over and squeezed her hand. "Of course you feel unsure about him. That's to be expected. Let's just get through this. We'll find out everything, I'm sure."

She squeezed his hand and nodded.

"Someone is trying very hard to get the VIN for the car," Randolph said. To Ricky, he asked, "Is there any way you can remove the VIN tag when we get it home? We'll put that into the safe deposit box with the title. I doubt if he can break into the bank's vault."

"I can take it off," Ricky said. "I can order those special starburst rivets so I can put it back so that it looks original. In case you ever want to show it."

"What about the top? Can that be fixed?" Rhetta asked.

"I'll ask Mr. Montero, my upholsterer, if he can fix this one. I'm pretty sure he can. He can fix anything."

By the time they reached Saint Louis, the temperature had warmed enough to melt any snow that remained. According to the weather app on Rhetta's iPhone, Saint Louis had barely received an inch of snow, and none had fallen in Cape Girardeau. The roads were all clear.

Buoyed by the improvement in the weather, Ricky said, "Let's just drive straight on home. I don't want to stop to eat, and take any more chances on getting attacked." She checked the fuel gauge. "Well, except we need to get gas. We'll probably need to stop at Perryville. We can pick up some snacks."

Randolph agreed.

Billy Dan piped up. "I am about to pass out from a nicotine craving, so Perryville is a must-stop."

"Okay, okay, we can do this," Randolph said. "Let me have your .38 when we stop, Rhetta. This time, I'll be the lookout. And we stay in pairs."

An hour and a half later, they pulled in to the brightly lit filling station at the Perryville exit on Interstate 55. Night had fallen, but the service station glowed eerily from the blue vapor lights that bathed the pump area in light brighter than daytime. The air was cool, but the ground was dry.

Randolph filled the tank while Billy Dan and Ricky headed inside. When they returned, Randolph handed Billy Dan the gun, and he and Rhetta took their turn inside. Rhetta bought some fruit, snacks and coffee to tide them over. They returned and settled back into the truck, heading down Interstate 55 on the final fifty miles home. Ricky insisted on driving.

Rhetta's eyes were tired and gritty from staring at every vehicle on the road.

Ricky wheeled the truck and trailer into her driveway. Her shop was located in a converted wooden barn that sat about fifty feet from an old farmhouse that she had inherited and painstakingly restored. She'd installed a green, metal-roofed breezeway that connected the house and shop; the breezeway matched both for one continuous roof. She pulled up alongside the first garage door.

"I'll go and turn off the alarm." She jumped down from the truck and disappeared inside her shop. In a moment, bright overhead lights lit up the doorway and driveway.

"It won't take but a few minutes to unload the car into the shop. I'll take off the VIN tag, and you can take it home with you."

Ricky unwrapped the car. Rhetta climbed up the trailer and squeezed through the driver door. She steered as Randolph and Billy Dan pushed the car while Ricky let the winch out. The car glided soundlessly down the ramp.

Once unloaded, the men pushed the car into the shop. Ricky pulled the doors down and locked them securely. Five minutes later, she handed the VIN tag to Rhetta.

"Here it is. Now, keep it safe." Rhetta's hand closed over it. Her heart sped up.

After pulling the trailer to its parking spot, Ricky and Billy Dan unhooked it, and took out their bags. "If we left anything behind, I'll pick it up at your office," Ricky said.

"I'll drive Ricky over to get her truck tomorrow," Billy Dan said, draping his arm across Ricky's shoulders.

Rhetta and Ricky hugged, and the men shook hands. Randolph tucked in behind the wheel and fired up his pickup. Rhetta buckled in and turned the heater on high.

As they backed out of the driveway, Rhetta's iPhone rang. She didn't recognize the number.

"This is Rhetta McCarter," she said, checking the time. It was almost six o'clock. Her stomach rumbled as a reminder that they hadn't eaten any supper. They were all so determined to get the Camaro home before any more trouble came their way that they didn't stop to eat. She thought she and Randolph could hit a Subway and grab something after leaving Ricky's. She was tired, and didn't feel like cooking. Besides, she craved a large fresh salad.

"Mrs. McCarter, this is Katelyn Montgomery from Family Outreach at Saint Mark's Hospital in Cape Girardeau. It's about Frank Caldwell."

Chapter 52

Saturday evening, January 19

"Mr. Caldwell provided us with this number when he was admitted three days ago."

"Three days ago? Why are you just now calling me?"

"Mr. Caldwell left specific instructions. We were to notify you only in the event he passed away."

Rhetta's ears began ringing. "Is he…has he…passed? Away?" Rhetta asked. The hunger pangs were gone. In their place a ball of acid began making its way north from her stomach.

"Yes, I'm very sorry. Mr. Caldwell is gone. He passed thirty minutes ago. I just received the notification. You are listed here as his only next of kin. We were instructed to notify you."

"Yes, I'm his daughter. I'm on my way."

Rhetta covered the mouthpiece and spoke to Randolph. "It's Frank. Head to Saint Mark's." Randolph nodded, then arrowed down Route K out of Gordonville where Ricky lived, and barreled toward the hospital.

"Please come to the Outreach Center on the lower level. Do you know where it is? I will meet you there," Katelyn Montgomery said.

"Uh, no, actually, I don't," Rhetta said. She glanced out of the side window. Night had fallen, and the streetlights along Route K glittered.

"When you come in through the main doors of the hospital complex take the C elevator down to the lower level. Then, turn right and follow the corridor all the way to the end. There will be a security door there. That's where I will meet you."

"Thank you." Rhetta disconnected. She stared at her phone. "He's gone." She turned toward Randolph. "I didn't know he was in the hospital. I presumed he was already dead. I guess we shouldn't have gone to Kansas City. I could have come up here to see him."

"Why didn't the hospital call you before he passed?" Randolph said, glancing at her. He stopped in the left turn lane on to Saint Mark's Drive. The light changed and he rolled into the parking lot.

"This woman, Katelyn Montgomery, said that Frank had instructed them not to call me until...he passed." Rhetta said. "By the way, I don't like that term. Why can't they just say, died?"

Randolph pulled into a parking spot near the door. "I guess they think that passing sounds better than dying. Who knows? More political correctness, I suppose."

Randolph reached for Rhetta's hand as they entered the building. "Are you all right?" he asked. She nodded, and squeezed his hand.

"I'm sad, only because there is so much about him that I would have liked to have known. I guess now I never will." She started to open the door. "You know, I spent a lot of time hating him. I guess now I just feel numb. It's hard to process how I feel."

Randolph reached over and cupped her chin, and kissed her.

"I'm the luckiest woman in the world to have you, Sweets."

After locking up the SUV, they made their way to the Outreach Center. Katelyn Montgomery was good for her word. She was waiting for them. The sturdy brunette wearing a white lab coat over dark blue slacks, also wore a nametag that identified her position as *Patient Outreach*. Rhetta wasn't sure where in the realm of patient outreach that the job of identifying or viewing a person who had passed would fall.

"I'm Katelyn," said the woman, probably mid-forties, Rhetta guessed, as she reached out to shake Rhetta's hand.

After the introductions, Katelyn peered over her reading glasses at Rhetta. "Do you want to view Mr. Caldwell?"

Rhetta let out a whoosh of air. "Yes, please."

"Please come with me. Mr. Caldwell is just over here." She led them into a room lined on three sides with stainless steel vault doors. Gurneys lined the fourth wall. Katelyn stopped at the foot of the only gurney that seemed to have an occupant. A morgue attendant dressed in blue scrubs stood by silently. The person on the gurney was completely covered by a pale blue sheet. Katelyn turned to Rhetta. "Are you sure you want to see him?"

"Yes. I'm sure." Rhetta took a deep breath as Katelyn nodded to the morgue attendant. He slowly pulled back the sheet.

Frank's face was calmer in death than Rhetta had ever remembered seeing it in life.

In spite of herself, a tear trickled down her cheek. A tear for all that could have been. It was apparent by everything that had happened recently that Frank Caldwell had indeed loved his only child. Her. His daughter. His life choices had prevented him from being a part of Rhetta's life, and her mother's, too. For that, Rhetta felt profoundly sad. The tear dripped down her cheek. She wiped it aside.

As she glanced at her father, covered up to his shoulders with the sheet, she remembered the strange tattoo. His arms were at his side, also covered.

"May I see his right arm?" The attendant looked up.

"His right arm, ma'am?"

"Yes." Rhetta held her iPhone at the ready.

The attendant bared Frank's arm and gently laid it by his side, on top of the sheet.

Rhetta went to the edge of the gurney, and snapped pictures of his arm and the unusual tattoo. Then she snapped pictures of his face.

The tattoo was clear, as was the mask of death he wore. Although she knew that she would receive a death certificate, she thought she might need more proof to show whomever about the trust.

She didn't explain to the two puzzled-looking hospital employees why she needed the pictures.

Chapter 53

B Y THE TIME SHE HAD signed all the paperwork and had notified the hospital that she would have the funeral home come and get her father, Rhetta had lost her appetite. Randolph suggested they still stop by Subway. They could get something fresh that would keep, and eat it later.

Before they had left, Katelyn Montgomery had handed Rhetta the few meager possessions that Frank still had on him when he was admitted—his wallet, some keys and a military ring.

Although she remembered Frank telling her that she wouldn't have to make any funeral arrangements, the staff at the hospital knew nothing. She presumed that the woman who burned up in the fire, Rushia Coughenour or Rushia Caldwell, Frank's wife, was the confidant who was supposed to have all the information. Rhetta realized then, that she didn't know what had happened to Rushia's remains. She would find out from the county, and if no one had claimed her, then she would bury her, too.

She called the same funeral director who had handled George Erickson's funeral, and turned everything over to him. She promised to come by tomorrow and make the final preparations. That meant, pay for the funeral. She would do that, and make sure that Frank would be buried with honor. She scheduled the burial for Tuesday, along with Rushia's, if no one had claimed her.

Rhetta emerged from the shower with a towel wrapped around her head, and wearing a thick white terry robe. Randolph took his turn at a hot shower, and soon joined Rhetta at the kitchen island.

"Do you want me to make you some coffee?" he asked as he sat next to her, kissing her cheek.

"Nope. I don't want any more jitters than I already have. This whole business of my father, and his death and the trust and the car…" She didn't finish, just shook her head and opened the refrigerator, brought out the food they had picked up, and set it on plates. Instead of coffee, she poured them each a glass of white wine.

"It will take about a week to get a death certificate," Randolph said.

"Uh, huh. I'm sure that's right. Maybe longer. Why?" She poured Ranch dressing on her salad. Randolph unwrapped his sandwich.

"You'll need to take it with you when you go to collect the trust." He took a bite into the six-inch turkey on wheat, then sipped his wine.

"Wait. What do you mean, when I go to collect the trust. You mean, we, don't you?" Her fork stayed poised in mid-air, a chunk of chicken impaled on the end.

"Of course." Randolph set aside his sandwich and pulled out his phone. He showed her his calendar. "Starting around the first weekend in February, I have exhibits and art shows nearly every weekend. I suggest we leave as soon as the certificate comes in. We shouldn't wait any longer. Especially if someone else is trying to get to that money."

She set her fork down in the salad, the chicken chunk intact. "I don't want to go to Vera Mardola. But I guess I owe it to Frank." She reached for her wine.

"And to George Erickson and everyone else in the trust who died. That was their agreement. Your father went through a lot of effort to make sure you get this. It appears that someone thinks it's significant enough to kill for, if someone struck down George Erickson on purpose.

I think the same someone could be after you. I'm definitely going with you."

"I could ask Ricky to go, if you want to stay here and get ready for your shows." Rhetta said this half-heartedly. She really didn't want to go to Vera Mardola at all. But, if she had to go, she sure wanted Randolph to go with her.

Randolph took Rhetta in his arms and hugged her. "There's no way I wouldn't go with you. Have Mrs. Koblyk feed the cats." A tear trickled down her cheek. She batted it away.

He kissed Rhetta soundly. "I love you, Rhetta. I'll be there with you."

Chapter 54

Tuesday morning, eight-thirty, January 22

ALTHOUGH THE WEEKEND HAD BEEN mild, *First News* had a predicted a snowstorm for Monday. The snow, however, had waited until this morning. Rhetta had taken Monday off, and wasn't disappointed there was no snow. She had all the funeral arrangements to finalize.

Now, giant flakes fell as Rhetta and Randolph eased Streak down the lane to the county road. There was no accumulation, yet. The weather had been mild until the jet stream decided to dip way south and capture all of Missouri in its icy grip.

"With any luck, the roads are still too warm for the snow to stick," Randolph said. "That is, if we don't get too much."

"I guess Mr. DeBrock won't be thrilled to be out on a day like this for the interment. I guess we could have waited until tomorrow," Rhetta said, turning up the heater.

"We're better off today. If this storm does get worse, tomorrow we may get six inches."

"When I called the coroner's office yesterday, Matt was sure that no one was going to step up and claim Rushia's remains, since no one had yet done so. In about another week, the county would have had to take care of burying her. I'm glad we were able to get a plot next to my father's so they could be together."

Rhetta had not held a visitation for her father or Rushia. She had insisted on her father's casket being closed and wanted no visitors. Understandably, Rushia's casket was closed. There was no preparation necessary for either of the two bodies—Rushia's because of her charred remains, and Frank because embalming wasn't mandatory.

Mr. DeBrock was cooperative. Especially when Rhetta explained briefly that she wasn't close to her father, and had no other family in the area. It helped that she personally went in and wrote a check for both funerals.

When they arrived at the cemetery, Rhetta spotted two caskets set up side by side beside two burial excavations. Overhead, the black canvas canopy flapped in the gusting wind. Two figures huddled near the first grave. "Looks like Woody and LuEllen didn't believe me when I told them they didn't have to come."

Randolph pointed to another figure bundled up in a long coat and wearing a scarf wrapped around her red hair. Next to her, Billy Dan held Ricky's gloved hand in his.

Rhetta wiped an errant tear away and blew her nose before getting out of Streak. "I'm so lucky to have such dear friends," she snuffled.

Randolph parked the Trailblazer as close as he could to the site, then wrapped his arm around Rhetta's shoulders as they walked the fifty feet to the waiting group. Off to one side, four members of the local Veterans of Foreign Wars stood at attention. One held a bugle.

Mr. DeBrock greeted them, then glanced around. "Will anyone else be attending?"

"This is it." Rhetta said, receiving hugs from her friends. She grasped Randolph's hand as they waited for the service to begin.

It took about five minutes for Mr. DeBrock to say a prayer for the departed. Then he stepped aside. A lone bugler played "Taps" as DeBrock positioned her father's flag-draped casket to lower into its permanent resting place. When the bugler finished, he joined three other

V.F.W. members. The team folded the flag smartly, then turned and saluted, maintaining the salute as the casket descended. When it reached the bottom, they turned and saluted her. One man stepped forward and handed her the folded flag.

In spite of herself, she choked up. These four men had not known her father, yet they came out on a day like this and honored one of their own upon his death.

"Thank you so much," she said, as she accepted the symbol of her father's patriotism.

Mr. DeBrock also thanked the four men.

Rhetta moved to stand by Rushia's casket. "I didn't know you, Rushia, but obviously you and my father meant a lot to each other. For that, I thank you." Rhetta touched the casket, and then nodded to DeBrock. The funeral director again recited a prayer for the departed. He pressed the button to begin lowering the casket. When it was below ground, everyone turned to leave.

Rhetta stopped Mr. DeBrock. "Thank you for arranging for the V.F.W members to be here. I know that the Vietnam War was unpopular. I'm glad the Veterans of Foreign Wars value their fallen." They shook hands.

"Actually, Mrs. McCarter, it was Mr. Zelinski there," he nodded toward Woody, "who made the arrangements for the honor team to be here."

Rhetta turned and hugged Woody. "Thanks, Woody."

"I wanted him to have the honor of a military funeral. He deserved that much." Woody cleared his throat.

Rhetta nodded.

As they made their way back to the cars, Rhetta pointed to a man walking away. She remembered seeing a figure standing at the edge of the cemetery. Now, she recognized his face.

"Woody, look over there. Isn't that Evan?"

Chapter 55

Tuesday morning, January 22

AFTER THE SERVICES, WOODY AND LuEllen returned to the office, while Randolph and Rhetta aimed Streak for home.

"I wish I'd had a chance to know Frank." Rhetta fingered the folded flag that lay alongside her on the seat. "I have absolutely zero memories of him. I remember my mom sobbing late at night, but she never really said much about him. Just that he had left us, and would never be back."

"Did your mom ever have any relationships after him that you recall? Did she ever find anyone to love after your father?" Randolph adjusted the heater controls. Rhetta had been shivering.

"You know, I don't think my mother ever stopped loving my father. I remember a couple of nice men that she dated off and on, but she never got serious with any of them." Rhetta turned down the heater a notch. The Trailblazer had warmed up, and her hat was making her head itch.

"I thought you told me once that your father said that he and your mother were never divorced. So how did he marry Rushia Coughenour?"

"I don't know. He said he kept up with me, so he probably knew that my mother had died. Frankly, since everyone is dead and gone, I really don't care. Obviously, my father needed someone, and if Rushia was there for him, who am I to question?" Rhetta pulled the hat off. She couldn't stand wearing it any longer. She ran her fingers through her hair. Her bruised head was tender but definitely healing.

"You're right. I guess we'll never know and it doesn't matter. They didn't have any children, so where's the harm?" Randolph turned off the gravel road and into the driveway. This time, Mrs. Koblyk didn't greet them.

Rhetta frowned. "I guess we need to plan the trip, although I wish we were going to the Mediterranean for a more pleasant reason, like a vacation." She turned to Randolph. "Why was Evan at the funeral? He doesn't go to the support meetings that Woody goes to, and he sure doesn't know me well enough to attend my father's funeral. Why would he come?"

Randolph eased Streak into the garage. "Do you think he may have known your father during the Vietnam War?" He put Streak into park, and turned off the motor. The garage door rumbled downward. None of the cats had sneaked into the garage. Rhetta stared about, looking for anything out of place, a habit she had developed since the break-in.

"He outright said he didn't know my father. Maybe Evan was only there because he heard that my father was a Vietnam vet, too. But you know," she placed her hand on Randolph's arm just as he was opening the SUV's door, "as far as he knew, my father was already dead. I remember telling him that when we talked. That's when he claimed he didn't know my father."

They both got out, and went into the house from the garage. "Oh well, I'm not going to worry about it. I'm sure Woody told him about my father, and he decided to pay his respects. I know those Vietnam vets are all close, even if they don't know each other."

Randolph nodded. "I'm sure you're right. Poor old guy, I feel sorry for him."

"So do I. He doesn't have a home anywhere. Who knows what problems he might have? It's very kind of Jeff to give him a job and a place to stay."

She trotted to the bedroom. "I'm going to freshen up, then go into the office. I have a closing this afternoon. I should be home at a decent time. I'll fix some grilled chicken breasts and rice, and a nice salad.

"Sounds great," Randolph said, as he headed out the back door toward his studio. Rhetta watched him as he descended the deck steps. Four felines followed him. She loved that man so much.

Rhetta guided Streak into the last remaining parking slot out front. The cable television company must be having meetings again, since there were little "bug fart" cars in all the slots in front of the office. She labeled those small economy cars, "bug farts" because when they accelerated, the noise they emitted sounded like a bug passing gas. Not, in her opinion, the way a real car sounded. Bug farts included small Kias, Hondas, Fords, Chevys. She wasn't prejudiced against any car, but she found the little square ones with baby stroller tires particularly offensive.

I never thought I was a car snob. I don't understand why these younger guys, especially if they're the greenie conservation gas-economy types can't opt for a little exercise and park farther down the parking lot and walk. All of our offices suffer with no customer parking while they're in here for their rah-rah meetings.

To Rhetta, sales meetings were a lot like cheerleading camp.

She spotted Philip Corini sitting in his white car just as she parked. She wasn't sure if it was an Impala or a Taurus or even a Camry. All of the cars looked too much alike, and the majority of them were white. Back in the sixties and seventies, cars had looks, colors and personalities.

She assumed he was getting ready to leave. He glanced in the rear view mirror then looked around before he even started his car. He sat in it a moment, his head swiveling around. Then he opened the car door. He wasn't leaving after all. He stepped out and walked over to a dark blue truck parked two spaces down.

Rhetta leaned over the passenger seat and pretended to look for something on Streak's floor. She faked a search in hopes of discovering what Corini was doing. She still didn't trust him. He was much too slick talking to suit her. And why was he going toward the blue truck? *Blue truck!*

Her heart began jittering. When she eased upright, she spotted the back of Corini as he aimed his keys at the truck. The lights flashed, and Corini returned to his car. As he bent over to retrieve something off the floor of the car, his suit jacket parted at the slit in the back. It closed up again as he slid behind the wheel. He closed the door and started up the car. But not before Rhetta spotted his waistband accessory. A 9-millimeter "Baby" Glock 26, if she was not mistaken.

Chapter 56

AFTER CORINI LEFT, RHETTA RAN up the sidewalk and burst into the office. She stopped at Woody's desk. "You'll never guess who I just saw with a Baby Glock tucked in his waistband." She panted. "And who has two vehicles here, one of them a blue truck!"

Woody turned away from the computer and stared at her. "I give up. Who?"

"Philip Corini," Rhetta said, her heart still thumping wildly. "I'm going to call the police."

Woody placed a hand on her arm. "Wait a minute. What are you going to tell them? It's not illegal to carry a weapon. If you have a concealed carry permit, you can hide it in your waistband. It's also not illegal to have two vehicles."

She shook off Woody's hand. She drilled a stare into Woody. "I know that, Woody. I have a concealed carry permit, and we have more than two vehicles. It's just that one of his is a blue truck, for heaven's sake. Maybe he's who ran over George Erickson." She ran to her desk, and grabbed the phone.

"Corini drove his pickup in the day we had the bad weather. So what are you going to report? " He followed her and stood alongside her desk.

Properly soothed about the truck, Rhetta muttered, "Maybe I'll just call Randolph first, and tell him. He can call the police in Columbia."

"Hold on, Rhetta, I haven't the first notion of what you're talking about." He shook his head, then rubbed it. "I'm missing something. What about Columbia?"

She threw her coat on the back of her chair before plopping down into it. Woody dropped into her customer chair. "I think you better tell me what happened in Columbia."

She did.

When she finished telling him everything that happened on the trip to get the Camaro, Woody stood and began to pace. He rubbed his head. Then he sat again.

"So, do you think the dude who robbed you and messed with the Camaro in Columbia are one and the same? And that he may have been who ran over George Erickson?"

"I definitely do. Maybe it's Corini" She shook her head. "Now I don't know what to think, for sure. I'm really freaking about all of this." She fingered the cord of the phone until it tangled. She spun it the other way, then returned the headset to the cradle. "I guess I don't need to call anyone."

She opened the drawer, glanced at the envelope still inside. "I stopped this morning on my way here and put the VIN plate into my safe deposit box, along with the thousand dollar bills."

"Good." He fingered his chin whiskers. "When are you going overseas?"

"It depends on how long it will take to get the death certificate back."

Rhetta got up, went to the kitchen and retrieved a very large cup of coffee. She brought it back and sat at her desk, both hands clutching the oversized mug, grateful for the warmth.

Woody rose, then sat again. "I don't understand this. If your father was already dead according to records, how come you need another death certificate?"

"The Tontine Trust was established after they all supposedly died. Their rule for inheritance meant that each time someone really died, my father, who was custodian, had to provide proof of death. Makes sense." She sipped the hot liquid carefully.

"I get it. So now that he's the last, and he's gone, you need his death certificate."

She nodded. "I need the official death certificate as proof positive. I have George Erickson's."

"Who do you think is after the money or the car?" Woody got up and returned to his desk. He sat, then swiveled around to face her to continue the conversation.

"I don't know. I can't figure this out. My father said for sure he was the last survivor. So who's left that thinks he's got a claim? I just can't fathom any of it."

"What were those men's names who belonged to the Trust? If you want, I'll try to find out if they had any families." He turned to face his computer and opened a browser window.

"Do you really think you can find these people?" Rhetta wrote down all the names on a piece of paper, then walked to his desk and handed it to him.

"It's worth a try." He turned to his monitor and began typing furiously.

"While you're doing that, I'm going to try to make flight reservations. Mr. DeBrock said he should have the death certificate in seven business days." She stared at her computer. "But first, I have to figure out how to even get to Vera Mardola."

Chapter 57

Tuesday night, January 22

AFTER FEEDING THE CATS, THEN finishing the grilled chicken breasts and brown rice she fixed for supper, she sat at the kitchen counter and opened her iPad. Randolph loaded the dishwasher.

"I made flight reservations for Friday, February first. We leave from Cape airport on Cape Air at two o'clock to St. Louis. Then at six, we board a non-stop American Airlines overnight flight from Saint Louis to Barcelona."

She glanced toward Randolph, who was neatly arranging the last of the dirty dishes on the lower rack, then tapped her screen. "That's almost four thousand miles. Anyway, since we can't fly directly to Vera Mardola, once we get to Barcelona, we'll take the train to Cadaqués, a little Catalán hamlet. Then we'll take a ferryboat to Vera Mardola." She scrutinized the tentative schedule. "Does that sound all right with you?"

"So if we fly out of Cape we have about a two-hour wait in Saint Louis?" Randolph asked, pushing the buttons to start the dishwasher.

"Yep. Unless we drive to the Saint Louis airport and leave Streak in the long-term parking, which I don't want to do. The two-hour plus drive to the airport going won't be too bad, but coming home, we may be really tired, and then we'd still have two more hours to go before getting to the house. I'd rather park in the long term at the Cape airport.

At the end of a long trip, fifteen minutes of driving home in no traffic beats a minimum of two hours, or probably longer, if there's snarly Saint Louis traffic to deal with."

"I agree," he said. "You're a better trip planner than I am. I'd have just booked from Saint Louis."

Rhetta scanned her e-book app. "Once we get settled in at our gate, we can catch up on our reading. I'm bringing my books electronically. We can't take much luggage, so I'm not packing any real books. Mine will be on my iPad."

"That doesn't necessarily mean that your suitcases will be any lighter," Randolph said as he sidled to the counter, putting his arms around Rhetta and peering over her shoulder to peek at her iPad screen. "Do you think you'll have room in your carry-on for at least one book for me? I haven't got a fancy e-reader yet."

"I'll squeeze a book in for you, don't worry." She turned and gave him her evil eye. "I'll have you know, my suitcases definitely won't be over forty-five pounds, because I'm not paying extra freight for them."

He smiled. "I have never gone anywhere yet with you that carrying your suitcases wasn't a major workout. Somehow I don't think this trip will be any exception."

She made a face at him, then turned back to the screen and pointed, resuming her travelogue. "We'll be arriving at Barcelona around ten in the morning, local time. We lose about six hours. We can only reserve passage on the boat once we're there. I figured we'd want to stay overnight in Barcelona, then go to Vera Mardola the next day. We'll be pretty tired unless we can actually sleep on the flight over."

"I think it's a good idea to have a base hotel in Barcelona. That will be a perfect place to leave our luggage. We don't want to lug it all to Vera Mardola. Plus, if we are just totally exhausted, we know we can rest a day before tackling the problems at the bank."

"I agree, Sweets. I doubt whether either of us will sleep much on the plane. Once we arrive we can get a good meal, rest up, and be fresh when we visit the *Banc Réal de Santo Domingo*." She said it with the best Catalán accent she could fake. Since she'd never heard any spoken Catalán, she tried for semi-Spanish. She closed the iPad cover and plugged it into the charger. "Why do you think we'll have problems at the bank? You're making me nervous."

He tilted her chin to him. "My darling wife, do you think this trip will be uneventful given all that you've been through recently?" She shook her head.

"Right," she said, as he pulled up a stool to sit next to her. "I sure wish I could take my .38 with us." Randolph gave her his judge look.

The phone rang. An excited Woody was on the line. "Guess what I just found out?"

"I have no idea, Woody. Spill it."

"One of the members of the Tontine has a son named Stanton Worthington."

"Okay. Am I supposed to know who that is?"

"He's an actor. And according to the cast list, he's coming to Cape Girardeau next spring when they film that movie."

"Holy smokes, I know who that is. He was in *Chasing Charlotte* a couple of years ago. I bet that's who we saw at the airport."

"Right. Quite a coincidence."

Exactly. "Wonder what he's been doing here?"

Chapter 58

Friday morning, February 1

ALTHOUGH RHETTA HAD AWAKENED WITH a headache, she felt nearly human again by the time the Bootheel Area Rapid Transportation shuttle came around to pick them up at ten fifteen. Randolph had offered to heft the suitcases into the luggage area in the back, but the driver insisted on doing it, hustling Randolph and Rhetta towards the open sliding door. Although the driver, a slightly built man with a thick white mustache and matching hair springing out from his BART cap looked frail enough to need help, he easily tossed the bags into the rear compartment.

Randolph had decided to take the shuttle instead of driving to Saint Louis to the airport. They could have used the Cape airport to fly and connect in Saint Louis, but the flights didn't work well with the international flights. With only two flights per day, it meant either a thirteen-hour wait or barely an hour. Counting on arriving with less than one hour was cutting it too close, so he opted for the shuttle.

Randolph slid in next to Rhetta while the driver made sure the luggage was stacked properly. Rhetta and Randolph claimed the entire third row seat in the luxury van when the driver told them they were his last pick up. In the second row, a handsome man Rhetta thought to be in his early forties, dressed in a snappy business suit and topcoat sat next to a teenaged girl who was a younger female version of the man. Undoubtedly his daughter. The girl wore ear buds under her red wool hat, a trendy scarf and a blue jean jacket over a long white sweater that topped black leggings. Her hands flew across the keypad of her smartphone.

A grey-haired woman in a green wool coat sat in the front, in the passenger seat. Her fingers worked in precision teamwork as she crocheted a scarf.

"I'm so glad I'm feeling almost human again," Rhetta said as she laid her head against Randolph's shoulder.

"Me, too. And that we got a ride on this shuttle." He patted her arm and buckled them in. "Close your eyes. Maybe you can nap on the way up."

Mrs. Koblyk waved at them as the van turned carefully onto the gravel road. The crochet lady in the front seat joined Rhetta and Randolph in waving. The girl didn't glance up from texting, while her father's eyes were glued to his iPad. Neither of them even noticed Mrs. Koblyk.

Rhetta had tucked her purse inside her carry-on tote, along with their passports, printed tickets, iPad, her medications, and all the documentation she thought she'd need at the bank. She had received two certified death certificates for her father two days earlier. She put one in the bank box for storage and tucked the other one in with her passport. She had memorized the car's VIN, and additionally, she'd made a file and had it stored on the Cloud backup, which she could access from her iPhone or iPad. She didn't bring the car title with her. It and the car's VIN tag were locked away in the safe deposit box at the bank. She had arranged with her cell phone provider so that she would have cell phone service in Europe. She patted her tote reassuringly and clutched it close to her.

Ricky had called last night to wish her a safe trip and to assure her that her father's Camaro was resting peacefully. No one had been around bothering her or the garage. Woody and Billy Dan called shortly after.

She promised Billy Dan that they would all get together for a fishing trip and barbeque at his place first thing this spring. Woody promised to take care of everything at the office.

Bumping down the gravel road jostled her head, nearly persuading the headache to re-bloom, but finally the ride smoothed out on the paved state highway. They glided up the ramp onto Interstate 55 northbound to Saint Louis.

Rhetta bolted up. A dark blue truck matched their speed in the adjacent lane. It wasn't Philip Corini. But was it Stanton Worthington? She leaned around Randolph to stare at the truck.

"Sweets, I swear that's Stanton Worthington. Look over there at the driver of that truck."

By the time Randolph did, the truck pulled over into the right lane and headed down the next exit ramp.

Rhetta leaned back. "Oh, God. Now I'm seeing Stanton Worthington everywhere. I really need to get hold of myself."

Randolph stared after the truck a moment longer.

"Hmm. I didn't see him."

Just then, another blue truck passed the van in the outside lane. A man who looked to be in his twenties was driving. Randolph pointed at it. "There must be a million trucks like that. Maybe we're both seeing bad guys."

Chapter 59

Later Friday afternoon, February 1

THE VAN BEGAN DISCHARGING ITS passengers by first stopping at the Southwest terminal for the father-daughter team. Southwest Airlines had its own fancy new terminal just north of Lambert Saint Louis International airport. Then, BART took to the highway for the half-mile circular ride to Lambert, where the crochet lady was discharged at the Delta terminal. "I'm going to visit my daughter for two weeks," she said, grinning, as the driver unloaded her two suitcases. A porter appeared and trucked the bags on his handy two-wheeler.

A half-block farther down, the van stopped at the American Airlines terminal. The driver bounded out and around to the van door and slid it open for Randolph, who climbed out first and turned to help Rhetta. Somehow, she managed to exit backward with her rear end emerging first. "How the heck did I get in so easily, but now I practically have to fall out?" she grumbled as Randolph cleared his throat. She knew he was swallowing his comment. And probably a chuckle.

As quickly as the driver stacked their suitcases on the sidewalk, a porter materialized and, after determining their destination, led the way to the international concourse. He stopped at a counter. Next to it was a cart as big as a pool table piled high with look-alike bags.

"Here you are," the porter, spiffy in a dark blue uniform said, beaming at them. "Enjoy your vacation. This young man will get your ticket information and check your bags through to customs." He tilted his head towards a harried-looking youth that Rhetta guessed was about twelve, who manned the busy counter by himself. On the wall above his head, a banner proclaimed, "SECURITY" in foot-high letters.

Randolph tipped the porter, who in turn tipped his hat, flashed a huge smile and deftly pocketed the bill.

Rhetta and Randolph stood in a short line and waited their turn for the young man to check their tickets and mark their bags.

"You'll need to meet your bags at Security Area 2, over there," he pointed across the room, "after they're scanned into the system."

Rhetta understood immediately that "scanned into the system" probably meant, "scanned for explosives," but didn't comment.

The young man tapped a keyboard, then asked them the usual questions about packing their bags and what they contained. When they'd apparently answered satisfactorily, the clerk printed out a card, tore part of it off and handed it to them, and began attaching the other end to one of the bags.

"Why aren't there four cards, since we have four bags?" Rhetta asked.

"One card per unit. Both of you constitute a unit," he answered, finishing and turning back. "You get to identify your bags over there." He pointed again. "Then you check your bags in."

"Ah. I see," Rhetta said. She didn't see, but she'd co-operate. She didn't want to lose their suitcases before they left the airport.

Following instructions, they proceeded to Security Area 2, answered a million more questions, identified their bags, then waited while a TSA lady opened one suitcase and rummaged through it. A second agent, a short, square man stood watch nearby. When both agents were satisfied, which Rhetta ascertained by their head nodding, they followed more instructions and trundled their bags over to the ticket counter and waited to check in.

"Why did that very large TSA woman have to open the bag that had all my undies in it?" Rhetta lamented.

"Better than opening the one with my undies in it," Randolph said, then grinned.

"Did she have to hold them up in her giant latex-gloved hands and wave them around? Sheesh." Rhetta stopped and bent down to double check her suitcases and make sure none of those undies were hanging out of the sides.

"Just part of the new and improved security system the government has provided for us post nine-eleven." Randolph lifted their bags onto the scales by the check-in clerk. Rhetta kept her word. Neither of her bags was overweight. However, one of Randolph's exceeded the weight limit, but not by a whole pound, so the clerk let it slide through. The pretty brunette smiled and tagged their bags.

"Must be that book I tossed in there at the last minute," he told the American Airlines agent.

"I already feel so much safer watching Henrietta the Hun waving my panties in front of everyone at the airport. That probably scared off at least a dozen terrorists. And no, it wasn't your book, because I have it in my carry on." Rhetta patted the tote.

The agent verified their computer tickets and matched them to their passports, issued boarding passes for their flight, number 998, and tucked the passes into a neat folder. Smiling broadly, she wished them a wonderful flight and handed the folders to Randolph. Who handed them to his wife, who tucked them into her tote.

Rhetta stared at their luggage as the suitcases bounced along the conveyor belt, sidled through the split rubber curtain and disappeared. She prayed she'd reunite with the bags in Barcelona, as the agent had promised. She'd heard how international bags often got lost or waylaid. She hoped fervently that she wouldn't lose the luggage lottery today.

Chapter 60

Saturday, February 2, 9:00 am Barcelona time

AFTER DROPPING OUT OF A gloriously blue Mediterranean sky, the Boeing 757 touched down flawlessly on the Barcelona runway. Rhetta had stared out the window as the plane dipped over crystal blue-green water bordered by gently swaying palm trees. Although initially dreading the trip, her heart now fluttered with anticipation. They were in Spain! And the winter weather was apparently gorgeous.

While Barcelona was a popular international destination, the weekend must have been a favorable time to land. Once on the ground, the jet glided effortlessly to the gate, and deplaning was quick and simple. The passengers were orderly and the process went smoothly. Only a couple of babies cried, and one elderly gentleman couldn't locate his wheelchair. Rhetta thought she overheard the flight attendant wonder if it made the journey. *Guess he lost the luggage lottery today.*

Their own bags turned up on the carousel as promised, and clearing customs went smoothly. When asked the purpose of their visit, they looked at the man straight in the eye and lied effortlessly. "Vacation," Rhetta said and smiled. No large agents ruffled through her bags and waved her undies around. That treatment was only necessary by the homeland team.

At the curb outside the terminal, Rhetta inhaled deeply. "It's beautiful, Sweets. I never imagined Barcelona would look like this." She tucked her arm into her husband's while waiting for the hotel van to pick them up. "Hey, I just thought of something. Wouldn't it be wild if we run into Jeff and his wife? LuEllen said they're vacationing here."

"Hmm. I guess. But it's a pretty big country. I don't know about you, but I could use a shower. Then we could eat lunch and get our bodies used to the local time." Randolph leaned over and kissed her cheek. "I know this isn't exactly a pleasure trip, but at least the weather is good."

"I'm grateful our luggage made the same trip we did." Rhetta's head swiveled, taking in all the sights. Except for the palm trees, and rows and rows of lusciously blooming flowers of every color and fragrance, the airport looked like most airports she'd been to in the US—lots of concrete floors and plenty of cars and taxis. She spotted a car rental booth nearby.

"Sweets, why don't we rent a car? That way we wouldn't have to rely on the hotel van or a taxi to get us to the train. We could drive ourselves to Cadaqués to catch the ferry to Vera Mardola. We'd have a car with us.

"Is the ferry a car ferry or just a people ferry?" Randolph began pulling out the handles of the suitcases.

"Both. I read all about it. I have the booklet." She patted her tote bag. "It leaves every forty-five minutes for Vera Mardola, from seven in the morning going over, to the last trip back to Cadaqués at nine o'clock at night. Daily except Sundays. It only runs Sunday afternoons." She rattled the schedule off like a seasoned tour guide.

"What about the bank? Is it open today? Or are we going to have to wait until Monday?"

"I checked online, and they're open all day Saturday, until eight PM, but not open on Sunday. That's different than our banks at home, that's for sure."

They began tugging their wheeled luggage toward the car rental kiosk. "According to the map, Cadaqués is about a two hours' drive, and the ferry ride is only an hour. I'd like to go today and get this over with." She checked her phone for the time. The little iPhone genie had changed the time to local Spanish time. "We can definitely make it today. Even with lunch, we can make it before the bank closes."

Randolph scooped her up in his arms. "I'm with you, Rhetta. Let's have lunch and a shower and we'll drive to Cadaqués."

A little over an hour later, most of which time was spent stuffing their four suitcases into the baby buggy that passed for a car, they zipped their way along the *Avenue Onze de Setembre* to the *Hotel Iberia Ruiz del Prat*.

Randolph quickly mastered the shifting pattern of the little car and drove it handily. It wasn't equipped with air conditioning, but the mild day was definitely an improvement over the weather they'd left behind in Missouri, so none was needed. The temperature displayed on a nearby sign read 22 degrees. Assuming, since they weren't freezing, that the display was in Celsius, Rhetta figured it was probably somewhere between seventy and seventy-five degrees Fahrenheit.

"Why are we the only country in the world too stubborn to convert to metric?" Rhetta asked after completing the quick calculation to determine whether 22 meant cold or warm.

Randolph nodded. "There are only three countries in the world that don't use the metric system so that's a really good question. I always thought we were a tad arrogant to think that the rest of the world would prefer our complicated way of measuring, especially when, along with the Canadians, we were the leaders in using metric in our money, many years ago. The Canadians changed to metric for everything sometime in the seventies and left us in the dust. Our military uses metric. The change should be an easy one. Shame on us for being late to the party."

"So which countries are left in the dust? Besides us." Rhetta pulled down the visor and was shocked at the reflection she saw looking back from the tiny, lighted mirror. She thought all her suitcases were in the baggage area, but apparently a few had traveled with her under her eyes. She flipped the mirror closed.

"Just Burma, or Myanmar as it's called, and Liberia." Randolph stopped for a red light.

Rhetta grumbled, "The Spanish may use metric, but we have better cars. I bet I wouldn't have had as much trouble fitting our suitcases into Cami as what we went through trying to stuff them into this glorified baby buggy. Or should I say *pram*, since we're in Europe?"

For a panicked moment when they'd begun packing their stuff into the car, Rhetta thought they might have to unpack a couple of suitcases in order to get their stuff inside. Because they hadn't reserved a car, no full sized one was available. They had to settle for a Peugeot 207, which by Rhetta's calculations, was barely large enough for her and Randolph and her carry on, plus one suitcase. The attendant, however, was convinced they and their suitcases would all fit, even though the sign above the car showed an outline of a person with a number "2," and one of a suitcase with the number "3." To Rhetta, that meant three suitcases and both of them. Good thing they weren't big people. That was probably why Adolfo, the animated attendant was sure he could fit them all in.

They found their hotel easily, a mere four kilometers west at the very end of the *Avenue Onze de Setembre*. The Avenue didn't go any farther or they'd have landed in the Mediterranean Sea, which lapped the coast several hundred feet below. The three-story rock main building covered with flowering vines and secured by a tall wrought iron fence reminded Rhetta of Mediterranean castles she'd seen in pictures.

A handsome twenty-something greeter materialized by Randolph's door as soon as he stopped the car under the hotel portico. Jorge, according to the nametag he wore on his left shirt pocket. "I will take care of your luggages," he said, and beamed at them, "and also park the car for you." He motioned toward the double glass doors. "Please, I will meet you at the desk inside." Did he just wink at her? Rhetta also noticed his clothes fit him to perfection.

"No. we'll take our own *luggages* with us." Rhetta leaned toward Randolph and whispered, "I'm not letting our *luggages* out of my sight."

As they crossed the tile floor of the wide entry, a heavenly aroma of spices and noodles wafted their way from the indoor-outdoor restaurant that opened from the lobby. "I'm starved," Rhetta said.

"Lunch will begin serving at eleven o'clock," the perky desk clerk answered with a broad smile. Her golden hair was snugged into a bun at the nape of her neck, leaving two nearly white tendrils cascading down ivory cheeks. While definitely not American, her accent wasn't Spanish.

"Where are you from?" Rhetta asked as Randolph completed the registration process.

"Amsterdam," she said. "I speak six languages," she added. "That's why I am the day manager here. I can speak fluently to almost all of our guests in their own language."

By then, the gorgeous parking creature had returned with a luggage cart, and led them to the elevator.

"Your room is number 307, on the top floor, overlooking the gardens," Jorge said, pressing the call button. "There is also near you, the pool. It's on the roof." Again a megawatt smile.

Rhetta nudged her husband. "Did you hear that? The pool is on the roof."

The glass elevator glided swiftly to the third floor. Rhetta noted that all the interior room doors overlooked the spacious lobby below. The gardens must be the outside view.

Rhetta stopped and peered over the wrought-iron balcony railing to the lobby below. The entryway was filled with colorful pots filled with plants and trees, while flowers trailed from hanging containers. She glanced down the hallway and spotted the glass doors leading to the pool.

"Here we are," said Jorge, sliding the card key into the slot, then propping open the door. He pushed the luggage trolley in ahead of them.

Just as she started to follow Jorge and Randolph into the room, a man standing at the check-in counter caught her attention. She took a step to the railing and peered over. It was hard to tell from the top, looking down, but something about him was familiar. *Where have I seen him before?* He turned left toward the dining area and disappeared from view, so she turned her attention back to their room. She didn't know anyone in Spain. Did she?

Chapter 61

"THAT IS ABSOLUTELY THE BEST shrimp pasta I have ever eaten in my life!" Rhetta mopped up the remaining sauce from her plate with the last piece of baguette. She swallowed her wine, then dabbed her lips with the linen napkin.

There were only three other guests with them in the dining room enjoying an early lunch. Instead of wine, Randolph topped his meal off with strong local coffee. Although he had a past history of abusing fermented beverages, she knew he steered clear of imbibing much of any spirits any more. He used to partake daily of a gin and tonic or a highball or few at home while he painted, but after nearly being killed in a bad wreck where the police thought he had been driving drunk, he'd all but eliminated alcohol from his routine. Some days he joined Rhetta in a glass of wine after dinner, but generally no more than one glass.

Rhetta admired his willpower. He'd told her he was doing it for her, that if she was strong enough to quit smoking, he could quit drinking. The guilt pangs stabbed her again as she thought about what he said. She made up her mind that she really would quit this time. Besides, she hadn't brought any cigarettes with her on this trip, and they would be together, so she could resist the temptation to smoke. She only smoked when she felt stressed. Okay, maybe not always because she was stressed. She decided she'd better not think about cigarettes, because she could feel the craving coming on.

"Hello, earth to Rhetta. Are you somewhere without me?" He tilted his head sideways and smiled at her as he scribbled on the guest check and handed it back to the waiter.

She quickly cleared her head of her guilty thoughts. "Sorry Sweets. I guess I was thinking about how beautiful this place is. I wish we were here for a fun trip instead of this business. What did you say?"

He put his arm around her shoulders. "Maybe we can get all this over with and have some fun. This place is gorgeous. But we best hit the road if we're going to Vera Mardola. It's past noon, so we want to be sure we have plenty of time to get to the ferry."

"I need to brush my teeth. Let's go to our room and I'll make sure I have everything we need." She tapped the tote she still carried.

The elevator whisked them quickly up to the third floor. She found her key in her pocket instead of inside the oversized tote, and let herself in the room.

While Randolph took care of brushing his teeth, she dumped the contents of the tote onto the bed, selected all the documents she needed, and put them into a little shoulder pouch along with her cell phone and her smaller than normal purse that she selected especially for the trip. She hoisted the pouch on her shoulder and grabbed a light sweater to wear in case it turned chilly. It felt very strange to go from heavy winter clothes to wearing white cotton slacks and a short-sleeved top and sandals in the space of what, she glanced at her iPhone and did some math, maybe thirty hours. Give or take.

She had slept a little on the flight over but woke up often. She knew she would really sleep better, later. After the trip to Vera Mardola.

"I'm ready," Randolph said as he rummaged through their bags for a light jacket.

She brushed her teeth quickly, then double-checking everything she arranged all the paperwork in her purse again, then scanned the room one last time. Randolph locked the door. "Let's use the stairs. I want to work off some of the pasta."

At the bottom of the stairs, they rounded the corner and Rhetta scanned the portico area. She waved when she saw Jorge pull up with the car. Just as she passed under the arch of the portico, her pouch bumped a man walking toward her. Instinctively she hugged the pouch to her body. She'd heard about pickpocketing being a rampant problem for tourists in Europe. But the man hadn't bothered it. He also walked away so quickly that her apology fell on empty air.

As she watched him leave, she recognized him as the same man checking in, whom she thought she knew from somewhere. She watched as he disappeared around the corner. She shook her head. *I must be imagining things. He can't be anyone I know.*

"See that man over there? He was at the counter when we got upstairs. I saw him when I glanced down at the front desk."

"What about him?"

"I hate to say this, but I swear he looks familiar." Randolph stopped and looked around for the man.

He was gone.

Chapter 62

Saturday afternoon, February 2, 1:15 Barcelona time

WITH A BIG SMILE, JORGE held the car door open as they tucked themselves in, Randolph again behind the wheel. The gorgeous creature had provided them with verbal directions, so they aimed for the highway to Cadaqués.

"I asked Jorge where the car was parked," Randolph said. "The parking lot is off-site, next door. I made a mental note how to find the car the next time. The tipping is already getting out of hand."

"Well, we are tourists," Rhetta answered.

"Not exactly," Randolph reminded her. "When we get back from Cadaqués, we can be tourists."

"You're right, Sweets. I really want this to be over with." Her stomach tightened up again, nerves beginning to quiver with dread. She clutched her purse tightly. "This whole thing is still so bizarre to me. And, just to add to this, I could have sworn I recognized that man at the hotel lobby. I'm being so paranoid," she added.

"I didn't get much of a look at him."

"I'm sure he wasn't anyone I know. How could he be? It's just that he looked vaguely familiar." She patted his arm. "How could I possibly know anyone here?"

Randolph glanced around at the other cars. "Do you see anyone in any car near us that looks like him?"

Rhetta sat up and looked out. "No, I don't. But I'll keep watching. Do you think we're being followed?"

"I don't know, but I don't want to assume we're not. With all that's happened ever since Frank called you, I don't want to take anything for granted."

"Actually, it all started with George getting killed, if you think about it."

The more she thought about it, the worse she needed a cigarette!

They pulled onto the four-lane highway that Jorge had said was engineered to accommodate speeds in excess of the eighty that was posted. Of course, in home talk, eighty was barely over fifty miles per hour. Besides that, Rhetta didn't trust the little car. She was positive the unfamiliar sounding whine of the Peugeot's motor signaled an impending disaster. She didn't know how these cars were supposed to sound, so she immediately thought of a worst-case scenario. Was it going to break down? And if it did, did they have the equivalent of Triple A here? Maybe they should have gone back and rented a different car.

"What do we do if we need roadside assistance?" Rhetta asked, as she gazed about the interior. It looked slightly bigger now without all their "luggages."

"There's an information packet in the glove box, but don't worry. The car is new and it's full of gas, and it's fine." Randolph reached over and patted her knee.

Despite her misgivings about the car, Randolph shifted gears perfectly and it hugged the hilly road like a seasoned mountain climber. She was glad she wasn't driving. This little car worried her. It just didn't sound right. Of course, she didn't remember ever hearing a Peugeot before. In fact, she didn't remember ever even seeing one before her arrival in Spain. Since nobody looked at them funny when they stopped at the intersections on the way to the four-lane, it must have sounded normal, so she tried to relax. All was well. She withdrew her iPhone from her bag, and checked the signal. Some unfamiliar service name popped up in place of the normal ATT, but she couldn't read it without her glasses on. She fished around her purse for her glasses.

"I wonder if I should call someone to see if the phone works." Another expedition through her purse produced the dialing instruction card that the clerk at ATT had given her. She began to read it.

She glanced at the road signs as they climbed a steep incline leading onto the highway. "We're going the right way. That sign said, *Cadaques, 80 kilometers.*" Her stomach began to flutter. She'd checked the map. The highway followed the outside of a mountain wall. She looked out at the disappearing canyons on one side and the sheer rock face of the mountain on the other. Luckily, the road was new, and as Jorge had bragged, engineered for more than a donkey's gait.

"I guess you could call Woody and see how everything is at the office," Randolph said.

Rhetta studied her watch. "I better wait a little while. It's only a little after six in the morning in Missouri. Woody's probably not up, or at least if he is, he probably hasn't had enough coffee yet. He's pretty grumpy before his caffeine and breakfast."

Rhetta slid her phone back into her purse. "I don't know anyone over here, except Jorge. I guess I could call him at the hotel." She nudged her husband as she said it.

He raised his eyebrows, but merely smiled. "So, dear wife, do you have everything you need in that purse of doom to convince the bankers that you're Frank Caldwell's only daughter? And that he is deceased?"

"I have an original of his death certificate, I know the account number if Frank was right and it's the VIN on the Camaro." Rhetta quickly recited the number from memory. "I have pictures of him, and his arm with the tattoo. And of George Erickson's tattoo also, thanks to Matt Clippard, although Frank said he'd informed the bank of Erickson's death." She hugged the bag close to her. "Along with my passport, I also brought my birth certificate, but of course it doesn't say if Frank had any other children."

Randolph downshifted. "This is a pretty steep hill," he said. The little engine whined in protest, but the car slowed.

"Sweets, do you think someone was after Frank's Camaro for the VIN for the account number? Do you think there's someone else out there who thinks they have a claim on the trust?"

"After everything that happened to you, I believe there's more than a coincidental connection." Randolph shifted again as the road leveled out.

"You don't think that my assault at the office was connected, do you? The cops think they have that guy. I think someone may have heard us talking when we were in the cave, and they're after the money that was in the glove compartment. I don't think anyone is after the trust. How could they be? I'm the last survivor's only child."

Before Randolph could answer, Rhetta went on. "I don't trust that weird Philip Corini. I spotted him with a 9 millimeter tucked into his waistband. Why would an accountant need that? And, if you'll remember, he found my purse. He may be a bookkeeper for the mob, for all I know. He may know who conked me on the head."

Randolph shook his head. "I don't like the looks of Corini either, but it just doesn't fit together that it would be him. Do you think he followed you to Kansas City? When you call Woody today, put him on the case and see if he can find out if Corini was gone at the same time we were."

"Good idea, Sweets. I'll check with AskWoodydotcom." She glanced at her watch. Woody would be up now. With the card in hand, she followed the dialing instructions.

"Rhetta? What's wrong?" Woody was not only up, he recognized her phone number. Even though she was overseas, the number display must not have changed. Of course it hadn't. She hadn't gotten a different number. She really didn't know much about overseas cell phone usage. If she became a world traveler, she'd figure it all out.

"Hi, Woody. Nothing's wrong. We're great. We're nearly to Cadaqués, where we'll get the ferry to Vera Mardola. I need you to check something for me, okay?"

"Sure. What?"

"Find out where Corini was when we went to Kansas City to get the Camaro. I'm suspicious of him."

"Uh, okay."

"Email me, because I don't know if you can reach me on this phone. I can check my email anywhere there's a wireless connection, and they're everywhere here."

"Sure thing. Tell Randolph hi for me."

"Likewise to Jenn. Gotta go now. Bye." She slid the disconnect button.

Randolph slowed the car, and downshifted again.

"Hey, Sweets, you're pretty good with that four speed," Rhetta said.

"It's a five speed, I'll have you know. And yes, by golly, I am pretty good with it." He grinned. "When my dad taught me to drive, he told me to downshift as much as possible to slow down. It saves your brakes."

"I learned to drive in my mom's Camaro," Rhetta said. "It was a four speed, like Cami."

Remembering her mother, Rhetta wondered what she'd make of all this foolishness with the Tontine Trust and Frank Caldwell. A pang of loneliness stabbed her then, as it always did when she missed her mother. She fingered her mother's locket in its usual place on the chain snugged around her neck. "The sixty-seven Camaro is a four speed, too," she whispered.

"Look at that sign, Rhetta." He pointed ahead. "We're coming into Cadaqués."

Chapter 63

AFTER THEY TOPPED THE MOUNTAIN, Rhetta stared at the sea below. "Wow, I never realized how vast the Mediterranean Sea is. Look at that color. It's azure." She shook her head in wonder. "It's awesome."

"It is, indeed," Randolph said. "The next time we come over here, I'll paint some of these beautiful scenes."

They started down the hill, gaining speed as they descended the steep, winding slope.

The highway was still four-lane, but thankfully, they were alone on this part of the road. Randolph hugged the slower lane, trying to utilize downshifting as much as possible to keep their speed down. When he did, the car's engine wound up pretty tightly, so he began tapping the brakes. The car responded. Rhetta breathed easier.

"I wonder if they have turnouts here like they have in Colorado so we can pull over and cool our brakes."

"I don't see any, but we're doing fine. There isn't too much farther to go." As he said it, the four-lane ended. They bounced onto a two-lane road for the rest of the five kilometers into Cadaqués.

"I know, but it's so steep." The car picked up more speed. "Randolph, please, slow down. We're going too fast."

"I'm trying to slow us down, but I don't want to ride the brakes. It s okay, honey, we're fine. Not much further."

Rhetta clutched the overhead grip handle with one hand and braced against the dash with the other. "I'm not used to these steep hills and this little box of a car."

Randolph smiled. "I know, I…"

He didn't finish. He mashed the brake pedal, but it only bounced back at him He reached for the shifter, but couldn't downshift. He floored the clutch. There was no resistance. There was no fluid, no clutch pressure. The car began picking up speed.

"Sweets, please slow down. This isn't funny." Rhetta clutched the grip handle even harder.

"I can't," he said, as he gripped the wheel, doing all he could to steer the careening car. "We have no brakes. Or clutch." He stepped on the emergency brake pedal. It wobbled under his foot. "No emergency brake, either!"

"What?" Rhetta didn't want to think about how fast they were going, either in miles per hour or kilometers per hour. The view out the side window was a blur. *What? Did he say no brakes?*

"Almost there. Hang on!" Randolph shouted, as he gripped the wheel and careened around the last curve. Where they met a lorry lumbering up the hill, occupying all of its lane and most of theirs.

Rhetta squeezed her eyes shut. This was it.

Oh, crap!

Chapter 64

Saturday afternoon, February 2

SHE WAS PRETTY SURE SHE wasn't dead. But, she was definitely upside down. So was Randolph.

When she saw the lorry, Rhetta had squeezed her eyes shut but they shot open again when, instead of a collision, she felt their car go airborne over the side of the hill. The Peugeot sailed out about twenty feet then dropped nose-down onto an outcrop of trees and bushes on the hillside. The heavy brush served to break their fall. They landed upside down on the canopy.

"Oh, God, Randolph, are you okay? Where are you?" Rhetta blinked and tried to see around the exploded air bag, and the cloud of white cottony smoke that filled the car. The seat belt and shoulder harness held her suspended upside down, held fast by her own weight. As much as she fumbled with the buckle, she couldn't unsnap it. Her fingers caught in the seat belt, and she let out a yelp.

"I'm okay. Rhetta are you all right?" Randolph had succeeded in freeing himself from both his seat belt and the air bag. He crawled out, then staggered along the hillside over to Rhetta's side of the car, and began tugging. Her door wouldn't open. He moved slowly, afraid to send the car plummeting the rest of the way down the hill. Because it had landed more on the passenger side atop a parasol pine tree, he'd managed to push open his driver door and roll out. Now, the car shifted precariously. With each movement, stones tumbled down to the bottom of the hill. Rhetta ceased trying to get out. When the car began rocking all she could see under her was air. The passenger air bag had exploded toward her, but had deflated. Her chest hurt, but otherwise she thought she was okay. Her hand was pinched in the seat belt, but she finally freed it. She needed to get out of the car before it fell the rest of the way down the hill. But how? She couldn't free herself. Randolph tugged at her door, but couldn't get it to open. He began to scramble back toward the driver side.

At the sound of a gaggle of voices shouting from the top of the hill, Randolph stood, leaning against the hill to support himself away from the car, and shouted back. "My wife is still in the car. Please, help me get her out!" Three young men scrambled over the side of the hill, slipping and sliding down to where the car rested. Their movement made the car tremble again. Rhetta sucked in a breath, and stared through the windshield at them. Randolph gestured to them and they nodded. They spoke and gestured to each other and she saw a couple of shoulders shrug.

She couldn't understand them, but she heard the fear in their voices.

Randolph signaled to them to help him free her, and they nodded vigorously. Two of the bigger men braced against the car as the third one helped Randolph pull the door open. As soon as they succeeded, the man produced a jackknife, slit the belt and Rhetta dropped to the ground. Randolph scooped her up, and the men cheered.

She hugged her husband's neck. She began to laugh. She wasn't sure why, but it was one of those, either-you-laugh-or-you-cry moments, and so, she laughed. Randolph began to laugh and even the men, who at first looked puzzled, as though they missed the joke, finally joined in. She laughed until the tears finally started. "Oh crap, that was close. What happened?"

"Let's get out of here and we'll figure this out." Randolph said, and began to ease her away from the car.

"Wait," she shouted. "I have to get the bag, it has my purse and all the paperwork!" She turned toward the trap where she'd just been held.

"Stay here, I'll get it," Randolph said, and inched his way to the car. He peered in. "I don't see it." The air bags had spewed their contents throughout the small interior. "This is like that movie where the submarine was upside down," he said. He finally located the bag in the back seat, but on the inside of the roof, the strap caught on the clothes hanger. He leaned way in, closed his hand around the strap and pulled the prize toward him. The car lurched and began falling. Randolph threw himself aside as the car toppled the rest of the way down the hill. He lay on the ground, panting, her purse clutched to his chest. Rhetta rushed to him, slipping on the rocks, and landing on her butt alongside him.

"Oh God, Sweets, are you all right?" She took his face in her hands. He was scratched and dirty, but she didn't see any blood. She gently brushed dirt and leaves from his face.

"I'm fine. But like you said, that was close." The rescuers scrambled to them and grasping their arms, helped them first to stand, then to scramble to the top of the hill and over the low demolished barricade, and finally, onto the road. Two men who had been leaning over to watch had scurried forward and grasped their hands to help them the last steps and to hoist them over the top. Rhetta couldn't understand a word they chattered, but was grateful for the concern in their voices.

A crowd had gathered, with many onlookers stopping their cars to watch the rescue. Among those cars was a small white one with a black band around the middle, and the words *Policia* in bright green two-foot high letters on each side.

For once, Rhetta was happy to see cops.

Chapter 65

Saturday afternoon, February 2 5:45 PM Barcelona time

BOTH RHETTA AND RANDOLPH INSISTED that neither of them was injured from the wreck, save for some scrapes and bruises from climbing back up to the road. The young constable, who told them he was stationed in Cadaqués, spoke surprisingly good English.

Rhetta told him they didn't want to go to a hospital. She explained that it was urgent that they continue on to Vera Mardola. However, they desperately needed new transportation. With his help, they were able to call the car rental company and report their accident. The constable was familiar with a car rental office in Cadaqués, and generously drove them to pick up another car. He stayed with them and helped to translate their request. After much paper shuffling, and credit card scanning, they were installed in yet another small white vehicle. According to the paperwork, this one was a Fiat, although Rhetta swore it looked just like the Peugeot.

The constable shook their hands and wished them a safe journey. He informed them that he would have his report done and to the rental company in Barcelona by Monday.

"Do you think his report will indicate that we lost brakes and clutch?" Rhetta asked, as they buckled in and reconnoitered the interior of their new ride. "And obviously someone cut the emergency brake cable, too. I know he was listening very carefully to your account. He took notes, too." Rhetta watched him jot in a black notebook embossed with a police emblem in gold on the cover.

"I hope so. Otherwise, we may have just purchased a wrecked Spanish Peugeot."

"What about the insurance? Won't it pay?"

"I would assume the rental insurance would cover the replacement, but frankly, I can't read Spanish, so I'm not sure what the agreement actually says. I kept the paperwork so we can check in with the company when we get back, which is what the clerk on the phone instructed. He said they would follow up and get the police report."

Within fifteen minutes, they were in line at the ferry dock. Before she got out of the car, Rhetta had dared a look at herself in the mirror, and saw that now, in addition to the "baggages" under her eyes, she had white airbag powder smeared on her face and on her clothes. Her Capris were streaked shrub green and dirt brown, and she'd broken a strap on her sandal. Her hair, well, it was short, spikey and messy. It looked all right.

They climbed out and leaned against the Fiat, watching the ferry as it chugged up to the quay. She eyed her husband. Green and brown stains also streaked his jeans, and his shirtsleeve was torn. His tousled hair fell across a bruised eye.

"Sweets, I think you hurt your eye," Rhetta said as she gently moved a strand away and inspected the wound carefully. He must have had a close encounter with a rock when he rolled away from the car.

He touched it and grimaced slightly. "I hadn't really paid any attention. I guess I did." He grasped both her hands in his. "I can't believe we didn't get killed. The brakes and clutch went out at the same time. I find that more than suspicious. I think somebody cut the lines."

"That's what I was thinking, too, but I didn't want you to think I was being paranoid again."

"Not paranoia this time. This was very real." He wrapped his arms around her. "We have to be very careful. There is someone who doesn't want us to get to Vera Mardola." He hugged her and whispered. "Do you see the man anywhere that you thought looked familiar from the hotel? There are two guys standing over there, looking us over."

Rhetta eyed the two men, but neither looked like the man she saw. "I think they are just giving us the once over because we look so rough."

Randolph smiled. "I guess we don't look like the regular tourists or whoever comes over here. You're probably right. We look like we've just been through a wreck."

"I can't understand what's going on, Sweets. Who could this person be?"

"Someone who thinks they have the right to the trust money. I have no idea who."

Rhetta replayed everything in her head, again, for what she felt was the hundredth time. *Who else thinks they should get the money? That's who's after us. And, that's who killed George Erickson.* Rhetta shivered. The adrenaline rush from the wreck was subsiding, and left her chilled. Or, was that fear that left her chilled?

A bell clanged the ferry's arrival as the boat bumped up against the dock. Two deck hands leaped down from the deck to secure the rectangular, flat-bottomed boat by snubbing heavy ropes to posts on the dock. Next, they lowered the metal ramp to allow the cars to leave. It dropped with a resounding clang. Within minutes, eight cars had sped down the ramp, off the ferry and away into town.

Rhetta and Randolph clambered back into their car as they heard the other cars start their engines. They were the third in line to board, with two cars and two small commercial vans behind them. The first two cars in line ahead of them drove up toward the front where the deck hand guided them to a stopping point, making them the head of each row, which to Rhetta, looked perilously close to the edge. She was glad she and Randolph weren't first in line.

Loading the ferry took just a little over five minutes. After more bell-ringing, the ropes were untied and the boat was underway to its destination at Vera Mardola. Rhetta swayed toward a wooden bench alongside the rail and she and Randolph joined the other passengers to sit the trip out. Some of the men took the opportunity to light up a cigarette, or to chat. She glanced over the rail at oily green water eddying around the boat and her stomach began swirling in rhythm to the engine's chugging sound. Although the ferry appeared quaint in the brochure, in reality it was small, crowded and stunk of diesel fuel. Rhetta's stomach fluttered dangerously. She abandoned her seat on the bench in favor of sitting inside the car. At least there, it didn't smell so foul.

Randolph joined her. "So, want to take a vacation cruise after we get home?" he asked.

She shot him a look. "I believe this is enough ship for me. I'll do my cruising in Cami from now on, thanks."

Mercifully, the trip was over within a few minutes, and Rhetta had managed not to get sick. As the ferry docked at Vera Mardola, Rhetta reached over and grasped Randolph's hand, and squeezed. She pointed to what appeared to be a rock fortress in the middle of the town square. Most European squares boasted cathedrals or churches, but here money was religion. She suspected the rock structure to be their destination. The elegantly scripted sign above the building, *Banc Real de Santo Domingo* confirmed it.

She tucked her arm through Randolph's, squared her shoulders, then sucked in a deep breath. "Here we go."

Chapter 66

Saturday evening, February 2, 6:55 PM Barcelona time

THEY LEFT THE RENTAL CAR at the quay parking, and headed on foot toward the center of the medieval style village. The modern housing boom had completely bypassed Vera Mardola. The upper balconies of two and three story rock and stucco houses leaned well over the narrow cobblestone streets built hundreds of years ago when the main transportation involved horses or donkeys, or an occasional ox. The pathways were barely wide enough to accommodate one modern-day vehicle, which resulted in all of the streets being one way. The cobblestone path they'd chosen circled its way uphill toward the center of town.

"I'm glad we didn't try to drive and find a parking place. This looks impossible," Rhetta said as she gazed around the Mediterranean style homes and buildings, most of which were made of rock and shuttered tightly against the afternoon sunlight. "Do people actually live here?" she added as she glanced at an inscription on the cornerstone of a building. The only part she could make out was the date, 1497. "Look here. This cornerstone was laid in 1497. Wow, now that's what I call an old building."

"Just think, that was a mere five years after Columbus discovered North America. We certainly don't have anything old like that in the

Midwest," Randolph said. "I think there are some late sixteen hundred and early seventeen hundred buildings around the original French settlement at Sainte Geneviève. Farther west, nothing is older than the eighteen hundreds. The east coast has some old buildings, but none this old." He stopped and gazed up at the narrow two-story building.

"All of these houses have shutters and most of them are closed up tight. I find that so strange." Rhetta said, as she joined Randolph in staring up at the windows.

He glanced around at the neighboring houses. "I'm sure one reason is because they don't have air conditioning, and they want to keep the interiors cool. Another reason might be that they don't want people staring inside."

The day, which had started out mild, but a little chilly, had turned out to be rather warm. Or, at least to Rhetta it felt warm. The thermometer outside the *fleca*, or bakery that they'd just passed, said 25. Now if she was in Missouri, she'd be mighty chilly at 25, but the Celsius indicator meant that according to her quick approximate calculations, the temperature was around 75 Fahrenheit. The Mediterranean winter was certainly milder than the one they left in Missouri. She knew that *fleca* meant bakery, not because of her skill in Catalán, but because her nose detected the delicious aroma of fresh bread.

Overhead, the clear sky had not a single cloud to mar the brilliant blue. The gentle ocean breeze teased her nostrils, evoking memories of the Florida beaches she'd visited with her mother when she was a child. The thoughts of her mother skittered away and were replaced with recent memories of her father. She wouldn't be here on this strange little island had it not been for Frank Caldwell and a string of bizarre events.

She threaded her arm through Randolph's and they continued the climb to the town square in silence.

When they reached the foot of the steps to the building, she stared at the massive double wood doors to the *Banc Real de Santo Domingo*. She riffled through the bag and fingered the envelope with her proof and evidence. "I even brought the pictures of George Erickson that Matt

Clippard took. He was interested in the tattoo, thinking he could use it to help identify the body. I also have a copy of his death certificate."

Randolph arched his eyebrows. "And how did you acquire that?"

Rhetta patted the envelope. "It's pretty handy having Matt for a friend." She grinned.

They climbed the six steps, and Randolph pulled open the ornate wood door. "I guess they don't have the equivalent of the Americans with Disabilities Act here. One certainly couldn't climb those steps or get that blasted heavy door open if one was handicapped. It was all I could do to open it."

Once inside, a young man in a military style uniform greeted them. "*Bona tarda. Benvingut al Banc Real de Santo Domingo.*"

Rhetta smiled. "Do you speak English? I'm sorry, I don't speak Catalán."

The blond security guard returned her smile and switched to an accented but clear English greeting. "Of course. Welcome to the *Banc Real de Santo Domingo.* How may we assist you?"

She sucked in a deep breath. "I need to speak to someone about Garibaldi."

His face paled. "Another?" Apparently catching himself misspeaking, he wrung his hands and said quickly, "But of course, please, come with me." He led them across the carpeted floor to a mahogany desk where he spoke rapidly to a young lady there.

She answered, then punched a button on a phone. Rhetta couldn't begin to understand the rapid-fire speech.

The guard turned, smiled, then backed away.

The pretty blonde at the desk eyed them as she spoke into the receiver. All Rhetta caught were the words, *American,* and *Garibaldi.*

The door to an office behind the young woman opened and a short, dark man wearing thick round glasses that made his eyes appear overlarge, stepped into the lobby.

Forgoing any greeting, he said, "Follow me."

They did, across the lobby to another door, which the man opened and then motioned them through. They entered a tiny room with a single table. Behind them, he closed the door, and Rhetta heard lock tumblers engage.

She spun around. And was greeted by the biggest thing in the room—a pistol pointed at her head.

Chapter 67

Saturday evening, February 2

"WHAT KIND OF FOOLISHNESS IS this, *Madame*?" the man said, wiping his brow with one hand, while keeping the gun trained on her with the other.

"I don't know why you have a gun pointed at my wife, sir, but I would request that you put the weapon down." Randolph's tone was stern, but calm.

The banker swung the gun away from Rhetta and parked it directly in front of Randolph's face.

"I have instructed the security guard to call the police, and they will be here shortly."

The man spoke English very well, Rhetta thought. Why on earth she would think about his ability to speak English when said person was holding them at gunpoint, she just didn't know. Her brain fired crazy thoughts when she was under stress. Crazy stress thoughts. That was it.

"I'm not sure what the problem is, sir, but I was given instructions to come here and ask about Garibaldi Tontine, and that is what we are doing." She wiped her forehead. If the bank had air conditioning, this little room did not. Her forehead began dripping.

"The problem, *Madame*, is that a gentleman claimed the Garibaldi just a few moments ago. Therefore, you must be imposters, and I will have you arrested." The banker withdrew a handkerchief and wiped his own brow.

Rhetta had spotted a single chair so she sat. "What man? How could he have claimed the Garibaldi? I am the daughter of the last of the Garibaldi, and I have all the evidence with me to prove that." She sat the bag on the table and reached to open it.

"Stop right there. Do not open that bag. We will wait for the police and you can explain to me and them at the same time."

As though on cue, a knock interrupted their conversation.

Again, Rhetta heard chatter in rapid-fire Catalán. She caught one word, *policia*.

The constables had arrived.

The bespectacled banker unlocked the door and with his weapon still trained on them, motioned for them to step through to the lobby ahead of him.

Four local *policia* holding automatic weapons greeted them.

Instinctively, or whether she had watched too many television shows, Rhetta put her hands up. Her purse slid to the floor.

Randolph followed her example and raised his hands. "Sir, we aren't armed. There's no need to hold us at gunpoint. We haven't done anything except ask about the Garibaldi Tontine Trust." Randolph's voice sounded so calm to Rhetta.

"That's right. I'm the rightful owner of the trust. You have some explaining to do, sir." Rhetta stared at the banker. Her voice cracked and she didn't sound a bit calm to herself.

She was bordering on getting very annoyed. In fact, she had sailed past annoyed and was tacking into full blown mad. She thought her voice might give her away. She took a deep breath to calm herself.

"Then, let us go to my office and you can attempt to explain yourself." The banker lowered his weapon, and pointed to a large office behind the receptionist's desk. The pretty blonde had abandoned her post. Probably when the *policia* arrived.

Rhetta sat in one green leather chair in front of the desk, while Randolph selected the one next to her. "May I?" she said and pointed to her bag.

The banker sat behind the desk, wiped his forehead again, and nodded. "You say you have proof?"

"Indeed I do, but first I would like to know who came and claimed the trust?"

The banker shook his head vigorously. "I don't have to tell you that, *Madame*. It is up to you to show me your proof."

Rhetta removed the large envelope from her bag, and spread the contents on the desktop. Once by one she showed the banker, whose name she learned was Cabriolet, everything in the envelope. *Did he say Cabriolet? Like the car? Yikes. More crazy stress thoughts.*

Mr. Cabriolet picked up the morgue picture of George Erickson, and the death certificate.

He wiped his brow again, removed his glasses, and cleaned them with the same handkerchief. He replaced them on his nose.

"*Madame*, this cannot be." Cabriolet tapped the death certificate. "The gentleman told me he is George Erickson, and he proved to me that he is the last survivor."

Rhetta pointed to a copy of Erickson's death certificate. "George Erickson died before my father did. My father gave me all this before he passed away. He didn't have time to send you the death certificate before he fell so ill himself." She waved her hand across the contents of the pouch Frank gave her. "I saw George Erickson get struck by a truck and die. My father died a few weeks later. Here is everything." She slid it toward the banker. "So there's no way the man who came here could have been George Erickson. He's an imposter."

The banker scrutinized the death certificates, then shook his head. "Impossible. Mr. Erickson was in here not thirty minutes ago, and he was very much alive. He had his birth certificate, his passport, all of the necessary identification for the trust."

"Mr. Cabriolet, I believe you have just been swindled. Do you possibly have any video of this Mr. Erickson?" Randolph asked.

"But, of course!" He picked up the phone and issued instructions into the receiver.

In a few minutes, a young woman knocked and was ushered in. She handed the banker a thumb drive, which he inserted immediately into his computer.

When it began playing, he swiveled the screen towards Rhetta and Randolph.

"There. This is Mr. Erickson. You see, he shows me his tattoo, and he has all the papers, too. Including the death certificate for Mr. Caldwell, your father, *Madame*. We initiated the wire into his account."

Rhetta made a sound, a cross between a curse and a yelp. "Crap, Sweets. I know this guy!"

Chapter 68

Saturday evening, February 2

RHETTA FLEW TO HER FEET. "Mr. Cabriolet, I know this man. He's not George Erickson. I know him as Evan Something-or-other, and he works in the building where I have my office. That would be in Cape Girardeau, Missouri." She grabbed Randolph's arm and began leading him to the door. "We have to stop him. The ferry doesn't leave for fifteen minutes. He's still on the island. We have to get to the ferry. Come on!"

Randolph began to follow her, but turned back to the banker. "Sir, I suggest you stop that wire. You just got robbed." He left the banker picking up his dropped jaw.

Rhetta was already out the front door. She stood on the top step and scanned the area in the square. Of course there was no sign of Evan. Randolph pushed open the door and joined her, handing over her purse with the paperwork.

"Let's go right to the ferry. I'm sure he'll try to get back to Spain as fast as he can. He's probably hotfooting it down to the quay right now." Rhetta took her bag from Randolph and slung it over her head, letting the straps cross her chest. "Are the police going after him?" she asked as she scurried down the steps.

"They were trying to decide what to do when I left. I'm not so sure Mr. Cabriolet believes us."

"I hope he at least stopped the wire. Otherwise, that money is gone for good. And, to make it worse, to a thief, and probably a murderer! Evan is not only an imposter but a murderer too. I bet he's the one who killed George."

She studied the area around the bank. She didn't see any police giving chase. In fact, she didn't see any police at all.

"I don't see any cops, Sweets. It's up to us to stop him. Let's go." She galloped toward the street.

Randolph snatched Rhetta's arm and stopped her from crossing just as a scooter roared by. "Slow down, Rhetta. You nearly got run over."

Rhetta shook off the warning and kept running, turning back briefly to shout, "Hurry, Randolph, if he gets on the ferry and we miss it, we'll never catch him."

He caught up to her and they sprinted toward the quay. It was all downhill. Their regular routine of running paid off. They weren't even winded when they pulled up and stood at the edge of the water. The ferry was chugging its way toward them. Four cars waited in line to board.

"You walk between these two cars and I'll go this way." Randolph pointed to the cars lined up. Their rental car was parked in the lot adjacent to the dock. They began working their way towards the lot.

Rhetta strolled alongside two of the vehicles. One contained a businessman in a suit, talking on his cell phone. He didn't even glance at her as she passed by. The next car had two occupants, young women. Rhetta barely glanced their way.

She and Randolph met at the end of the small line of cars.

"I don't see anyone in these cars who looks out of place. Maybe he's on foot, and will catch his ride when he gets to the mainland," Rhetta said, glancing around again to see who might be on foot waiting for the ferry. There was no one.

"Let's get on the boat. We can always wait at the other quay for him." Randolph said.

"Let's do that. You get the car. I'll wait here and check out the people on foot who board. I know what he looks like." She handed Randolph the bag, but kept her purse. "Would you take this to the car? I want to make sure the papers stay safe."

Randolph took it from her and trotted toward the car.

The ferry arrived with horns blaring. Rhetta studied everyone who was waiting either in a car, or on foot. An older lady carrying a shopping bag walked up and waved to the young man on the ferry who was throwing the ropes to tie the boat. He smiled and waved back. She was probably someone who came over every day and was going home from work.

She studied a lone man, sandy haired, wearing a lightweight leather jacket. Definitely not Evan. After scrutinizing everyone, she concluded that Evan wasn't among the folks waiting to cross. Perhaps he'd caught an earlier ferry? No, she had the schedule memorized. There wasn't a ferry leaving in the time span the banker said. Unless the banker was wrong. Maybe Evan had been in there earlier and had made an earlier ferry. No, she'd seen the time stamp on the video. This would be the first ferry. She watched as the arriving cars unloaded and sped off. Then she studied the departing cars as they loaded. Randolph drove their car on to the ferry, and was the second last in line. She ambled toward the gangplank. Randolph was still in the car.

Just as she stepped onto the footbridge, she heard the roar of a motor start up. A blue speedboat with two men aboard raced past. One was steering the little boat, the other, an older man, stood grasping the handrail. She recognized him.

She shouted to Randolph and pointed. "Evan's in that boat!" Randolph didn't see or hear her. He was handing his boarding information to the boat crew.

She started up the walkway, her eyes glued to the speedboat. It veered off. It wasn't going to the mainland. If she and Randolph stayed on the ferry, Evan would get away.

She spotted another small powerboat idling at the wharf, preparing to launch. She made up her mind. She stepped off the gangway and sprinted toward it, waving and shouting, "Wait, please. Wait!"

He looked up, held his hand to shield his eyes. He waved, a signal to Rhetta that he heard her.

She knew what she had to do.

Chapter 69

Saturday evening, February 2

RHETTA SHOUTED ABOVE THE ROAR of the motor. "I need to follow them." She pointed to the departing speedboat bouncing across the water. The boat owner, dark haired and wind tanned, had a bare working knowledge of English, but nodded vigorously when Rhetta reached into her purse, snatched a fistful of money from her wallet and waved it. She pointed toward the fleeing speedboat. He threw her a life jacket, pointed at the grip bar and shouted, "Hold there." She secured the life jacket, jammed her wallet back in her pocket, and gripped the bar.

They launched with a roar, her head snapping backward as they accelerated. The little boat bounced and dipped, spewing a large fan of water in their wake. She'd snagged the right boat. It was plenty fast. The wind slapping her face made her eyes water, so she scrunched them nearly closed against the wind. She quickly realized the life jacket wasn't keeping her very warm. The sun had begun to set, and the brisk air turned downright cold on the water. To avoid getting tossed overboard she clung to the grab bar with both hands. Seawater foamed across the bow and arced behind them, like a giant rooster tail. She shuddered, thinking about how cold the water would be. She gripped the bar and sucked in a breath. Damn, they were going fast! He had understood to catch the boat, and that was exactly what they were going to do.

She forced her eyes open, and spotted their quarry ahead. She doubted if Evan knew he was being followed. His boat didn't seem to be going as fast as they were, but it was hard to tell for sure. Night was descending quickly. She glued her eyes to the running lights on the boat ahead. She had hoped she could follow discreetly. From the way her driver was roaring forward, lights ablaze, hope for discretion was evaporating quickly. She hadn't explained why she wanted to follow the boat. He probably wouldn't have understood her, anyway. If she did catch up to the boat, and Evan spotted her, he'd try to get away. She wasn't sure what to do. She only knew she had to follow him. She dared turn her head sideways, and spotted the ferry chugging across the water. She hoped Randolph wasn't frantic. She could call him, but there was no way she was turning loose of the grip bar, at least until the rocketing boat slowed down.

What would she do when they caught up? Motion for Evan to pull over and stop? It wasn't likely Evan would do that. Surely he wasn't armed, since handguns weren't allowed in Spain. Were they? At least he wouldn't be shooting at her. Small comfort.

She hadn't thought her plan through. She really wanted merely to drop back and just follow.

Fat chance of that as her boat sped up. Where did all that power come from? She began to feel her stomach toss. Nerves and seasickness joined forces. She swallowed hard and closed her eyes.

Ahead, the motorboat with Evan seemed to be slowing down as it approached an island, or a peninsula. Rhetta wasn't sure which, only that the land jutted out, and she could tell there was water on each side. For that matter, it could be a cove. There was no more daylight so it was difficult to tell, exactly. There was a scattering of lights surrounded by inky dark, which she took for water.

The motorboat veered to the right and headed for the cove.

She and her pilot followed. She ducked down on the pretense of examining her shoe. She didn't want Evan to turn around and recognize her. Perhaps in the dim light, he probably couldn't even see her very well. Still, she took no chances.

Up ahead, Evan's boat pulled alongside the wharf. The motor cut down to idle. He leapt from the boat to the dock. Once on the wharf, he turned and waved the boat away. He trotted along the dilapidated wood structure to where another boat, larger, more like a small cruiser, sat moored. He jumped aboard and disappeared below deck.

How was Evan able to do all that leaping and jumping? He could barely walk around their building. He'd told her he had suffered a leg injury. Now he was miraculously cured. Must be the Mediterranean air.

Rhetta's launch idled up to the wharf. She reached into her purse and handed several fifties to the boat driver. She peeled off her vest and handed it over. He pointed, and over the noise of the motor, shouted something to her about France, then smiled, tipped his cap and helped her onto the wharf. He turned his speedboat around and roared away

Night had fully descended, and with it, a late winter chill. The moon had risen, sending silver streaks across the dark water. She stepped carefully along the wharf, hoping to sneak up to the boat she had just watched Evan board. Maybe she could hear something.

She needed to tell Randolph where she was. Of course, she didn't know for sure exactly where she was, but she'd try to call him. She groped in her purse for her phone. Her broken sandal strap tangled in a loose plank and she went down hard on one knee.

"Ow," she muttered, and collected herself enough to stand. Her knee throbbed and when she examined her pant leg, it was torn. "Great." She limped away, head down, rummaging in her purse.

Chapter 70

Saturday night, February 2

"*MADAME, VOUS N'AVEZ PAS LE DROIT.*" The uniformed man waggled his index finger in front of Rhetta as he blocked her path. She didn't understand him, but was certain from his tone that she had done something wrong. Although she had no idea what the man was saying, or in what language, she didn't need an interpreter to tell he wasn't happy to see her.

"I'm sorry, but I'm afraid I don't understand you, sir." She decided to be very polite. This encounter had not started out well.

He switched to heavily accented English. "*Madame*, I said, you are not permitted to be here. Have you your passport?" He held his hand out to receive it from her.

"I, uh, sure. Yes. Right here." *Oh crap. I think this guy is border patrol, and my passport is in the bag that I gave to Randolph.* She tried smiling. "Is there a problem?"

He glowered at her. "You cannot come here via the water, *Madame*. You must enter this part of France by land. This is not a valid port of entry."

France? Port of entry? This isn't sounding good. Oh, no, that's what the boat driver was trying to tell me. "I'm sorry, I didn't know I was in France. Sir, may I please tell you why I'm here? I was following a man who—"

He held up his hand as though stopping traffic. "That would be an excellent idea. I will listen as I check your passport." He turned his hand over, palm up and waited.

Rhetta tossed her purse. No passport. Of course, not. It was in the bag, in the car, on the ferry with Randolph. Who was probably by now going berserk worrying about her.

"I can't seem to locate my passport. I think it's with my husband on the ferry." She gestured toward the direction she'd just come.

"The ferry from Vera Mardola?" the border guard asked.

"Yes, he's with the car. I gave him the bag with all our paperwork."

"And you are here, not there, because?"

Rhetta pointed toward the cruiser. "As I said, I was following a man. He stole money from the *Banc Real de Santo Domingo* at *Vera Mardola*. He's an American, too, and he's on that boat." She didn't add that he probably hadn't shown any passport to anyone either.

"And you are the police?"

"No, I'm the victim. He forged papers and stole my money, and I believe he probably killed a man to steal his identity in order to do this. Please, we have to stop him."

Just then, the cruiser's motor started up. Two men tossed ropes from the wharf to the boat, then jumped aboard.

"Please sir, don't let that boat leave. There's a possible killer on board."

The border guard shrugged. "I fear you have a vivid imagination. That boat belongs to a well-known American actor. I do not know why you are sneaking into France by boat, when land access is very easy and simple. Any country in the European Union has easy border crossings. So, I think you must be up to no good, as you say in America. Therefore, I must place you under arrest. Come with me." He reached for her arm, and began to steer her away from the wharf.

The cruiser chugged out to sea. Evan was getting away. She was getting arrested. This was definitely not going well.

Oh, crap.

Chapter 71

Late Saturday night, February 2

G RIPPING HER FIRMLY BY HER arm, the guard walked briskly, Rhetta stumbling along at his side, trying her best to keep his pace. Her sandals had taken a beating after the accident. The strap was long gone. She had to grip the bottom of the sandal with her toes, or walk right out of her shoe. He foot cramped. She glanced over her shoulder at the departing boat.

"Please, sir, my shoe is broken, and my foot hurts. Can we walk a bit slower?" There was no more urgency. Evan had escaped.

"We have arrived at the office. Now you can sit."

He led her through a metal door into a small concrete building that she figured was probably fifteen by twenty feet. It had two small offices, and a back door marked *toilette*. She guessed what that room was. She glanced at his badge as he led her to the table. The name read, P. Legrand.

Legrand was a short, slim man who wore his neatly creased uniform like a glove. A dark line above his lip turned out to be a thin mustache. His black shoes reflected the overhead light. He pointed her to a large metal desk, asked for her purse, told her to sit. She handed the purse to him and sat. He placed it gingerly on the desk, then picked up the phone, dialed a number, and spoke quickly. When he finished, he waggled a thin index finger at her purse. "As customs officer I must search your bag. Is there anything in there that is contraband or prohibited?"

"Uh, no, I don't think so. I don't know what's prohibited, so I can't answer for sure. I just have the usual stuff in there."

He removed a pair of latex gloves from his desk drawer, slipped them on then opened her bag. He searched methodically, removing her wallet and her cell phone, and laying them alongside the bag. The latex gloves were probably to protect him from cooties. He closed the bag then sat across from her.

He folded his hands on the table, and leaned toward her. "Now, *Madame*, I suggest you start at the beginning and explain to me not only why you are here, but how you got here. Please start with your name?"

"My name is Rhetta McCarter, and yes, sir, I will be happy to tell you everything. But first, may I please call my husband?" She motioned to her phone. "He must be worried sick about me. He doesn't know where I am. He's probably back in Spain and has perhaps contacted the authorities there. Please, I need to tell him I'm safe." She glanced up at the border officer. "I am safe, right?" She shivered, although it wasn't cold in here with the wall heater glowing. She always shivered when she was scared. Sometimes she got physically ill and threw up. She prayed she wouldn't now, although her stomach wasn't cooperating. Acid bubbled and she gulped back the queasiness.

He handed her the iPhone.

She stared at it, willing herself to remember the dialing code. She tapped the numbers, but all she heard was a recorded message in a language she didn't understand. She tried again. Still, the call wouldn't go through.

"I have a card in there with dialing instructions. May I please see it?"

The officer handed her purse to her.

She fished inside the purse but couldn't locate the card.

"Do you know how to dial to an American cell phone?" she asked as she tore the contents of her purse apart. He shook his head. He drummed the desktop with his fingers.

She finally found the card. She held it in front of her. She couldn't make out the numbers without her glasses. Another foray through the purse produced her glasses. She squinted at the card, and followed the instructions. This time, the call went through.

As soon as Randolph answered, Rhetta blurted, "I'm safe. I'm in France, but I'm under arrest."

"Oh God, Rhetta, what did you do?"

"I followed Evan, and now he's gone, and I'm being held because I entered France illegally. I think I'm in trouble. I'm going to tell this nice man all about it, but can you come and get me?" She smiled at the customs agent. He didn't smile back.

"Where are you?"

"Uh, just a minute, Sweets. I'll ask. I don't know what part of France I'm in, except I know it's not Paris."

To Legrand, she said, "Can you tell me where I am?"

"Oui, *Madame*, you are in Port Chartier, France."

She repeated it for Randolph.

She heard paper crinkling. "I just checked the map. Sit tight, it's about a two hour drive. I'm on my way."

She'd be sitting tight. What else could she do? Her nerves tingled, and she couldn't warm up. What she wouldn't give for a cup of coffee.

Maybe this nice customs agent would oblige. After all, he surely didn't meet many people in this lonely outpost. Of course, that made her wonder what he had done to deserve such a lowly posting. Or, was it a lofty post, maybe earned because he had so many years of service? He wasn't a young man, probably in his forties. Wait, she was in her forties and she considered herself still fairly young. At least she was a long way from over the hill. She felt her brain zig-zagging in all directions, something else she did when she was stressed.

She desperately craved a cigarette. She'd be damned if she'd ask for one. But if that customs officer pulled out a smoke, she'd tackle him for it. She prayed he wouldn't smoke. She prayed he would, then offer her one. Dear God.

She knew she was in big trouble, maybe about to get arrested and hauled off, never to be seen again. No, that only happened in movies. Of course, things like this whole Tontine Trust thing, the Evan thing, only happened in movies, too. Yet, here she was. And, what about Evan, anyway? How on earth was he involved? There went her brain again.

She said, "My husband is coming and bringing my passport and all my paperwork. In the meantime, do you think we could have some coffee while I tell you about this?"

Legrand stood, shook his head, and with a sigh, headed to the nearby counter. He made them coffee.

Chapter 72

Late Saturday night, February 2

RANDOLPH ARRIVED IN JUST UNDER two hours. She spotted his headlights coming towards them at the same time Legrand commented that a car was approaching.

"This must be your husband now," he said. She had not seen one other person since her own awkward arrival. She agreed that it must be Randolph. She wondered how much this border guard really had to do on this lonely stretch of coast. She didn't dare ask him. It might not be something he cared to discuss. Maybe her unseemly landing was the highlight of his day.

She had told Legrand everything about the circumstances that brought her to his outpost on a peninsula in the French Mediterranean. Whether or not he believed her, she couldn't really tell. He took notes, nodded a lot, and then made even more coffee. He did tell her that occasionally stray tourists made their way to Port Chartier by boat, and shrugged as though it was a minor offense. That gave her hope she wouldn't be incarcerated. Then he pointed out that those tourists typically carried their passports with them, while she, on the other hand, didn't have hers. That statement cancelled the hope.

Randolph parked next to the small building.

"Oh, Sweets, am I ever glad to see you!" Rhetta met him at the driver's door as he climbed out. She hugged his neck.

He kissed her. "I'm glad to see you too. You had me worried when you didn't make it on to the ferry. What, on earth happened? How did you get here?"

"Evan got away. I'll tell you all about it."

Legrand cleared his throat. "Please, *monsieur* and *madame*, come with me into the office." Turning to Rhetta he added, "I pray your husband brought your passport?" He motioned toward the building, indicating he would follow them.

Randolph reached in the car and came out with Rhetta's bag, and handed it to her. She slid it up her shoulder, clasped Randolph's hand in hers and led him to the building.

Inside, she laid the bag on the table and sifted through the contents. She located her passport along with the envelope containing all the paperwork for the bank. She presented the passport to Legrand. He examined it, then handed it back to her.

"It is in order, *madame*." He turned to Randolph. "May I please see yours, *monsieur*?"

Randolph produced his for scrutiny. Apparently satisfied, Legrand nodded and returned it. Randolph tucked it into his shirt pocket.

"Here's the rest of the stuff I was telling you about." Rhetta slid the envelope toward Legrand. "I can show you the evidence to back up what I told you about."

He waved it off. "It is not necessary. You are free to go. Please enjoy your stay in France."

"Thank you," Rhetta said, and gathered up her belongings. She knew for once when to shut up and quit talking. They bolted for the car. She tossed her stuff in the miniature back seat, buckled herself in, then cranked up the heater.

Randolph fiddled with the heater controls, checked the mirrors, then pulled away. "Let's head back to Cadaqués and spend the night and tomorrow there. We can go back to the bank on Vera Mardola first thing Monday morning, and see what they did about that wire. I pray to goodness that it got withdrawn."

Rhetta nodded, and rubbed her arms. "I'm freezing," she said, her teeth chattering. It wasn't all that cold out, but her adventure across the bay left her nervous and chilled. She looked at the weather app on her iPhone and it revealed the temperature to be fifty-four degrees Fahrenheit. "Thank God this phone tells me in Fahrenheit. That way I know whether I'm cold or not."

"That sounds like something Woody would say," Randolph said Rhetta smiled. Yes, it did.

"I found a room in a lovely little inn there while waiting for you. I thought you might be on the next ferry, and since it was getting so late, I figured there was no sense in driving back to Barcelona. We still need to sort this out at the bank. We can spend a leisurely day in Cadaqués, then go back to Vera Mardola first thing Monday."

"I'll be a sight myself come Monday. I don't have a change of clothes, my pants have a rip in the knee and my sandal is broken."

"No worries, the lovely lady who owns the inn said she'll launder our clothes first thing tomorrow morning while we enjoy breakfast in our room. She can probably fix that little tear, too, maybe even glue your sandal together. Don't worry." He patted her knee. "She said they will have dressing gowns and sleeping clothes for us." He grinned at her. "I can't wait to see you in whatever they find for you."

"Oh great. I can't wait." Rhetta rolled her eyes. At this point, though, she really didn't care about being a fashionista. She was exhausted.

She glanced at her phone. It was nearly eleven-thirty. "Speaking of Woody, I'm going to call him, see what he found out about Corini. It should be six-thirty back home. He'll be up." She scavenged again in her purse for the dialing instruction card and her glasses.

The call went through quickly.

"Rhetta, what's up? Are you okay?"

"We're fine, but I need to know if you found out anything about Evan, and if he's still around." She put the phone on speaker.

"Jeff's office didn't know too much about him, other than he's an injured Vietnam vet. They said Jeff hired him because his own dad served. Nobody has seen Evan for several days. They said that Tony hasn't heard from him for a few days and doesn't know where he is."

"I know exactly where he is, Woody. He's here. I followed him today. Well, more like chased him, you might say. He was at the bank claiming to be George Erickson."

"He's there? How can he be there? He said he's George Erickson? Rhetta, what's going on?"

"That's exactly what we're trying to figure out. When we went to the bank, they told us that George Erickson had already asked for the trust to be disbursed. When we told them George Erickson was dead, they showed us the surveillance video. The man claiming to be Erickson is Evan. He's posing as George Erickson. We urged the bank to stop the wire, but I'm not sure they were able to. Hope it's not too late. We tried to follow him, but he escaped. I don't know how we're going to catch him.

"We?" Who else is on this?"

She could visualize Woody rubbing his pate.

"We, as in Randolph and me, and they, as in local bank authorities. Evan is a fake, and I suspect is a killer. He probably ran down poor George. And he probably hit me on the head and dumped me in the Dumpster."

"How could he do that? He's an old guy who can barely walk."

From his tone of voice, which sounded stressed, Rhetta imagined Woody was now rubbing his head with both hands. Unless he was holding the phone with one of his hands.

"You should have seen him leaping onto boats and running away, Woody. He's a lot friskier here than he ever was at home."

"So not only was he posing as a vet by the name of George Erickson there, he may very well be posing as a handicapped old man here."

Rhetta stared at her phone, then at Randolph. *Of course!*

"Woody, that's it! You're a genius!"

Chapter 73

Sunday noon, February 3

R HETTA LONGED TO ENJOY THE quaint inn that Randolph had found, but without clean clothes and too exhausted to think, she wasn't up to much frivolity.

Randolph parked in the private lot across from the entryway. He clasped her hand as they trudged to the massive oak door. The cornerstone of the two-story rock building bore the date 1726. Inside was cozy and modernized, while retaining a provincial charm. The dark wood flooring blended into white plastered walls, while overhead, ancient hand-hewn beams held the old roof in place. Outside, the roof was covered in red clay tiles, although she suspected it may have once been thatched or made of wood planks.

Randolph had already checked in, so they went upstairs to their room, one with a balcony and a magnificent view of the Mediterranean. As promised, the room came supplied with all the essential care items they needed, so after brushing her teeth and a quick, hot shower, Rhetta crawled under the sheets dressed in a cotton nightgown provided by the matron, *Señora* Perrine. The apron-wearing matron had collected their clothes, provided them with sleepwear, then left with a promise to return their laundered and repaired clothes early Sunday afternoon.

Rhetta didn't wake until nearly noon. The time difference along with the previous day's excitement made for a deep, dreamless sleep.

Randolph, dressed only in a bath towel, stood on the balcony sipping coffee when she awoke. Next to him on the deck table was a tray loaded with pastries and a steaming pot of coffee.

"Well, did you decide to return to the land of the living?" he said, grinning at her and heading for the coffee pot, preparing her coffee while she visited the restroom.

She joined him on the balcony, leaned over the rail and inhaled the salty sea air. "This is such a beautiful place. We should come back here sometime so we can truly enjoy it." She looked longingly at the sugary white sands of the beach below. "I'd love to go swimming and play on the beach." Sampling the strong coffee, she added, "The Spanish really know how to make great coffee. This is heavenly."

Randolph pulled up a wood deck chair and joined her at the balcony table.

"Sweets, what do you think Evan is up to? And who, exactly is he?"

"I've been thinking about this. I suspect Evan knew someone involved with your father or some of the other members of the Tontine, someone who divulged its secret. So he figured out a plan to collect."

"Do you think he killed George Erickson to steal his identity?"

Randolph nodded. "Yes. He probably believed your father was already dead. You, however, became a liability to him when he found out your father was still alive. He's probably responsible for the fire that killed Rushia. He needed to kill Frank so that he could impersonate George Erickson and collect on the trust. I have no doubt that he conked you on the head, trying to get the last of the information he needed. I suspect he would have killed you too, if he needed to. Then he had to follow us to Columbia in order to get the VIN off the Camaro when he couldn't get to the title, which, you, my clever wife, locked away in the safe deposit box." He kissed the top of her head. She hugged his neck.

"I didn't recognize him until I saw him in the video. I can't believe Evan did this." Rhetta shivered. "I hope that tomorrow we find out that the wire was stopped. I don't think he should get away with murder. If the wire went through, I'm afraid there will be no catching him. We could turn it over to Interpol, or some such agency, but I doubt seriously if any cops would go after him." She selected a croissant from the heaping plate.

A knock at the door interrupted them.

Mrs. Perrine was all smiles when Randolph answered the door. She handed them their clothes, freshly laundered, repaired and hanging neatly on wood hangers. She had even glued Rhetta's hapless sandal back together.

"Sweets, ask her if there's a Walmart nearby. I'd like to buy some undies and maybe some hair spray."

Mrs. Perrine, who had a rather good command of English, looked puzzled at the request. "What is a Walmart?" she said.

Randolph answered, "It's a huge department store that sells everything from groceries to swimming pools."

Mrs. Perrine seemed confused, so Randolph asked, "Do you have any stores open on Sunday? My wife thinks she needs to shop for a few items."

She shook her head emphatically. "No, no, not on Sunday. It is day of church. Nobody shops today, except at *fleca*. We must always have fresh bread." She nodded solemnly toward the plate of baked goods. "Without the *fleca*, Sunday or no Sunday, we would have the civil unrest."

"Yes, of course. Silly me," Rhetta said, and stuffed another croissant into her mouth. What the heck. She wouldn't suffer any pangs of diet conscience today. If she had to wear the same clothes three days in a row, then by golly she'd gorge on croissants.

Chapter 74

Monday afternoon, February 4

THIS TIME, THE TRIP ON the ferry was routine—no Evan, nor anyone else who looked or acted suspicious.

Rhetta and Randolph arrived at the bank ten minutes before it opened. They sat on the steps and waited. Exactly on time, the large wood doors swung open. The same guard who had been on duty Saturday escorted them inside without giving them a second look, as though it was perfectly normal for Americans to come back the next working day attired in the same clothes they'd worn previously. At least Rhetta thought that's what he might be thinking. If in fact, he even remembered them at all. He didn't act like it. He probably could care less, as Woody would say.

He greeted them with the same plastic smile he wore on Saturday. *"Bona tarda. Benvingut al Banc Real de Santo Domingo."* His rote greeting confirmed her suspicion that he didn't remember them.

Rhetta nodded and pointed toward the blonde receptionist. "I need to speak with her, thanks." They marched past the guard and stopped at the mahogany desk.

"Please, I need to speak to Mister Cabriolet again about the Garibaldi Tontine."

The blonde eyed Rhetta, then tilted her head slightly to consider Randolph. Apparently satisfied, she picked up the phone, and again, all Rhetta caught was *Garibaldi Tontine*.

An office door flew open and once again they were eye to eye with the short, dark man, Mr. Cabriolet. This time, he motioned them to his large expansive office, not the cubbyhole they were in last Saturday.

Rhetta looked around quickly. This time there were no guns pointed at her. As she walked into the office, her sandal strap broke again. Mrs. Perrine's glue didn't hold up. She removed both her sandals and stood barefoot on the rich carpet. If Cabriolet noticed, he said nothing.

"Ah, sir and madam please, have a seat." He gestured toward the chairs in front of his shiny uncluttered mahogany desk. The only item on it was a modern phone. Rhetta instantly thought of her own cluttered desktop that always looked like the aftermath of a tornado. How did he work with nothing on his desk? And where was his computer? She glanced around. Didn't see it.

Cabriolet opened the conversation. "I took precautions after our little, ah, disturbance, and placed a hold on the wire to the account for Mister Erickson."

Rhetta's heart began to crash against her ribs.

"Mister Erickson has already telephoned this morning and is on his way here. I informed him that there was more paperwork I needed him to sign."

Cabriolet picked up his ringing desk phone. "Ah, he is here, now. In the lobby."

Rhetta thought she'd pass out. She gripped Randolph's hand. "What are you going to do, Mr. Cabriolet?"

"Why, I will invite him in here and ask how it is that you have his death certificate. I also have invited several *policia* to our little party." He spoke again into the phone. The outer door at the rear of his office opened and two uniformed cops entered. They took up positions at the side of the office, hands resting on their sidearms. Mr. Cabriolet rose, walked to the door, and left the room.

I didn't think European cops were armed. Wait, this isn't part of the EU, so I guess they can do what they want. Rhetta leaned over and whispered to Randolph. "I hope they're on our side."

"Me, too," Randolph answered, clutching her hand tightly.

The door opened and Mr. Cabriolet returned. Evan walked in behind him.

Rhetta stood, turned, faced him. "Hello, Evan."

"What…who is this?" Evan asked, his voice beginning to quaver. He pointed at Rhetta. "Why is she calling me Evan?"

"Unless you have a doppelganger, you're Evan, our handyman, from Cape Girardeau, Missouri. Care to tell us why you're posing as George Erickson? Is it because you know he's dead? And that you killed him?" Rhetta positioned herself directly in front of Evan. Within inches of his face, she pointed her finger at him. "You're a killer and a thief!"

In a flash, Evan turned and bolted toward the door. Rhetta was closest. She didn't hesitate. She sprang after him. The two cops joined in just as Rhetta leapt on Evan's back. They crashed across a chair, with Rhetta still pounding him, riding his back as the fell to the floor. Evan swore loudly, and with a shove, pushed her off him with surprising strength for an elderly man. Rhetta rolled away and the two cops snatched him by his jacket and hauled him to his feet.

Randolph reached the melee in time to help Rhetta to her feet. "You're not going anywhere, Evan. You tried to defraud this institution and steal Rhetta's money. I believe there's a jail cell somewhere that will accommodate you."

Rhetta brushed off her pants, then stared at Evan. He lowered his head and muttered, "You people are crazy. I didn't kill anyone." He raised his head and pointed at Rhetta. "Keep her away from me. She's nuts."

Rhetta lunged at him again, this time grabbing a handful of his scraggly beard. It came off in a wad in her hand. She yelled, "He's wearing a phony beard." She pointed to his hair. "And I bet that's not his real hair either."

Half of Evans's face was clean-shaven, but with studio glue smeared across his cheek. It was obvious he wasn't old. He reached up and removed his wig. Under it was a full head of dark hair tinged with grey. Evan then removed the rest of the beard. He stood up straight. Gone was the stooping old man, and as the cops began to lead him away, his limp disappeared, too.

"Oh dear God. I know him, Sweets, That's Stanton Worthington."

The two officers jerked his arms behind his back and handcuffed him.

Chapter 75

Late Monday morning, February 4

CABRIOLET WAS ALL SMILES WHEN he slid the paperwork over for Rhetta to examine.

"This is a numbered account only, no names. The money will stay here until you request it. As sole owner of the account, I now need your signature. We also have beneficiary forms to sign. The account will be a standard account. The Tontine Trust is no longer."

"What about taxes?" Rhetta asked. She glanced at Randolph. "How do we pay the taxes?"

Cabriolet smiled. "As long as the money is here, in Vera Mardola, there are no taxes. If you request any deposits into your American account, then, well, you will have to check with your country's regulations, yes?"

Rhetta nodded. "I guess it won't matter too much unless it's a lot of money."

Cabriolet's expression was unreadable. "I'm not sure where the tax threshold will apply. As I said, you must check with your country's tax laws."

Rhetta nodded. "I'll check with our accountant. Where do I need to sign?"

He pointed to a line. Above the line was a number. In United States Dollars.

She didn't have her glasses on, so she was sure she wasn't reading the number correctly. There seemed to be so many of them. Must all be running together. "Can you hand me my purse, Randolph? I need to get my glasses. I can't read that amount." Randolph handed his wife her purse. Rhetta changed her mind. "Better yet, Mister Cabriolet, can you read it for me?" She really didn't want to embarrass herself by reading it incorrectly.

"But of course. Twenty-seven million, seven hundred and eighty thousand, three hundred forty-seven and sixteen cents. In United States dollars."

Rhetta's stomach clenched, her gut ricocheted and her fist gripped the pen so hard it snapped. Pieces flew off and bounced to the floor. Rhetta clung to the useless, empty barrel. "What did you say? How much?"

He repeated it. So very calmly.

Rhetta's ears popped.

Chapter 76

Late afternoon, April 27

R HETTA READ THE NEWSPAPER ACCOUNT aloud to Randolph, Ricky and Billy Dan as they sat around the stone fire pit near the pond bank at Billy Dan's. The spring day had been just about perfect, with the temperature in the seventies. After nightfall, the air was crisper. The warmth from the crackling logs felt delicious on Rhetta's bare arms.

When they had left Vera Mardola, Rhetta and Randolph swore a pact of secrecy about the account. All the way home, Rhetta had fretted and stewed about the money.

"Why did Frank do that to me? I don't think I should have all of it. I want to track down the other members of the Garibaldi and find out if there are any children. We should share."

"Whatever you want. I know you'll do the right thing." Randolph had kissed her cheek. "Now try and get some rest. You didn't sleep at all last night."

Randolph had added, "I don't think we should tell anyone about this money, not even our friends. Especially until we know what you're going to do with it."

"I agree. I want to help Woody and the other vets with PTSD." She had gnawed on her fingernails. There were none left, but she continued to chew anyway. Sleep aboard the plane had been impossible. Children had fretted, lights had flickered, and the flight attendants had provided beverage service with noisy carts.

When they had finally got home, she had slept. For two days.

After a day spent fishing on Billy Dan's lake, Rhetta and Ricky had driven to Green's Grocery, the old fashioned country store down the road, and picked up a mountain of the "world's best" fried bologna sandwiches and a half gallon of potato salad to take back for supper. Rhetta had grabbed the early edition of the local Sunday paper when she spotted the headline, *American Actor Accused of Hit and Run in Cape Girardeau Found in Spain.*

Rhetta snatched the paper. "Hey guys, listen to this," she said, and began to read.

American film actor, Stanton Worthington, 48, shown here in the custody of federal agents, was returned to Cape Girardeau, MO to face criminal charges. Among the pending charges is one for a hit and run death last November 15, and an assault charge against local mortgage banker, Rhetta McCarter. According to a witness, the victim of the hit and run, George Erickson, was struck by a blue pickup truck. Erickson was pronounced dead at Saint Mark's hospital later that evening. Worthington has a 2010 blue Ford pickup registered to him, according to the Missouri Department of Motor Vehicles. The truck has been impounded.

Worthington made international headlines in February when he was found bound and gagged on a wharf in Cadaqués, Spain. He claimed that the police in the nearby island country of Vera Mardola had tied him up and left him there. He was unable to explain the reason, and it was widely believed that he had been a victim of an assault and robbery. Spanish authorities immediately arrested Worthington on suspicion of theft. No charges ensued and he was released to American agents just yesterday. Worthington was part of the cast of the movie, Gone Lady to be filmed here later this summer.

Rhetta set the paper down. "It was Worthington, disguised as Evan, who conked me on the head and tossed me in the Dumpster. I'm glad he'll go to trial for killing George Erickson. Too bad they can't prove it was premeditated. No wonder he kept looking familiar, but I couldn't ever identify him. He's adept at changing his looks."

She tapped the paper. "That's why he was able to get on that boat in France. It was his, and he kept it there. You'd think if he had enough money to live like that he wouldn't have had to steal more."

Randolph skewered a couple of fat marshmallows on two sticks, and handed one to Rhetta. He laid his along the fire pit, and picked up his sandwich. "He may have had money, but it was apparent he thought he was going to get a king's ransom out of the trust. Maybe he was living on more than he earned. You know, even if you earn a million dollars, but spend a million and one, you're still broke."

"The bank at Vera Mardola would have to release information about the Tontine Trust to prove premeditated murder. And we both know that Mr. Cabriolet will not do that."

Randolph finished the last of his sandwich, popped open a diet soda, and sat back in his chair. "Stanton Worthington is the son of Cooper Worthington, one of the original seven who formed the trust with Rhetta's father. Stanton somehow found out about it. Maybe his father told him before he died, who knows? Anyway, the idea that there was big money in the trust must have given Worthington the idea he could get it. He impersonated the man he ran over in his attempt to prove he was the last man. Because he's an actor, he figured it would be easiest to impersonate the dead man. He didn't have everything worked out though, because he thought Rhetta's father was already dead. Mr. Cabriolet told us that Evan or Worthington, in his disguise had shown up with a claim before Rhetta's father died, insisting he was the last. Mr. Cabriolet informed him that Frank Caldwell was still alive. That's when he began trying to get rid of not only Frank, but Rhetta too. He knew that the money would go to the last surviving heir or heirs." Randolph patted Rhetta's arm. "Of course that was Rhetta, since Frank was truly the last one to die."

Rhetta shuddered. "Evan, or Worthington I should say, was probably in Vera Mardola the first time nobody could find him around the place. Pretty sneaky, dressing up like an old dude and spying on us at MCB."

"He must have needed the correct account number too, since he followed us to Columbia and got the number out of the Camaro," Ricky chimed in.

"Not to pry, but was the account that valuable, after all was said and done?" asked Billy Dan.

"No, not really. The men had pulled a lot out over the years," Rhetta said. She didn't look at Randolph. She fiddled with her marshmallow stick.

"How will they prove he ran over George Erickson?" asked Ricky.

Rhetta thought about it a moment. "I had already told Sergeant Delmonti about the Tontine Trust, and my father's involvement, and I have all the paperwork my father gave me. It will prove the account existed. That, combined with any evidence they may have from his truck should be enough. Apparently, there were paint scrapes on George's clothing. If they match the truck, well, that ought to do it." Rhetta moved to the arm of Randolph's chair. He slid his arm around her waist.

She turned to her husband. "What I don't understand, though, Sweets, is how Worthington got to Cadaqués? When we left Vera Mardola, the *policia* had him in handcuffs."

Randolph grinned. "That, my dear, is what we in the judicial system call, a 'Midnight Extradition.' I'm sure Vera Mardola didn't want him there. No one had ever attempted to rob their bank before, and I'm sure that they were ticked off, to say the least. Since Vera Mardola has no extradition policy, they took matters into their own hands. And *pronto*, he shows up in Spain."

Everyone laughed.

"Hey, anyone up for some chocolate fudge ice cream?" Billy Dan asked.

Rhetta and Ricky groaned in unison. Then they both said, "Absolutely!" Billy Dan ran up the porch steps to his kitchen to get the dessert.

"Now, I need to know something," Randolph said, turning to Rhetta. "What on earth made you grab Evan's beard?"

"When I looked over at him, it was sideways! Woody had made a few remarks about his pathetic beard, and it struck me right then that it was phony. So I yanked on it and sure enough!"

Billy Dan stopped midway down the steps. He set aside the large tray holding ice cream, dishes and spoons and jogged back up the stairs, disappearing around the corner of the house. Rhetta soon heard the reason Billy Dan interrupted his descent. A four-wheeler roared into the driveway, spewing up gravel before stopping at the side entrance to the house. Rhetta stood and watched Billy Dan speak to the young driver. In a moment, the man left, and Bill Dan loped across the porch and down the steps to where everyone sat. He'd left the ice cream.

"That was Jimmy White Cloud. There's been an accident at that new bazillion dollar religious camp where that Oklahoma developer is building back in the woods." Billy Dan pointed to an area down the road. "Some construction workers found a body. They think he was murdered."

THE END

ABOUT THE AUTHOR

SHARON WOODS HOPKINS

*K*ILLERTRUST, THE THIRD BOOK IN the mystery series featuring mortgage banker Rhetta McCarter hits close to home. Sharon is a branch manager for a mortgage office of a Missouri bank. She also owns the original Cami, the car featured in the book.

Besides writing, Sharon's hobbies include painting, fishing, photography, flower gardening, and restoring muscle cars with her son, Jeff.

She is a member of the Mystery Writers of America, Sisters in Crime, the Southeast Missouri Writers' Guild, and the Missouri Writers' Guild. Her short story, "DEATH BEE HUMBLE," appeared in the SEMO Writer's Guild Anthology for 2012. Her first Rhetta McCarter book, **KILLERWATT**, was nominated for a 2011 Lovey award for Best First

Novel, and was an Indie Excellence Award Finalist in 2012 in the Mystery Category.

Her second book in the series, **KILLERFIND**, was a 2012 Lovey award nominee for best series, and was also an Indie Excellence Award Finalist in 2012. **KILLERFIND** won First Place in the Show-me Best Book Awards at the Missouri Writers Guild for 2013.

Sharon has been a regular contributor to www.wheel-emag.com and was a regular contributor to the Appaloosa Journal. She spent 30 years as an Appaloosa Horse Club judge, where she was privileged to judge all over the US, Canada, Mexico, and Europe.

She also spent time in the air as a flight attendant for American Airlines, fifteen years as a real estate broker, and ten years in retail management.

Sharon lives on the family compound near Marble Hill, Missouri, with her husband, Bill, next door to her son, Jeff, his wife, Wendy, and her grandson, Dylan, plus two cats, one dog, and assorted second generation Camaros.

Watch for Rhetta McCarter and the fourth book in the series, **KILLERGROUND**, coming soon.

WEBSITE QR CODES

SHARON WOODS HOPKINS
Author of the
Rhetta McCarter Mysteries

BILL HOPKINS
Author of the
Judge Rosswell Carew Mysteries

DEADLY WRITES
PUBLISHING, LLC

ELLIE SEARL,
PUBLISHISTA

www.ingramcontent.com/pod-product-compliance
Lightning Source LLC
Chambersburg PA
CBHW021209250626
47155CB00008B/2742